Praise for A WORLD OF SILENCE

'A dark and twisty novel about entangled lives, interlaced with mistakes, that will leave you thinking about the behaviour you are willing (and unwilling) to walk past every day.'
—Casey Nott, Author

'Raw and real. The ambiguous and so often unseen nature of domestic abuse is explored in this gripping tale of three women. Skinner deftly draws a slice of life narrative that, uncomfortable though it may be, hits home how vital it is for us to use our voice.'
—Sarah Todman, Author

'… explores coercive control, yet you'll be uplifted by the friendships. Skinner's skill in showing how inconspicuous events leading up to harm can be when lived in real time, verges on breathtaking. 5 stars.'
—Cate Sawyer, Author

'Raw, unflinching, this novel deftly tackles the danger of staying silent about one of the most insidious and challenging issues of our time.'
—Claudine Tinellis, Author, Podcaster, Course Presenter

'Pitch-perfect in its depiction of young mothers in the pretty suburbs, juggling married life, kids, jobs, friendships. The pace quickens as the mysteries deepen and violence escalates. Ordinary life illuminated with great insight. Skinner is a new powerful voice worth listening to.'
—Mary, Book Reviewer & Social Worker

'Entwining storylines, driven by years of secrets and regret, propel the plot towards a heart-wrenching climax. An essential read for those seeking stories of empowerment and recovery.'
—Jack Roney, Author, Podcaster, and retired Police Officer

Praise for A WORLD OF SILENCE

'Secrets in suburbia, the complexities of female friendship and motherhood, and the myriad guises of violence against women are explored in Jo Skinner's gripping second novel, *A World of Silence*, a compassionate and sharp commentary of life in middle-class Brisbane.'
—Poppy Gee, Award-winning Crime Writer

'Seen through the eyes of best friends Kate and Tori, we discover the hidden truths and uneasy pacts which can lurk beneath the surface of even the most perfect-looking of families. Unflinching yet empathetic, fast-paced yet lyrical, *A World of Silence* will linger in your mind long after you've turned the last page.'
—Kyra Geddes, Author

'Skinner does not shy away from the taboo topics of domestic violence and coercive control. This book explores the personal side to these stories, illustrating that there is no one type of perpetrator, and no one type of victim. With relatable characters who don't always make the wisest decisions under pressure, Skinner presents an accurate snapshot of suburban Australian life and the importance of speaking up.'
—Eileen O'Hely, Author

'Set in Brisbane, Australia, this novel brings colour to the too-often overlooked lives of everyday women, revealing that there is always more to a person than meets the eye. Readers are immersed in the lives of psychologist Kate and single mother Tori through Skinner's seamless perspective switches.'
—Lara McCormack, Reviewer

A World of Silence

Jo Skinner

HAWKEYE
PUBLISHING

First published in Australia in 2025 by Hawkeye Publishing.

Cover Design by Kaity Tran

This book is a work of fiction, and the characters are entirely fictional.

A catalogue record of this book is available from the National Library of Australia.

ISBN 9781923105447

Proudly printed in Australia.

www.hawkeyebooks.com.au

These pages contain discussion and instances of animal cruelty,
sexual assault, murder, and suicide, which may be triggering.

To my soulmate Michael, and our three children, Lara, Eva, and Jonathan,
you inspire me daily and fill my life with joy.

And to my first bestie, Tammie Goedecke, who read this book long before I had a
publishing contract. Your enthusiasm was the encouragement I needed to
send my words out into the world.

1

DARKNESS swallowed the grey-bellied clouds that hung in the disappearing dusk. Kate dimmed the lights, stacked the magazines, and glanced at her schedule for the next day. She startled at a rustle outside, saw a shadow pause. Kate called out, 'Hello?'

'Are you closed?' A strained voice.

Kate unlocked the door to red rimmed eyes.

'Bea?' It must have been two years since she had been in for counselling. 'Come in.'

The loud sound of rush hour assaulted Kate's ears. She pulled the door shut, locked it, grateful for the carefully chosen green hues and quiet of the clinic.

'Have a seat. Can I get you a glass of water, a cup of tea?'

Bea shook her head, perched on the edge of the chair, one short, black boot jiggling.

Kate kept her voice soft. 'What's happened?'

A siren shrieked outside, a flash of red in the window. It reached fever pitch then died away, leaving the background drone of traffic. Bea's hair fell across the side of her face while she whispered into her handbag. 'Jake's out.'

Kate swallowed hard.

'I came home to a knife stuck in the front door.'

'Have you reported it?'

'I rang that number you gave me.'

'And?'

'The woman said I was overreacting. It could have been anybody.'

Kate leant over and touched Bea's arm, felt her wince.

A drenching rain drowned Kate's efforts to soothe, so she put her arm around Bea's shoulder, squeezed and waited for the squall to soften. Water slid in great sheets down the windows, the wind a high-pitched wail. Bea started to shake. Tears rolled down her cheeks. 'Artemis is missing.'

'Artemis?'

Bea pulled up a picture of a cat on her phone. Sleek, long whiskered, sitting like the sphinx.

'She's beautiful.'

Still quivering, Bea gulped. 'And so smart. She knows when I get home, waits for me at the front window…'

Sobbing, she stroked the image with a trembling finger. 'And today the sill was empty. I called and called, put out her favourite food, but she's gone.'

After the storm reduced to a steady rain, Kate walked Bea to her car, the two of them huddled under an umbrella. The traffic had thinned, the lights of the Story Bridge a blurry flicker in the distance.

When Bea drove off, Kate returned inside, slumped behind her computer and listened to the flow of water down the gutter. She picked up her phone, dialled Dorothy's Place where she volunteered once a month, hoping her former supervisor was working tonight.

'Dorothy's Place. Can I help you?'

It was one of the young ones. Kate stared into the bleak, dark outside while explaining what happened; left out the bit about Artemis.

'Has she seen us before? Wait, let me check… got it. Get her to ring us, I'll pull out her file.'

The shuffle of paper. 'And move on. There's only so much you can do.'

Kate reported the incident to the police, typed up some notes and logged off. Driving home, the windscreen wipers squealed back and forth and struggled to keep her view clear.

✢

Tori stretched her tired muscles. She had been smiling and serving customers non-stop since seven o'clock in the morning. Not that she was complaining. Her vintage store The Treasure Chest was a local icon, a place where women loved to browse and imagine a life colourful with possibilities. It was rare for anyone to leave without some small item.

Kate had told her to get sales help, and Tori had resisted until now. She was reluctant to let someone into this world she had created. Since the online orders took off, she relented and found an employee. She took a final glance around the now quiet shop before she locked up and walked down the gravel path to the unit.

Tori pushed open the door and found Leo sitting at the table, his school bag spilling contents across the kitchen bench. She paused and absorbed his brown curls, childish and long, his intense concentration. It made the beat behind her sternum ache.

'Hi, Leo.'

He had not even noticed her come in, deeply immersed in a project, the tip of his tongue visible. He looked up, his big brown eyes wide, and quickly hid something behind his back. 'Mum, you're early. I was making something for you. I'm nearly finished.'

A warm rush of love filled Tori from someplace deep inside. 'How about I go get changed into some civvies and you just pretend I'm not here. Give me an oi when you're done.'

Despite her curiosity, she made a point of turning her head away, pulled the bedroom door shut, and slipped into slouchy gear.

A few moments later, Leo called out, 'Finished!'

When she returned to the kitchen, he held a tiny paper treasure chest aloft, a folded replica of her shop's logo. He handed it to her, and she held it with reverence, gazing at it from every angle and using one finger to open the lid. 'It's beautiful, I love it.'

'It's origami. We made some stuff at school in maths for geometry then I found this book and saw the chest.'

'It's so perfect. I'll keep it next to my bed where I can see it every day.'

That was when Tori saw the cream envelope, the name and address handwritten in black ink. *Victoria Stafford.* Her mouth went dry.

Leo stood at the fridge, pulled out the orange juice. 'There's a letter for you. I left it on the bench.'

He tipped up the juice bottle and took a slug. Some dripped down his chin.

'Don't do that. Get yourself a glass.' Her voice was sharper than she intended.

Leo's face fell. He put the juice back, disappeared to his room, pulled the door shut behind him.

Once he was gone, Tori slid a trembling finger under the seal. As she scanned the letter, her skin goosebumped and the hairs behind her neck stood up. She stared out the window, watched the gathering storm outside and jolted when lightning flashed across the blackness, snapping the world in two. The thunder that followed rumbled through her.

When the rain started, she stuffed the letter back into the envelope. She had not given him much thought since she left, pregnant with Leo, and they managed fine for twelve years without him. A chill moved through her like a cold breeze.

She gritted her teeth, looked around her place with its odd angles, slanted timber ceiling and low corners. It was decorated with vintage gear she had salvaged from her shop. A comfy sofa strewn with colourful pillows, bold throws, and a sturdy timber table with mismatched chairs. It still made her feel dizzy to think that this was hers. She wondered whether she should mention the letter to Kate.

2

KATE glanced around the dusty attic. Typical of Edie to forget to mention the family tree project for school until this morning. It would be a chaotic rush again. Ryan was no help. He woke up late and wasn't ready yet. Kate pulled out a handful of photographs then paused and felt a warm blush on her cheeks.

She slipped into her past as dust motes spun on a slat of light that fell across the cloistered space. She held the moment between her thumb and index finger; one faded photograph she had long forgotten about, the scent of her youth hidden under a layer of mothballs, dust, and tired leather.

It was the start of her second year at university; those early weeks without pressing deadlines when the sundrenched freedom of summer holidays still lingered. She was hanging out with Shelley, her friend from school who was beautiful but too anxious to be aware of it, and Victoria, who had moved up from Melbourne to study. Shelley begged the two of them to join her to watch a football match. Shelley had her eye on a rookie player, touted as having promise. She didn't want to go alone.

Kate wore a spaghetti strap sundress, bursting with red strawberries, ripe for picking. The football landed at her feet midgame, and she tossed it back, giggling. That was the first time she saw him. Daryl caught her eye and held her gaze. She looked away, suddenly aware of the swell of her breasts against the flimsy fabric. The game continued while Shelley chattered. Victoria sat with her arms folded, while Kate's pulse thrummed. Her cheeks burned crimson.

Daryl came off the field, grass-stained sweat glinting on the flex of his forearms. Shelley giggled, breathless; he gave her a wink before he turned his attention to Kate and grinned. *How about a drink?* Kate's heart pushed against her ribs. *Sure.* Could he see her heartbeat dancing behind the strawberries? Shelley looked away and left with Victoria.

Kate and Daryl continued with fish and chips by the river, his fingers feather light on her thigh. She had no memory of them talking, only the sensation of his lips, his breath on her skin, his hands on her body. The evening dissolved into the next day with the two of them tangled in crumpled sheets while dawn split the sky with a firework of oranges and pinks.

Then, eighteen months later, Shelley married him.

'Mum!' Edie screamed from someplace.

Back amongst the scatter of photographs, Kate slipped the ragged edged photo of her young self with Daryl into her pocket. She rummaged through the box and picked out a selection of shots of both families, including a solemn black and white one of her nanna and pop's wedding.

She glanced at her own bare fingers. Her heart dipped. It was not important, she knew that. Ryan loved her, they had two gorgeous kids and a mortgage big enough to drown them. All the things that mattered. She pulled herself away from her longings, shoved the rest of the pictures back into the dusty box and added, 'sort photos' to her endless to do list.

'Found them!' she called out and clattered downstairs, shuddering when she brushed a sticky tendril of web from her hair.

Noah was sprawled on the floor with his green slime. Kate stepped around him and glanced at the dirty bowls and plates scattered along the bench. She made a mental note to remind everyone to put dishes straight into the dishwasher then clenched her teeth and did it herself. She propped the collection of photographs on top of the pile of unopened bills, then stacked plates.

The smell of shaving cream alerted her that Ryan had finished getting ready and was standing behind her. 'Morning, beautiful.'

He reached for the sandwiches he must have cobbled together earlier. The bread and cheeseboard were, of course, still on the bench. Kate kept her voice calm.

'I need you to drop the kids off on your way to work.'

Without looking at her, he started to stuff sheet music into his satchel. 'Not today, sorry. I meant to tell you, I resigned from Soul Sounds. The band is finally going places, there's an opportunity coming up and we need to polish our songs. It's my big chance.'

Kate grabbed the counter, stared at him. 'We need the money. You can't just resign.'

He kept his back to her, and she turned away, making a point of clearing up very deliberately, when she saw an enormous grey huntsman spider near the sink. Her hand flew to her mouth, stifling a scream. Ryan stood close enough behind her that she could sense his grin.

He reached for a glass in the overhead cupboard and brushed against her to grab an envelope from the pile of unopened bills. In a swift action, he placed the jar over the offending creature and slid the envelope underneath before deftly tipping it over, spider safely enclosed. When he tried to head outside, the sliding door caught; another job that needed doing. Kate leant against the kitchen bench, her arms folded, pressing against the tight anger in her chest. A minute later, Ryan came back inside, whistling, leaving the screen door open. He grabbed his bulging, frayed satchel, and leaned in to give her a kiss. She turned her face away and felt the brush of his lips on her cheek. He headed for the front door, keeping his voice light. 'Have a good day. Don't worry, we'll talk when I get back tonight.'

Standing in the chaos of the kitchen, Kate put her hand in the pocket of her old cardigan and touched the photo again, feeling its creases and frayed corners. Glancing around to see if the kids were there, she quickly slipped it into the zip up pouch in her handbag and squared her jaw when she recalled how Shelley hitched up with Daryl the minute they broke up.

Kate looked at the time. She shoved Edie's photographs into an envelope and zipped them into the front of her bag. After school drop off, Kate looked forward to making herself a cuppa, shutting herself in the office and getting her clients' notes up to date. Most of all, she wanted to touch base with Bea and check if she was okay, see if Artemis had turned up.

'Edie, Noah. Clean your teeth, pack your lunch boxes, and get your shoes on. Now!'

Kate sighed with relief when the two of them ran past the gate to the sound of the warning bell. She wondered whether to treat herself to a café coffee from that new revamped place, then remembered Ryan's casual confession this morning. Perhaps she needed to cut back.

Kate's phone pinged. A message from Georgie.

Coffee with the girls. Usual spot?

3

TORI sat in her kitchen, checking the online orders when her phone lit up with Georgie's message inviting her to coffee. The familiar chime announcing the arrival of the first customer to the shop drifted through the window. It was Indigo's first morning opening the shop alone and Tori had to stop herself from heading over and checking up on her new employee.

She punched a text to Georgie. *See you soon.*

Tori stood in her bedroom and rummaged through the trunk where she tossed clothes still to be sorted. She had sent Indigo to her first deceased estate sale last week. Her discerning eye resulted in some real gems. After declining to get help for so long, the decision to employ Indigo had been easy. It was not only her experience with furniture restoration, but her self-containment. Tori remembered seeing Indigo for the first time, her strong gaze, firm handshake. Unlike the first two candidates, she wore casual clothes. Black jeans and a soft grey shirt unbuttoned at the top. Not a skerrick of artifice about her.

Tori pulled out a beaded belt and some chunky jewellery. The best part of her job was getting first dibs at the gear. Nothing like a great outfit to disguise a crappy mood or colour a bleak day. Tori tugged on her jeans. They were so loose. She threaded the belt through the loops and pulled it tight over the hollow of her belly, frowning at herself in the mirror. Now with Indigo to help, it was time to reduce her hours and look after herself better, spend more time with Leo. She reached for the tiny origami chest, caressed it then placed it back on her bedside table where she could see it when she woke up.

As far as Leo was concerned, he didn't have a father. He occasionally asked, but Tori always shrugged, determined to keep Leo protected from her past. She longed for a glass of wine but had promised herself not to drink until after five and to have a couple of alcohol-free days every week.

She crunched down the gravel drive and decided to drop in on Indigo, just to say hi. Tori waited till Indigo finished serving a couple of customers. 'Hey, I'm just heading next door with a couple of friends to check out the revamped cafe. Leo's at school.'

Indigo looked up. 'Cheers.'

When she turned away to serve two young women, Tori shifted her brown canvas tote to her other shoulder, pulled her gaze away and headed to the café.

The minute Georgie saw Tori she stood up and beckoned, all smiling lipstick lips, fluttering, pink-tipped fingers. 'Hasn't the new guy Vincent done a fab job of refurbishing.'

New guy Vincent. Tori made a note to set ground rules early just in case he got any ideas. Heading past the tables towards Georgie, she absorbed the ambience of the place. It had been transformed with large golden sunflowers beaming from green fields; blue-summer skies stretched across the walls. Wooden chairs and benches were tossed with comfy, coloured cushions and small vases on the tables were filled with daisies. Her resistance softened. This new guy had a knack for décor. Maybe he was a decent sort and their businesses could collaborate and create a vibe for the Martha Street precinct. It would benefit both of them.

Tori slid her tote along a bench just as Kate arrived looking frazzled.

'Hey gals. I really need a strong coffee today. How did you manage to get away from your shop? There seems to be quite a crowd there.'

'Thanks to you, I've finally employed someone to help. It was the right call. Indigo owns her own minivan which is a great help. I have so much more time to create individualised orders for loyal customers.'

Tori poured herself a glass of water and glugged it down. Kate raised an eyebrow, waited till Georgie was distracted and mouthed, 'Are you okay?'

Without catching Kate's eye, Tori nodded. 'It's been bloody hectic. Hopefully, now I have help, I can slot in some time to look after myself better.'

After an approving scan of the café, Georgie pressed her manicured fingers to her mouth and blew them both a kiss. She tapped a fingernail on the timber before pointing it at Tori. 'That new lady in your shop, she's hard-line. One of the other mums went to buy a dress, added some accessories, and she wouldn't negotiate a discount.'

Tori felt herself colour, wanted to say something to defend Indigo, then wavered. 'Georgie-girl, if you want something, just ask me and I just might consider a bargain for a friend.'

Kate frowned. 'Hey, I might have to take you up on that. Ryan's resigned from Soul Sounds, so he only has his music students now. Since his brothers got the band together again, I hardly see him.'

Georgie looked like she was about to say something, then her hand flew to her mouth, eyes wide. The pause that followed stretched a fraction too long. She smiled too brightly. 'Ryan is such a talent. I *adore* his music.'

Tori nudged Kate's foot under the table, while Georgie continued, her voice babbling now. 'The new guy, Vincent, is just divine. Have you met him yet?'

They both knew Georgie didn't want an answer. She was all flapping hands and bubbling enthusiasm again. 'When I peeked at his website and saw he caters as well, I arranged for him to do Gaby's birthday party next weekend. You are both still coming?'

She looked stricken. 'You haven't forgotten?'

Tori enjoyed the extravagant parties at Georgie's place. The no expenses spared, glitzy events with free alcohol where Georgie and her husband, Mark, spent time networking for his financial planning and her wedding planner businesses. 'Wouldn't miss it for the world, Georgie-girl.'

It seemed like a good time to order. They each picked up a menu. The tattered cardboard ones had been replaced by slick solid plastic; the options printed over a background featuring Vincent Van Gogh's sunflowers. On cue, a young bloke, bearded, early to mid-thirties approached. 'Hi. Welcome to Vincent's. Can I get everyone a drink? Something to eat while you chat?'

4

KATE'S heart did a somersault. Somehow, Vincent's easy spontaneity reminded her of those early days with Ryan. A time when they were still besotted, days without commitments when they talked about everything. The blooms on the walls pulled Kate back to the day he drove her to Nobby and Allora to see the sunflower fields. Standing inside his embrace, watching a breeze ripple through a field of gold, she'd never imagined happiness could be pinched out like a candle, leaving only the drift of memories behind. Staring hard at the menu with its familiar artwork, she realised Vincent was right behind her.

'I've always been a huge fan of Van Gogh. Very grateful to Ma for my name. It was the obvious choice when I finally opened my very own café.'

After he disappeared with their orders, Georgie winked. 'He suggested a gourmet barbeque for Gaby's birthday.'

Kate glanced at Tori and noticed her eyebrows raised a notch. Trust Georgie to have a catered party for a ten-year old and lift the bar beyond anyone's reach. Vincent returned, balancing an impossible number of plates on his forearms.

Kate sipped the coffee, felt it course through her body. He made a good drop. Tori plunged her fork through the white cloud of a lemon meringue pie, releasing the tangy smell of citrus. Her shirt slipped off one shoulder and Kate was shocked to see collarbones stick out like a bird's wings.

13

'Wicked,' said Tori before stirring three sachets of sugar into her espresso.

A steady stream of takeaway coffees and food headed out the door while the pleasant hum of background chatter surrounded them. Vincent's place was doing well considering he had been here less than a month. Then Kate remembered last night. She'd promised to ask around about Artemis. 'One of my old clients came in after hours yesterday, distressed because her cat was missing.'

She pulled up the picture on her phone, showed the others. Georgie used her fingers to enlarge the image. 'Send it to me, I'll put up a couple of posters around the school.'

Looking at Artemis brought last night back in vivid detail. Kate's brow furrowed. 'I hadn't seen this client for ages. She stopped coming after her husband went to prison. He was sentenced for assaulting someone, rendering them unconscious. The irony is that he had been assaulting his wife for years with no consequences.'

Georgie finished her coffee. 'Why doesn't she just leave? I mean, if Mark hit me, I'd pack up, take the girls and go.'

Tori's mouth was a thin line. 'Why is it up to her to leave? Why should he just be able to get on with his life while she is forced to start afresh somewhere? It seems to be the wrong way around.'

'I'd rather start afresh than stay and get beaten up.'

Kate sighed. 'It's just never that easy.'

It was hard to imagine Georgie giving up everything and starting afresh. Kate deliberately changed the topic. 'How are the plans for the Music Fest going?'

'I was hoping to get Vincent to donate some vouchers for the raffle. It would be great publicity for him.'

Looking at the crowd here today, it didn't look like Vincent needed too much publicity. Kate drained her last mouthful of coffee and her eyes landed on the glint of Georgie's huge diamond engagement ring nestled secure behind the platinum circle of eternal love. Yearning tugged at her. Ryan had always been dismissive about the whole wedding business. She imagined a ceremony on a beach;

Byron where they met. Bare feet, the sound of the surf, a simple ceremony followed by prawns and champagne.

The scraping of Georgie's chair interrupted her thoughts. 'I better head off. We're taking the girls to the Whitsundays next holidays, and if I don't book soon, we might just miss out.'

Tori grabbed her tote. 'I better get back to the shop, give Indigo a hand.'

Kate paused a bit longer. A holiday, that was what they needed. Not their usual camping, but somewhere with a kids' club, meals included, deck chairs around a pool. It might be the very thing to help them reconnect and find that spark again.

5

EVIDENCE of last night's storm was visible in the puddled path strewn with branches and debris, and the turbulent rush of brown water down overflowing gutters. The air was thick with the scent of frangipani, water droplets glistening like diamonds on their long, leathery leaves. Kate fumbled with the key to her clinic when her phone rang.

Balancing her handbag and briefcase, she pressed the phone to her ear and used her shoulder to hold it there. 'Hello? Kate Simpson.'

There was the sound of a scuffle. The phone slipped from Kate's shoulder and landed on the pavement cracking the screen. 'Bugger,' she muttered under her breath, pushing the door with her foot and heading inside.

After dumping her gear, she realised the number was Bea's. Kate's gut dropped like an elevator plunging twenty floors. She scrambled to redial, listened to the dial tone until it rang out, then punched the number in again. No response.

Sweating, she made quick notes in Bea's file and called the police. There was not enough detail for them to respond. Kate paced, then rang Dorothy's Place again. It was a relief to hear the efficient voice of her old supervisor who promised to assign a case worker to Bea and to follow up.

For the rest of the day, Kate listened, probed, and guided her clients through grief, anxiety, relationship breakdown and the multitude of stressors that led them to seek support and counselling.

Before leaving, she tried to call Bea one more time, wondering if Artemis had turned up. No response. She crossed her fingers the feline had fled the oncoming storm and hidden somewhere till it was over. Animals were like that.

After Kate logged off, she sat for a moment, closed her eyes, and let her mind tunnel back to her childhood. She landed inside that night. It was so long ago. It was yesterday. Raised voices, slammed doors, smashed plates. Her mother calling out, *Kate,* her voice high-pitched and urgent. The numbing fear, drenching rain, the sudden bang of a door startling Kate, so she dropped her bear, Ted, whose pleading eyes stared out from the long grass while their car screeched away trailing a spray of dirty water.

Heart thudding, Kate opened her eyes again, the computer screen blank and the phone silent.

✦

After Kate picked Edie and Noah up from school, she delayed the witching hour chores and headed to the small front room she used as an office. Tonight, she planned to run her holiday plans past Ryan. Hang the cost. They needed a break. Family time to chill and reconnect. Scrolling through resorts, her mood dropped. It cost so much more than she imagined. Even the places offering special deals would stretch their already tight budget. Ryan would almost certainly suggest some camping spot, probably remote with cold running water if they were lucky. There would be a full day sorting out the camping gear, preparing food and precooking. By the time they arrived, she would be exhausted and expected to help with setting up. Holding tarps, handing him pegs, while he faffed around trying to remember how it all connected. Perhaps she would make something nice for dinner then drop her plan casually into the conversation after the kids went to bed.

Kate scrolled to another place on the Gold Coast when she heard a piercing scream from the lounge room and stood up so fast the chair crashed to the floor. She imagined broken limbs, blood. *Get a grip,* she muttered and stepped out of the office. Noah was red faced and yelling and Edie clutched the unicorn she had adored since she was a toddler, its rainbow mane matted and dirty, the tail held aloft in her other hand. The movie was loud and unwatched in the background.

'Can't you play for five minutes without fighting?'

Her heart pounded in her chest.

Tears streamed down Noah's face. 'I didn't mean it.'

Edie stood feet apart, clinging to ghoulish evidence of the crime. 'He broke it!'

The front door opened and Ryan stepped in. He raised an eyebrow, placed his guitar inside the door and ventured a smile. 'Big day?'

He held a bottle of champagne and Kate blinked away tears, wondering if she had forgotten some occasion while Edie and Noah ran over to greet him. Ryan stood loose-limbed and relaxed, his boyish brown hair flopping across his face. 'Today is a day for celebration. *The Bloody Blue Bloods* have officially been signed up for a series of gigs playing at The Spiked Echidna as well as a few weddings.'

He made a bow and Kate willed herself to hug and congratulate him but all she could see was every evening and weekend spool away from her grasp. Ryan stepped forward and embraced her. She felt her arms reach around to hug him back. Edie vied for Dad's attention. 'Dad! Dad!'

Ryan handed the chilled bottle to Kate then bent down and picked Edie up to swing her around.

'Me too!' screamed Noah, lifting sweaty hands in the air.

Ryan swept him up in his other arm and swirled them both in a full circle like the Hills Hoist on a windy day. Kate watched the three of them so happy. 'Well, I guess I should get going with dinner.'

Ryan reached over and tried to waltz her around the room. 'Let's keep things easy and get pizza. It's a celebration after all.'

Noah and Edie yelled out. 'Pizza! Pizza!'

Ryan winked at Kate. 'I'll get the crew sorted. You sit down with a glass of bubbles, and I'll pick up a couple of pizzas.'

He blew her a kiss. She turned away and didn't respond.

The house was finally quiet. Kate and Ryan stood in the kitchen with pizza boxes stacked next to the bin and dirty plates lined up in the dishwasher. Ryan shared the last of the bubbles between them. 'Come on, let's sit down.'

He reached for Kate's hand and led her to the sofa that sighed when they sank into its worn pillows. The bubbles made her head fizz. He should not have signed up for all these gigs without running it past her first. Ryan ran his arm along the length of sofa behind her and leant back, the evening infused with Fiona Boye's fingerpicking blues. Kate softened and slid closer to him. He gave her shoulder a squeeze. 'The Spiked Echidna has signed the band up for Friday nights and we have three weddings lined up over the next couple of months.'

His body pressed warm against hers, transporting her back to the days where she had travelled around the countryside with him whenever she could, helping with gigs and music festivals. The Murphy boys adopted her into the family like the sister their mother longed for. Late nights, blurred by cheap wine, raucous with loud humour and tall tales. Ryan's foot kept a steady beat to the music, his fingers played along her arm. She wondered if it would lead to more when his foot gave hers a playful nudge. 'Now that I have a steady income, we might even get a fence built so the kids can finally get the dog we promised them.'

She jerked away from him. 'A dog? I don't have time to look after a dog.'

'The kids will look after it.'

'For the first couple of weeks.'

Ryan's eyelids drooped; he raised one hand in a helpless gesture. Kate deliberately changed the topic. 'It's great news about the band.'

She reached for the final mouthful of now flat champagne on the coffee table. This was the right moment to mention her holiday plans, while Ryan was high on his own success. She swallowed the lukewarm liquid. 'I think we need a holiday. A proper holiday at a resort with a kids' club, a pool, meals included. Someplace where others do the work, and we can relax and spend time together.'

There was a long pause. Ryan left his hand on her shoulder, but he tensed. 'A resort? That seems extravagant. I know I'll be earning again but why don't we find a great camping spot. Away from everything, everyone. We'll keep it simple, get the kids to help with setting up. It'll be so good for them to be in the bush with us.'

Kate's throat tightened. 'Why can't we splash out a little now you're becoming a name on the music scene? Surely, we can loosen up a bit.'

She shifted away from him. 'I've had a look at some places online that sound perfect. Some even have great bargains for families.'

The music had finished a little while ago. There was a long, weighty pause. Ryan hunched over and rested his head in his hands while she stared at the curve of his back.

His voice sounded muffled, disappointed. 'Can we talk about this again later?'

Kate pressed her lips together. She stood, gathered the dirty glasses, and walked to the kitchen without saying another word.

6

IT was the Thursday before the Schneiders' party on Saturday and Tori was up early sitting at the kitchen table adding the final touches to a dress for a customer. There was something special about that quiet, still space before the noise of the day intruded, when it was possible to get lost in your thoughts without interruption. She heard sounds coming from Leo's room. The creak of his bed, the bang when he opened his wardrobe door and it hit the bookshelf. She smiled to herself, imagining him pulling on his uniform, all elbows and knees, the last remnants of the child he still was with glimpses of the teenager he was rapidly becoming.

'Morning, Mum.'

'How about I make you some brekky.'

'Nah, it's okay. I can do it.'

The clatter of a bowl and a spoon, the crinkle of the cereal packet, the flick of the kettle, the sound of the toaster being plunged down. She was proud of how independent he was becoming but anxious he was growing up so fast.

Only two more buttons to cover with fabric. Tori leant back into her task. Leo placed a mug of instant at her elbow, sloshing some onto the table. Then he brought her a couple of pieces of toast with a scrape of peanut butter. 'Hey, kiddo. Spoiling your Mum.'

Leo stood close. 'Mrs Potts said breakfast is the most important meal of the day.' He paused and chewed his lip. 'Promise you'll eat it?'

Tori shifted in her seat, aware of the press of the timber on her buttocks. She really needed to make more effort with self-care. It would be easier now with Indigo working at The Treasure Chest. 'I promise, buddy.'

He grabbed his own bowl and headed back to his room. She called to his back. 'And thanks.'

There was a knock at the door. Tori froze. Her first instinct was not to respond. She rolled her tight shoulders. It was probably Indigo who was driving up to Nambour today to pick up some furniture. Maybe she had forgotten something and was dropping past before heading off.

Another tap, a bit louder this time. 'Hello? You home?'

It was Kate. Tori's shoulders relaxed and she opened the door. 'Hey, what's up?'

'I just thought I might take you up on that offer of a dress from your collection to wear at the party.'

'Sure, give me a tick and we'll head over to the shop.'

Tori grabbed the toast, quietly poured the instant down the sink and washed the evidence away. She called out. 'See ya, Leo. I'm heading to the shop.'

Glancing at the now cold toast in her hand, she added. 'Love you.'

It was fifteen minutes before opening time at The Treasure Chest. Tori made sure she left the closed sign up and headed to a rack of dresses against one wall.

Kate looked around, wide eyed. 'It's all changed. It looks amazing. When do you get the time to do it all?'

'It's Indigo. You were absolutely right about getting help around here. It was the best decision I ever made.'

Tori paused and showed Kate an antique elm sideboard. 'Indigo spent a few hours doing restoration work on this piece. She transformed it.'

Kate ran her fingers along the timber. Tori chewed her lip. 'I was wondering…'

She stopped. 'Never mind.'

'Wondering what?'

'Do you think it would be okay if I asked Indigo to the party?'

'Of course, you should invite her. Georgie won't mind. There'll be so many people there, one extra won't matter.' Kate linked her arm through Tori's. 'What's she like?'

'Different, but easy to get along with. She works hard, only talks when she has something to say, and keeps her opinions to herself.'

'I'm looking forward to meeting her. I'm sure she'll have fun. The party will be a blast. The Schneiders' parties for their daughters always are.'

Kate wiggled a finger the way Mark did. 'Nothing but the best for my million-dollar babies.'

Tori shook her head. 'They don't spare the expense.'

'I suspect Georgie is thrilled to have her two girls. She had such a tough time falling pregnant. Remember the years of IVF she endured?'

Tori thought about her own unplanned pregnancy and shivered. The letter was hidden under her smalls where Leo wouldn't find it.

Kate ran her hands along the dresses and paused at a 1950s daisy print.

Tori pulled a couple more dresses off hangers and held them up against Kate.

'This one will show off your waist and bring out the colour in your eyes.'

Kate felt the fabric, put her face against it. 'It's a dream. I just don't know if I can pull it off. How about this one with the daisies?'

'That's one Indigo worked on. You go try them on while I open. Grab me when you've decided. I'll take twenty percent off.'

'Are you sure?'

'Positive. You seemed a bit stressed the other day. A new dress will be like a tonic.'

Half an hour later, Tori rang up the dress at the old-fashioned cash register. She watched customers browse the racks, run fingers along the fabrics, touch the scarves, fondle the jewellery. She enjoyed seeing a customer's eyes light up with an unexpected find. There was real pleasure seeing them stand taller wearing the perfect outfit or drooling over a piece of bling.

Kate left, shoulders back, swinging the bag with her new dress inside. Tori rang Georgie who sounded breathless.

'Of course, you should invite Indigo,' she gushed. 'The more the merrier.'

Kate drove home and parked on the kerb, grateful to see Ryan's car was gone, and relieved he had taken the kids to school. It was his turn after all. When she got out, she stood at the front gate hanging forlorn off one hinge and stared at their house. It was now the only one in the street that stood dilapidated and defiant in the face of progress. She frowned. The place really needed a lick of paint. She recalled her last conversation with Ryan about organising some maintenance. *Do you think we should look at tarting the place up a bit?'* Ryan had shrugged. *Nah. I'm happy to live in the worst house in the best street.*

Kate glanced across the road at Georgie's large, white place, absorbed its wrought iron fence, solid gate and tidy garden beds and thought back to when they first met. It was after Kate had signed up to the local gym on one of her missions to get fit. Georgie was in her spin class and chatting afterwards, realised they lived in old Queenslanders in the same street. Soon afterwards, Mark and Georgie bulldozed their place and built a sparkling new one with a pool and enormous bedrooms for the children they planned to have. Kate remembered Ryan had been horrified when the old home was demolished.

Time was slipping away. Kate hurried inside, rolled her eyes at the cereal boxes and bowls scattered across the bench, then decided to ignore them. Instead, she pulled her new dress out of the brown bag with The Treasure Chest emblem embossed in black on the front. Tori had folded it between soft sheets of tissue paper that rustled when Kate let them fall away. She held it against herself, then slipped it on. It was gorgeous. She loved the soft fall of the fabric against her skin, the way it swished against her leg. With regret, she changed back into

her work clothes, hung the new dress on a padded hanger, and went
to work.

7

SATURDAY was one of those blue-sky, crisp days, perfect for a party. Early autumn had tempered summer's intense heat and humidity to a mellow warmth, just right for Kate's new dress. She spent time getting ready, enjoyed a long shower, straightened the kinks in her hair, and applied a touch of make-up. Finally, she slipped on the dress, paused to admire her reflection, smiling at the daisies dancing across the fabric. She hoped Ryan might notice her efforts.

She stepped into disarray and clenched her jaw when she saw Ryan strumming away on the guitar, the swim gear not packed. 'It's the party, we're running late. Is it too much to ask you to pack the towels and togs?'

'Chill. It's rude to turn up exactly on time.'

'No risk of that.'

Kate stepped into the laundry and jammed towels, togs and Noah's goggles into the swim bag.

Finally, only forty-five minutes late, they were ready to leave. Edie wore faded shorts and a sparkly tank. Kate frowned and opened her mouth to suggest Edie change into her new dress, when on cue Ryan gave her that look. The *Just leave it, Kate* one he used when he anticipated her launch into a confrontation with Edie. Then Ryan disappeared inside again.

'What now?'

Kate wondered if she should just leave him behind and head across the road with the kids when he emerged with the pool noodles.

Kate shook her head, and they walked across to the Schneider's place, today festooned with balloons and streamers with music threading its way out to the pavement. Edie and Noah ran ahead, stopped to stare at the huge glittery banner announcing, *Happy Birthday Gabriella.*

Ryan hummed along to the music and held the front gate open for Kate. She walked past, narrowed her eyes at him, then saw the table on the front deck sagging with parcels. She deposited Gabriella's gift, hoping that the handbag with reverse colour sequins was the right choice.

Georgie swept out to greet them, all froth and soft pastels with a large bloom in her hair. 'Oh, don't you just adore a great party?' She glanced at her reflection in the hallway mirror, smoothed her dress. 'I arranged a magic show for the kids downstairs, so grab a drink and relax out the back.'

She indicated the sweeping staircase with her hand while holding a champagne flute aloft, but Edie and Noah had already disappeared. Georgie giggled. 'My way of ensuring we have a bit of adult time around the pool before the kids jump in.'

'Sorry we're late,' mumbled Kate, glaring at the ridiculous way the pool noodles drooped out of the bag slung over Ryan's shoulder.

Georgie laughed. 'You are not the last.' She bent closer, one finger to her lips. 'We actually have one more family arriving. Well-known celebrities. They were enrolling their kids at the school while I was there sorting things for the music committee. I invited them along, thought it would be a relaxed way for them to meet other kids and parents.'

She winked and blew Kate a red lipstick kiss before proffering her cheek to Ryan. She beckoned. 'Come on and get a drink. Vincent will sort you out. He has a couple of fellows walking around with nibbles too.'

Georgie swept ahead. Kate followed Ryan and the bag of swimming gear. Her hand flew to her mouth when one of the pool noodles brushed the elaborate flower arrangement on the side table. Ryan kept moving, the noodles bobbing behind him.

There were several clutches of people around the pool with conversations in full swing. Kate glanced with longing at the bar. At that very moment, Vincent presented one of the women with a foam topped pink drink in a martini glass garnished with a maraschino cherry. She vowed to try one of those before the evening ended and wondered if Tori had invited Indigo.

Georgie sipped her champagne and smiled at Ryan. 'By the way, we were thrilled that you were able to do Fridays at The Spiked Echidna and help out with those functions. I'll keep your boys in mind for future gigs if things go well.'

With that, Georgie drifted back to her other guests, leaving a trail of Chanel Number 5 in her wake. Kate narrowed her eyes at Ryan. 'What was that about?'

He looked past her. 'She's quite something that Georgie.' He bent and kissed Kate's cheek then headed to the pool, grabbing a beer on the way. Her nails bit into her palm while she watched him dump the pool bag, before joining a huddle of dads. She snatched a flute of champagne from a passing tray and scanned the chairs around the pool and on the lawn until she spotted Tori on one of the cushioned lounges at the far side. Beside her was a lean dark-haired woman who must be Indigo. Tori stood up when she saw Kate and beckoned her over. She took a deep breath and downed some bubbles.

'Hi, Tori.'

'Hi, Kate. You look great in that dress.' She turned to Indigo. 'It's the first one you transformed. Doesn't it look fab?'

Kate held the skirt out with her free hand, nodded at Tori. 'I really appreciated that discount too.'

Indigo's forehead creased. She shot Tori a quick look.

Kate bit her lower lip, then held out her hand. 'By the way, I'm Kate, the local shrink. It's lovely to meet you.'

She used one hand to toy with the skirt of the dress. 'And I just adore this dress.'

'Glad you like it.'

Kate snapped up a couple of cheese pastries making the rounds and popped one in her mouth. After pulling up a chair, she kicked off her sandals and stretched her legs in front of her. 'It's so good to just sit down and relax.'

Georgie emerged from the house and joined them. Tori gestured with her arm. 'Georgie, I'd like you to meet my new partner at the shop, Indigo.'

Indigo raised a hand in greeting. 'Quite a place you have here.'

'We built it ourselves,' gushed Georgie. 'If you like, I can take you on a tour of the inside later.'

'All good. Thanks, anyway.'

Indigo stood. 'Anyone keen to share a joint?'

There was the sort of silence you could drive a semi-trailer through. Tori sat very still not looking at anyone. Kate nearly choked on her second cheese pastry. She stared at Indigo while her nostrils took her back to the earthy skunk of a hundred festivals. The diesel fug of smoke merged with the beat, sweaty bodies swaying, cheap wine in plastic cups. Georgie's voice sliced through sharp with fury. 'How dare you bring drugs to my home. There are kids here, families.'

Indigo raised an eyebrow, the offending item between her fingers pointed across the water. 'Maybe you need to explain it to that lot.'

Four men stood flushed with alcohol, their voices bawdy and raucous. Kate couldn't help thinking that Indigo had a point, but Georgie refused to look. She pointed her manicured finger to the gate. 'I want you to leave.'

Indigo seemed non plussed. 'Jesus. Don't get bloody worked up. I asked. Tried to be friendly and share. I'm not dealing, just having a casual smoke.'

She took her time, walked over to where she had dumped her black canvas bag and slung it over one shoulder. Tori got up to go as well. Kate suppressed an urge to defend Indigo and reassure Georgie. Indigo pointed the joint at Tori. 'Stay. I'll let myself out.'

There was an awkward gap where Georgie stayed standing, her arms crossed, cheek muscle twitching. Kate wanted to step in and make everything alright again. A young fellow was heading towards them with a tray of feta beetroot blinis, and she stood up quickly to intercept him, hoping to defuse the tension with food. She miscalculated. The fellow tripped and Georgie wore a tray of feta, beetroot, and Kate's champagne.

Kate's hand flew to her mouth 'God, I'm so sorry.'

The sight of perfect Georgie standing blotched with beetroot, while feta and oil dripped from her hair, unleashed something in Kate. She started to giggle. Mortified, she repeated herself. 'I really am sorry.'

Georgie's voice was shrill. 'My dress!'

Tori stepped up. 'Let me donate one. I'll bring a few around during the week and let you choose.'

She looked away but not before Kate noticed the smirk of a suppressed laugh.

Kate grabbed Georgie's arm. 'Hey, let's get ourselves a couple of those pink cocktails.'

She turned to Tori. 'Another drink?'

Tori shook her head and looked poised to leave. A chunk of feta slowly slid down Georgie's bob and landed in a white splotch on her shoulder. She flicked it off. 'Aagghh, that is so disgusting.'

Kate and Tori didn't dare look at each other in case they started laughing. To their relief, Georgie giggled. 'I might just have a shower.' She pointed a finger at Tori. 'It had better be a gorgeous dress,' then disappeared.

Kate paused a moment. 'Indigo seems nice. Don't worry about Georgie.'

Reaching for her empty flute, she headed towards the bar, skirting the pool and squeezing past the clusters of people chatting and drinking. Just before she joined the queue waiting for drinks, Kate stopped suddenly.

Standing apart from the crowd, stood a slight blonde, hair caught up in a ponytail. She shifted from one high heel to the other, her sky-blue dress shimmering. There was a rockstar quality to the way her bracelets jangled along her arm, the way she wore her glittering strapless dress. She turned and faced Kate, her profile silhouetted against the burnished sky. Kate sucked in her breath. Her glass slipped from her hand, shattering on the tiles. The noise echoed. Every head turned towards Kate and those closest edged away to avoid the tiny splinters lying in wait for bare feet. *What the hell is Shelley doing here?*

8

MARK emerged with a dustpan and swept up glass while one of the other dads herded children to the other end of the pool. Soon the air filled with squeals and splashes again.

The last contact Kate had had with Shelley was the wedding invitation. Shelley and Daryl's society wedding. Kate had not even bothered to respond. Not so much as a card of congratulations. Shelley's dream of a big, white wedding, her happily ever after, had come true.

Georgie reappeared, wearing a pale green dress this time, her hair pulled back sixties style in a matching bandana. She had even found time to change her lipstick to a glossy pink. Georgie's polish lost its shine next to Shelley.

'Kate, I want you to meet Shelley Brady.'

She gave a knowing nod. 'You know, Daryl Brady's wife.'

Kate willed herself to say something. How did you greet a friend you grew up with when you parted on such bitter terms nearly thirteen years ago?

Georgie took advantage of the pause in conversation. 'They bought the big place in Coorparoo Heights. You know, the one with the great views of the city from the front deck?'

Georgie was babbling, her hands fiddling with her pearls.

A pebble sat on Kate's vocal cords. Her eyes darted around the pool, wondering where Daryl was. She had not seen him in person since he became a football star. The Brady wedding had been written up in the social pages of the local paper and was given a spread in the *Women's Weekly*. His face often appeared on the news when they discussed sport. Kate had a sudden urge to retrieve her handbag, to rid it of the photograph she had slipped in there earlier.

Shelley opened her mouth to say something, then Georgie looped arms with her, like they'd been buddies for years. 'Kate's daughter Edie will be in the same class as your Melody.'

Kate's eyes fixed on Shelley's dress and absorbed its intense blue. It reminded Kate of taut summer skies and lazy, sticky days at the beach with melting ice creams. She thought with a pang of those sleepovers at Nanna's beach place where little sleep had happened. Nights on a lumpy mattress where Shelley's sunburn felt hot under a shared sheet while they read books in the tented dark with torches and shared secrets, promising to be best friends forever. Kate still remembered the first time she pleaded with Mum if Shelley could come to Nanna's at Bribie. They spent every summer there after that.

Kate remembered exactly where she was when she read that Daryl was snapped up by the Wild Dogs. Standing in a queue at the Norman Park newsagency, reading the headlines while waiting to pay for the paper. He was engaged to Shelley by then. His every move, including marriage to Shelley, was fit for speculation.

'Shelley, it's been a long time.'

Georgie's voice was a squeak. 'So, you know each other?'

Without looking at Georgie, Kate nodded. 'You could say that, although it's been a while.'

She bit her lip, could not bring herself to look Shelley in the eye. 'We must get together over coffee or a drink.'

Shelley wore a glittering diamond the size of a large pebble on her left ring finger and her dress was special. It must have cost a fortune. Kate waited for Shelley to say something, half expected her to turn on her pretty spiked heels and walk away.

The noise of drunken laughter and loud chatter echoed around them. Kids splashed in the pool and shrieked at each other.

Kate wished Georgie would give them five minutes alone. Her

forced smile did little to hide her disappointment that Kate already knew the Bradys. 'I guess I'll see you back by the pool.'

To Kate's immense relief, Georgie slipped away.

The air loosened. Kate blinked back tears, remembering how they'd clung to each other after every summer holiday when it was time to go back to their own homes. She leant forward. 'Shelley, you look incredible.'

Shelley did not quite meet her eyes. 'It's a relief to see a familiar face.'

Her voice had not changed. Still the hint of apology, uncertainty that belied her fame. The knot in Kate's chest loosened a little. She shifted closer to her old friend and whispered, 'Just be careful. Georgie has a heart of gold, but she will use that celebrity of yours if it raises funds for her precious school committee.'

Shelley gave a small nod. 'I figured.'

Their heads stayed bent together as the squeals and laughter around them faded. Kate felt something fall back into place between them. 'I was just on my way to get one of those pink ladies. Can I get you one? I've been assured they're delicious.'

Shelley shook her perfect blonde head. She stared down at her manicured toenails peeping through the front of her high, strappy sandals. 'I might just have a sparkling water, thanks.'

Kate was surprised. Who drank mineral water at a party with a free bar? Then again, Shelley was new around here. She might want to keep her wits about her.

'One mineral water it is,' she responded. 'You head over to the other side of the pool and join Georgie and Tori.'

Shelley hesitated. She had always been shy. Or maybe she was just thinking about their childhood. Her own rags to riches story that made her seem like a princess to the media. Kate smiled encouragement. 'I won't be long, promise.'

Kate joined the queue at the bar again and glanced at Shelley's retreating back. There was a loud splash and Kate was slapped into the present by a drenching. One of the men had jumped into the pool fully clothed followed by loud cheers and laughter. She stepped back a moment too late and a familiar face emerged from the water. She ducked behind the potted fern at the front of the bar, only to watch Daryl shake his head like a dog emerging from a bath.

'What would you like?'

She was at the front of the queue and turned away, relieved Daryl had not seen her. She found herself face to face with Vincent and blurted out, 'One sparkling water and a pink lady thanks.'

She watched the deft way he added ingredients, shook and mixed her drink, his movements fluid and elegant. He handed them to her and smiled. 'Enjoy.'

Kate scanned the pool and the BBQ before she headed back to the girls. Vincent and the young fellow started tending a huge selection of skewered and marinated meats, the smell of herbs and garlic pungent.

Kate handed Shelley her drink then took a sip of her own. It tasted divine. Tori was hunched over, sitting at the edge of her seat, arms clenched around her knees.

Shelley hesitated, blushed. 'Victoria? Do you remember me from uni? I just love your shop. I often scroll through your website.'

'Don't call me that. It's Tori.' Her voice was curt.

Shelley shrank back. 'Sorry, Tori.'

Kate wanted to say something, was surprised at Tori's rudeness. She held back and took a long sip of her heavenly drink instead.

Then Tori stood. 'I don't feel so good. If you don't mind, I might find Leo and head off.'

Georgie touched her on the shoulder. 'Can I get you a glass of water? Some Panadol?'

'No. Thanks anyway.'

Tori walked away without turning around. Kate half stood up, to follow and check on her friend, but changed her mind and edged closer to Shelley. She kept her voice light, wanting to paper over the tension left in Tori's wake. 'What's Daryl up to these days?'

Georgie's eyes were wide. She leaned in close.

Shelley toyed with her bracelets. They caught the light and made her sparkle. 'He's had a few injuries and needed several surgeries. Two knee reconstructions and a shoulder reconstruction.'

She glanced around and lowered her voice. 'It's not official yet, but he needs to retire. He kept putting it off, but I think in the next month or so it will be official. For now, he's injured and on leave.'

Georgie put a hand over her mouth. 'Oh, the poor man. How awful for him.'

Shelley stared at the ground, one toe making little jabs in the lawn.

Kate pulled her knees up onto the lounge, hugged them to her chest. 'What's he planning to do?'

'Start his own business. Do some coaching at the local club and maybe some promotional work.'

Kate stole a look over at the pool and suddenly felt nauseous. There was Daryl, now changed into dry clothes, standing next to Ryan. She shifted back to the edge of the lounge partly hidden by the shrubs, polished off her cocktail then snatched up another champagne. The alcohol did little to dull the anxiety that danced in her gut.

The rest of the evening passed in a blur of too much food and booze interspersed with fuzzy conversation. Kate couldn't remember any of it.

It was close to midnight when they trudged home carrying Edie and Noah between them. Kate's head throbbed and she downed a few glasses of water. She decided to surprise Ryan and slip between the sheets naked. But when she joined him in bed, he was already asleep.

Her thoughts went back to Daryl and a warmth pooled in her pelvis. She glanced over at Ryan curled up next to her, tried to remember the last time they'd had sex. Her fingers reached down to touch herself and she came quickly, then rolled away from him and closed her eyes.

KATE woke with a pounding head, her mouth thick and stale. Sunday morning sounds and smells drifted through the house: the clatter of cutlery, Edie giggling, the aroma of freshly brewed coffee. So different from her own Sundays growing up.

She pulled the doona over her head, curled up and followed the ugly trail of her thoughts to a dark place. That night where her Mum gathered the courage to leave, Kate sat in the back of the car, staring out the window. Dad stumbling outside silhouetted in the porch light, the rain making him indistinct and wavy. In the moment before the car jerked to life, Kate pressed her finger to the window and blacked him out. It seemed like hours later they pulled up at Nan's where Kate curled up in the small, safe bed with sheets that smelt of lavender, and slept.

A week later, they returned. The new girl next door came over when she saw Kate in the front yard searching.

I'm Shelley.

She still remembered Shelley's eyes when she handed over a damp Ted, one of his eyes hanging loose. A silent witness. Shelley's unspoken message, *I know, I understand.* They stared at each other; eyes full of things unsaid. Their pact not to speak about it.

A loud bang jerked Kate to the present, set her pulses racing. Then Ryan's voice. 'Shh, Mum's having a lie in.'

Kate dragged herself into the shower then peered in the mirror. Brownish, wavy hair, grey eyes, a scatter of freckles, the weight of worry etching lines into her forehead.

She rummaged through her jumble of clothes, wishing she was more like Georgie with her slick, coordinated wardrobe. One where everything fitted, and you created a look. She slipped on her red shirt dress and on impulse, grabbed her lipstick, stretched her mouth into an 'O,' and coloured her lips bold. What she needed was a bit of bling, something to sit in that hollow of her neck. She fumbled though the wooden box where she kept her jewellery and swore she would clear it out and get organised. Then at the bottom it winked at her, the tiny silver ball studded with stars and a crescent moon. A little gift she bought herself when she learnt she was pregnant for the first time. The only acknowledgement of the tiny life growing inside her. After she lost the baby, she packed it away and forgot about it. She held it up against the V of her dress. It was perfect.

In the kitchen, Kate found Ryan helping Noah pour batter into the pan of melted butter. It sizzled and Noah pulled his hand back when it spat. A chaos of dirty dishes was piled in the sink and some batter dripped in slow motion onto the floor. Ryan turned and gave her one of his endearing lopsided grins. He used his free hand to pour a coffee into her special sunflower mug and held it out without leaving his pancake post.

'Morning, beautiful. Big night with the girls.'

He turned away and she gratefully wrapped her hands around the mug and took a sip. 'Thanks. I need my caffeine this morning.'

He slid odd-shaped pancakes onto a plate and turned off the gas. 'Quite the party last night.'

Ryan handed the plate of pancakes and a bottle of maple syrup to Noah who headed to the table to join Edie. Kate hugged her mug, inhaled its scent. 'Well, you know the Schneiders.'

Ryan rolled a pancake and ate it in two big bites. 'That new bloke, what's his name? The footballer? His ego matched his biceps.'

Kate swigged black coffee just in time to stop herself defending Daryl. It tasted bitter. Trust Ryan not to know who Daryl was. Everyone knew Daryl Brady. She had a sudden image of her fingers knotted through his dark chest hair, his hands firm around her buttocks, wondered what her life would have been if she'd stayed with him.

Ryan ran water into the pan and it hissed. He left it sitting there with the pile of dishes. Such a bloody mess for a few pancakes. She plonked herself on one of the bar stools, her legs unsteady, and wondered if she should tell Ryan about Shelley. She hesitated, and the moment slipped between the folds of another ordinary morning.

Ryan walked away, leaving the detritus of his kitchen efforts in his wake. 'I'm heading to another rehearsal with the boys after lunch. Just want to make sure things are on track for our first gig this week.'

The casual way he announced his absence hit a raw nerve and reminded her of Georgie's casual comment. Kate slammed her coffee onto the bench. She needed a day off. A day just to faff, read her book and gather her thoughts. It was just not fair.

Edie paused, a chunk of pancake halfway to her mouth. Noah looked down onto his plate, his sleepy time hair in tufts at the back of his head. Kate's words exploded out of her mouth. 'So, you plan to be away every weekend then?'

Ryan opened his arms in a helpless gesture of surprise. 'Hey, I thought you'd be pleased that I'll be earning a regular income now. How about I cook tonight?'

'How about you start by clearing this up.' Kate gestured to the kitchen with one hand. She knew that she should stop and count to ten before she said anything else. Instead, she blurted out, 'How come Georgie knew about your gigs before I did? I thought we usually talked about big changes, discussed how it might work for the family, for me.'

Her voice had gone up a notch. In the strained quiet, uneaten pancakes went limp. Kate regretted her outburst. She always vowed her own children's home would be calm and relaxed. No raised voices, broken plates, slammed doors, or fear curled inside wardrobes.

Ryan leant back against the sink, his arms stretched behind him, hands resting on the bench, oblivious to the splodge of pancake batter pooled there. 'You always supported my music. You assured me that you wanted to work and were pleased that I stayed home and managed the kids, while you studied and set up your practice. You knew that one day I would start playing gigs again.'

'You never even discussed it with me. I was presented with a *fait accompli* with no plans about how we would arrange our family life around this new schedule of yours. You obviously had time to discuss it with Georgie but couldn't take a moment out of your precious band rehearsal to run it past me.'

Ryan stayed infuriatingly calm. He picked up a tea towel and wiped his fingers clean of batter. 'Mark is the financial planner for The Spiked Echidna. They decided to have live music on Fridays and maybe other nights if it goes well. Your friend Georgie recommended me. She then suggested that I could play for some of those toffy weddings she arranges.'

Kate's anger deflated, a tight balloon losing air. She slumped over the slosh of coffee left in her mug and stared at the smear of red on the rim. Georgie should have run it past Kate first. Georgie was, after all, *her* friend, not Ryan's.

'I see.'

She lifted her old handbag from the bench, the leather creased and cracked, the insides bursting with crap. 'I just need to sort out a few things at work.'

She walked to the front door, her heels punching the floor with each step. She felt the family's eyes follow her, swiped the car keys from the side table and put her hand firmly on the knob. 'I'll see you later.'

She pulled the door shut behind her, harder than she intended, and enjoyed the satisfying shudder of timber. The old Corolla was dented, faded and on its last legs. Kate snapped her seatbelt into place, backed out of the driveway then put her foot hard on the accelerator, wondering what model Daryl drove. She imagined Shelley beside him with a perfectly organised Gucci handbag poised on her lap.

Kate headed to her clinic to write up her notes and finally get herself up-to-date for the week ahead. Somehow there were never enough hours in the week to get on top of the paperwork. Once inside, her shoulders unclenched. In the small tearoom, she poured herself a glass of water, found an old packet of paracetamol and swallowed two of them before logging onto her computer. Her work diary bulged with scribbles that really should have been transcribed into her clients' files weeks ago.

She opened Bea's file first, hoped she had found Artemis, and wondered whether the case worker had been around yet. Kate dialled Bea's number and was just about to give up when she heard Bea's voice. A hesitant, 'Hello?'

Kate swallowed, made her voice calm, professional. 'Kate Simpson. Just touching base to see how things are going.'

Bea hesitated. 'It's sorted.'

Kate heard a male voice somewhere in the background and was filled with a mix of anger and dread.

'Are you back together?'

Bea whispered. 'Don't worry. Things have changed.'

Kate's fingers tightened around her phone. She wondered how to keep Bea talking.

'I gotta go.'

Silence.

Kate's heart hammered. Things were not all right. She called the police, hoping Bea had gone ahead with the domestic violence order.

'I want to report an incident. I'm concerned about a client's safety.'

'Do you want to make a statement?'

Kate shared information about her concerns and requested they flag her address for any calls for service. After she hung up, the room felt stuffy and small. The police did not act on gut feelings whatever the guy's history.

Kate's thoughts turned to Shelley and the party last night. Her fingers hovered over the computer while memories muscled to the fore. She found herself back inside the day Daryl invited her to Cairns for a week after four crazy months together. She missed a week full of tutorials and lectures. She even neglected to hand in one of her assessments for the first time. Nothing mattered except being with Daryl. He confided that his mother ran away when he was ten years old and left him with a father who searched for consolation in the arms of other women. His son was a hindrance and a disappointment. There was a fated balance to their relationship. He without a mother, she without a father.

Up north, he drove to Palm Cove where they stayed at a resort. When she realised she had forgotten to bring her contraceptive pill, she suggested getting condoms, but he scoffed, telling her that he did not want any barriers between them, that she was too beautiful. He loved her too much to compromise their pleasure. He guided her hand inside his jeans, and she relented, the week passing in a hedonistic blur of champagne, prawns, and sex. She would wake up to find him straddled over her and go to sleep curled up in the curve of his hard embrace. A month later, her breasts full and tender, she bought the pregnancy test and watched the faint second line emerge. She indulged in a small silver pendant, embedded with a crescent moon and stars, but didn't tell anyone her secret.

Kate ignored the subtle changes in her body and focused on her psychology degree, her career and future mapped out in her head. Daryl continued to ravish her at least every other night and she started to fall behind.

One afternoon, while she finished her overdue essay, he slid in behind her, slipped his hands under her shirt, and squeezed her breasts hard.

'You're hurting me.'

He ignored her, snuck his finger inside her pants and pushed against her.

When she resisted him, he pulled her onto the floor and rolled her over. 'Come away with me. We'll move up north, away from everyone. Just you and me, babe.'

He grabbed her under the hips, thrust himself inside and she cried out with pain, wanting him to stop. 'I want to stay here and finish my degree.'

He pushed harder, his fingers pressing into her skin. 'Forget about it, I'll look after you now.'

He grabbed her pendant, then moaned and collapsed on top of her. She felt raw inside and worried she might throw up.

Kate recalled her nineteen-year-old self in front of her lecturer.

'I've decided to head up north with my boyfriend.'

Her lecturer, Prof Blackwell, looked up, forehead creased. 'Kate, that's so sudden. Is everything alright? You were our highest performing student last term. Why would you throw it all in?'

Kate stood mute, unable to explain herself and the urgent need to be with Daryl. She didn't want to tell Prof she was pregnant.

Prof Blackwell gazed at her, tried to be helpful. 'I would be happy to arrange a deferment. Let me sort out the paperwork so that you can come back if you change your mind.'

Kate became aware of a clench in her gut, a warmth between her legs. 'I'm sorry,' she mumbled as she stumbled out of the office.

Once in the corridor she clutched her belly. The baby gripped Kate's uterus until she doubled over in pain. Alone in the white-tiled cubicle, the baby let go and slid away.

Kate flushed the foetus away, the swirls of blood dying the toilet water red with loss. She curled up in bed, the cramps so severe she wondered if she would ever be able to stand again. She refused to let Daryl in, declining to tell him what was wrong, unable to face his demands for sex. By the time she had recovered, he was seeing Shelley. It was a betrayal that still felt tender, like pressure on a bruise.

Kate stared at the screen in front of her, fingers still on the keys. She noticed a message on the work phone and pressed to listen. The male voice was rough. 'Butt out, bitch.'

Her pulses accelerated. *Jake?*

It was Bea's number. She needed to report the call to the police. Make sure it was documented. A noise at the door made her freeze. *Who would it be on a Sunday?*

The door opened, the familiar jingle indicating someone had come in. She glanced around frantic, wondering how she could escape. The glass window in the consulting room only opened a few centimetres. The tearoom window was tiny. She was trapped.

'Hello?'

It was not Jake.

She glanced around the door into the waiting room. Her fingers flew to her throat. There he was, as if conjured by memories. Her gut contracted. Older, a few distinguished flecks of grey but Daryl, nonetheless.

He smiled at her in a familiar way that bridged thirteen years.

Kate stayed fixed to the spot her legs weak. 'What are you doing here?'

Her voice sounded high pitched.

He sat in a waiting room chair and dropped his head into his hands, shoulders hunched. She moved towards him, then stopped herself from putting her hand on his arm the way she normally would. His voice was low. 'I wanted to see where you worked. I saw a car out front and wondered if it was you.'

He looked up briefly, still hunched forward. 'You look gorgeous, Kate.'

She crossed her arms, hesitant to acknowledge his compliment.

He continued, after a big sigh, 'I want to start seeing you.'

She sucked in her breath and stepped back, ready to tell him that she was hitched with children and to remind him that he was too.

He continued, 'I want to sort myself out. We are having difficulties in our marriage and it's my fault.'

10

TORI sat on one of the kitchen chairs, her knees pulled up under a long tee. She regretted inviting Indigo to the party. People here were weekend piss pots not potheads. If only she had gone home with Indigo and not hung around until Shelley and her husband, Daryl, arrived. Leo wandered out, lanky and dishevelled, wearing his Totoro pyjamas. It made her heart trip.

'Mum, can I have a doughnut for brekky?'

'How about we go out together and have brekky at the café next door?'

He paused next to the doughnut box and looked at her, ran a hand through his hair. 'What about the shop?'

'We have Indigo helping now.'

Tori thought about the incident yesterday. Chances were, she'd seen the last of Indigo. The best bloody thing that had happened to Tori in years and she'd stuffed up.

'Tell you what, I'll sort something. We might have dinner at the new burger place if Indigo can't help out.'

Leo turned away. 'Can I have a doughnut then?'

Tori bit the inside of her mouth and nodded. He grabbed the last two and headed back to his room.

'Just grab a plate,' she called after him, but he had already shut the door.

Tori heard the distinctive chime from the shop. Her legs slid from under the stretched tee, and it crumpled like old skin. Indigo was here, no doubt to get her stuff and get as far away from The Treasure Chest and Tori as possible. She hurried to her room, pulled on some jeans, finger combed her hair, and readied herself to face Indigo.

'Just heading to the shop for a sec,' she called to Leo.

A minute later, she crunched down the gravel drive and saw Indigo through the window with what looked like a folded tea towel holding black curls off her face.

She had her back to Tori, shifting a mannequin to the display window. It didn't look like Indigo was going anywhere.

Tori stepped inside, hesitant. 'Morning. Are you alright?'

Indigo edged an antique sideboard onto an old piece of carpet and attempted to drag it across the floor. 'Not really. Can you give me a hand?'

Tori put her muscle behind Indigo's and pulled hard. When the piece was in place, Indigo wiped the sweat off her brow. 'This is an incredible piece. An Art Deco French style walnut sideboard. It should fetch up around eight thousand.'

Tori stared at the dark timber that curved in a thick coil around the top. 'You are planning to stay then?' She knotted her fingers together. 'I'm sorry about the party. Georgie can get edgy, but mostly she's fun.'

Indigo shrugged. 'If I want a smoke, I'll go and have one.'

Tori slumped into a nearby chair and gave a shaky laugh. 'It got worse after you left. A couple I knew from uni turned up. Not sure if you know Daryl Brady?'

Indigo leant against the sideboard. 'Can't say I do.'

Tori fidgeted with her hands again. 'You're lucky.' She stood up and ran her hands along the sideboard, admired it from several angles. 'You know that's more than I've ever managed to sell a piece for.'

Indigo wiped the mouth of her water bottle, handed it to Tori. 'You could probably get more but I prefer not to be greedy. I figure I'm bloody lucky to be doing something I love. I get to spend my time faffing with timber and making stuff. Can't put a price on that.'

'How about I leave you here in the shop for a couple of hours this morning while I treat Leo to brekky then give you the afternoon off to work on those pieces you brought back from Nambour?'

Indigo folded her arms. 'It's a deal.'

✢

On Monday morning, Kate scanned the cars pulling up at the school and hoped she was early enough to miss Shelley. She wondered if Daryl was the sort of dad who came to school drop-off on the first day. Kate's hands gripped the steering wheel, and she nearly shaved someone's side mirror off. If the Bradys were there, she would just act casual and be herself. The image of Daryl in her waiting room jarred with everything she had read about him. Every story included at least one shot of Shelley and their angelic daughters. Daryl, the sporting hero and family man.

Parents stood clutching takeaway coffees, relieved to pass their offspring into the care of others. There was the hint of autumn with some students already donning the grey jumper. Kate saw a park and pulled in. Before the kids were out of the car, Georgie ran up to the window and waved Kate over. Frankie and Gaby stood on the pavement, their hair done in elaborate French braids.

'Hi, Kate. Hi, kids.'

Georgie's lips were ruby red and matched the trim on her dress and shoes.

Noah pressed against Kate's legs, shy in public. He saw one of his friends and tore himself free. 'Bye, Mum.'

A large black Land Cruiser pulled into the recently vacated park behind her Corolla. The door opened and Shelley stepped out wearing skinny white jeans, high heels and a baby blue shirt knotted at the front. Gold bracelets jangled off one arm and her long blonde hair was pushed back by a pair of sunglasses. She dived into the car to pull out three shiny new schoolbags. Cherub-faced blonde twins hopped out followed by an older pouting girl. Kate's breath caught. She tried to forget about Daryl in her waiting room and beckoned to Edie. 'Why don't you walk Melody over and help her settle in?'

She watched the two girls head towards the quadrangle. Edie

scruffy, one sock around her ankles, Melody slouching, her new satchel half dragging on the ground. Kate leant closer to Shelley. 'Edie is a force to be reckoned with. Don't worry about Melody.'

Georgie bent down to Gaby and Fran and straightened a collar, then tucked a loose hair behind an ear before kissing them on the cheek and shooing them along. She beamed at Shelley. 'We are so thrilled to have your family move here. If you need a hand with anything, please ring. Mark and I are happy to help.'

She slipped her hand into her bag, pulled out a couple of business cards and handed them over.

Shelley had a protective arm around the twins. 'Thank you.'

Kate watched Georgie hurry away and found herself alone with Shelley and her two youngest. 'Are you right? Do they know where their classroom is?'

Shelley's grip loosened. 'Yes. We were given the tour last week and met the teacher.'

She knelt and gave them a hug, one in each arm. She held them for a long time. 'See you right here the minute school finishes.'

Kate noticed Shelley's eyes were wet. 'How about we have a coffee? There's a cool new place called Vincent's a few blocks from here, on the corner of Martha Street.'

'That would be lovely.'

Kate arrived first and waved Shelley over. She tottered over and kicked her spiky heels off the minute she sat down. 'It was such a relief to see you at that party. A familiar face.'

'It was a bit of a shock seeing you there. It caught me by surprise.'

Kate bit her lip, looked down at the table and brushed thoughts of Daryl aside. 'I want to say sorry. I know it's been years, but I should have come to your wedding.'

'Honestly, the whole day was such a blur. There were so many people, it didn't matter. I'm sorry too. I can understand why you were angry.'

Shelley fiddled with the little sachets of sugar. 'But I honestly thought it was over between you two. Daryl came and said you'd dumped him, that you never wanted to see him again.'

Kate thought back to those awful weeks after the miscarriage when she avoided Daryl completely. It didn't matter now. That was in the past. Shelley didn't need to know about the pregnancy and miscarriage.

'You know, it's okay. It was all a long time ago. Truce?'

They hooked their little fingers together, the way they used to do when they were buddies at school. A hip waitress hovered, and they ordered coffees.

'So, what brought you to this area. Did you move here for work?'

Shelley fiddled with the sugars again. 'It was Daryl. He's taken the injuries hard and misses playing. He wanted a fresh start.'

'And how are you with the move?'

'I miss my friends, my job. The kids were happy at their old school. I'll find my feet. It just takes time I guess.'

The coffees arrived and Shelley wrapped her hands around a mug. 'Georgie is so kind. She really made us feel welcome.'

Kate sipped her coffee. 'Georgie has a huge heart, but it's fine to say no if she starts leaning on you to help out at the school.'

'To be honest, I'd be happy to help. It will be a great excuse to get out of the house, to be involved and get to know everyone.'

'Well, just don't say that to Georgie.'

Kate glanced at the time. 'I'm sorry to rush off but I need to get to work. Just ring or text if you need anything. It can take a while to settle somewhere new.'

The minute Kate arrived at her clinic and unlocked the door, her phone started to ring. She looked at her screen. It was Daryl. She had to tell him it was impossible for her to see him. They had been a couple. Shelley was her oldest friend.

'Hello.' Kate kept her tone brusque.

'It's so good to hear your voice, Kate.'

'I'm sorry, Daryl, but I can't see you as a client. It would be inappropriate.'

There was a pause. She thought he might have hung up on her.

'I just need to talk to someone. I can't trust anyone to be discreet. You have no idea what it's like to be in the public eye. Everyone wants a piece of you. When you fuck up, they want to see you fail, then splash it in the papers. The next big headline. I trust you. Please help me.'

Kate leant against the doorframe. Surely there were no rules about chatting to a friend. He sounded so desperate.

Kate swallowed her uncertainty. 'How about we have lunch at a café? But it is strictly as an old friend. I want to be clear, I can't see you as a client.'

There was a long pause and Kate thought she had made him angry. That he'd hung up.

'Is that a yes?'

Kate's hand went up to her throat. 'I'll book somewhere and let you know.'

11

'DON'T forget your lunch!'

Tori chased Leo's pushbike down the gravel drive, waving Tupperware. Brakes squealed as he pulled up. Breathless, Tori caught up with him and stuffed the box into the satchel on his back.

'Ta.'

He took off again, standing up to pedal, and disappeared around the corner. Tori stood and watched long after he was gone. She missed those days when he reached up to her sticky fingered, a little kid dependent on her for everything. His increasing independence made her ache.

Inside, Tori boiled the kettle, plunged the toaster down, and logged on to check her website. She answered emails, then checked the flurry of orders since yesterday. At this rate, she might need another employee. The toast popped. While she was poised with the knife, her phone rang. There really was not a moment's peace when you ran your own business. Success could be bloody hard work.

'Hello. Victoria?'

Tori's knife clattered to the floor.

'How fucking dare you ring me.'

'Victoria, please. I just want to meet him and get to know him. I don't want to take him away.'

She wanted to hang up on him but didn't dare.

'Have you told him about me?'

'Told him what? That you wanted to pay for a termination?

Maybe I should mention that to him.'

'I was only thinking of you.'

'Jesus. Spare me.'

She leant against the counter, her legs shaking. 'What do you want from me?'

'I've changed. I'm not the same person I was. We won't tell him the truth, I promise. We both have secrets we'd rather not air in public. You were hardly a saint.'

Tori's back slid down the kitchen cupboard until she was sitting with her legs pulled up to her chest. She gripped the phone so hard she half expected the glass to crack. 'Please, just leave us alone. You and I, we made a mistake, it's in the past.'

He responded with silence.

A moment later, he ended the call.

Tori sat, drained like she had run a marathon. Her mistake had been going back, telling him she was pregnant. That evening twelve years ago burnt a deep ugly scar into her memory. Hearing his voice dredged it back from an archive she'd allowed to grow dusty.

'I'm pregnant.'

His panicked face, the way he grabbed her and pushed her up against the door.

'I'll pay for a termination. Just get rid of it.'

His breath stale, liquored, one hand on her throat, his power absolute. She knew in that moment that she would keep the baby and raise it alone. Leave. Not tell anyone.

'Don't worry. I'll sort it out.' Her voice was croaky under the pressure of his palm.

He banged her head against the door, the metal handle jamming into her side. He threw her onto the floor. Her head throbbed where it hit the tiles. It took a few minutes for her to orientate. His face was close to hers and his eyes wild with panic. 'Promise me you will get rid of it. It was just a night out, we can forget about it, no one need ever know.'

She turned her face away, refusing to give him the satisfaction of eye contact. She willed him to release her so she could get the hell out of there and never see him again. Her voice was muffled. 'Just let me go, I won't breathe a word, ever.'

He was not listening to her anymore. He pressed against her and for one terrifying moment she thought he might kill her, but he had used one hand to unzip his pants and held his hard penis like a weapon. She made up her mind to give him what he wanted, then get the fuck out of there. He straddled her, pushed her denim skirt up her hips and pushed into her, panting, while she stayed outside herself until he was finished.

While he stumbled to have a piss, she pulled down her torn skirt, and stood, unsteady. There was no time to lose. Her head pulsed and she wondered whether that tiny bean inside her had survived. Half sprinting, half hobbling to her car, she prayed it would start first time.

Second turn of the key, it grunted to life. Tori saw him stagger outside, saw his raised fist and his mouth move. She pressed on the accelerator and drove off without looking back, confident he wouldn't pursue her.

And now, here he was. She really thought that she would never see him again and wondered if it was too late to report him. She dropped that thought as quickly as it came into her head. There was Leo to think about.

After Kate booked a café at West End and shot Daryl a text, her throat constricted. When she logged on, she realised her hands were trembling and wondered if it was too late to ring and cancel, to tell him it was a mistake. The screen blurred and the jingle of the door announced the arrival of her first client.

Kate pushed herself away from the desk with both hands and stood up, reassuring herself. She was having lunch with a friend who was distressed. That's all.

Her first client was new. A suited woman. Kate pulled herself back into the moment, reached out to shake her hand, was shocked to find that her own was sweaty. She suppressed the urge to wipe it on her skirt.

The last client of the morning cancelled in the last minute. Kate arrived at the café first and found the reserved table in the far corner. She kept looking at the entrance. She half hoped Daryl would change his mind yet was curious about the details, with a voyeuristic desire to catch a glimpse of his real life behind the gloss in the papers. When he walked in, her heart skittered along her ribs. He was exactly on time.

She half stood and waved. 'Over here.'

He seemed smaller than she remembered. He pulled out a chair and sat down, elbows on his knees, face in his hands. Seeing him so broken, she wondered why she had she been so anxious about talking to him.

The lunchtime hum of the café fell away while she absorbed the slump of his shoulders and the way his eyes failed to meet hers. She resisted the urge to touch his arm and offer comfort, instead allowing the silence to fill the space between them until he was ready.

When he spoke, his voice was low. 'Thanks so much for seeing me.'

He stared at the floor. Kate watched him, aware that he was a man unaccustomed to revealing his inner world with its inevitable doubts and fears. He shifted in his chair but kept his head in his hands. Kate sat very still, aware how the spaces between words were often more important than anything that was said.

A young fellow came over and hovered, ready to take their orders. Kate frowned at him and gestured for him to come back later. She hoped he had not recognised Daryl.

Daryl's head remained flexed forward, his eyes fixed on the grain in the polished timber floor. 'I'm a terrible husband. I've failed Shelley.'

Kate was thrown by this admission and thought back to the party where Daryl had appeared so confident. She remembered the way he emerged from the pool to cheers and laughter. The centre of attention. He seemed like another man entirely today.

'Do you think you are being a little harsh on yourself?'

He gave a small shake of his head. 'I had an affair. Shelley doesn't know.'

His eyes suddenly looked up and penetrated hers. 'Please, don't say anything to her. I want to start afresh, become a better husband, and better father.'

Kate pictured Shelley in her tottering heels, her blue eyes full of trust, and her first thought was that of course she had to warn Shelley. After all, women had to stick together and support each other.

His voice sliced across her thoughts. 'I mean it. I want you to swear you won't tell anyone. It would kill my career.'

Kate thought about Shelley's whispered confidences at the party, Daryl's injuries and forced retirement. She reached over and touched him lightly. The contact was an electric charge up her arm and she withdrew her hand, shocked. His eyes landed on her bare ring finger, and she dropped it into her lap. She heard herself make a promise using the same words she used to reassure her clients. 'Anything you tell me will remain confidential.'

Daryl stared at her without blinking. Kate felt suddenly protective of Shelley and did not want her friend to be hurt but felt trapped by her promise. She repeated the words, even while regretting them. 'I meant it when I said that anything you tell me remains a secret between us.' She looked away.

The quiet between them felt uncomfortable this time. Kate picked up the menu and held it up like a barrier between them. 'Let's order, shall we?'

12

IT was Tori's morning to open the shop, and she was running late. That bloody phone call. She used a washer and cold water to rub her face, let water drip down her neck and back. Still damp, she slid into a sombre black dress, then pulled her hair back so hard it stretched the skin on her face. The gall of him to make contact after all this time.

When she left Melbourne a second time, just over a decade ago, she made sure to bury her past and left no traces of herself there. She was determined her son would not be tainted by the circumstances around his conception.

After the rape, Tori had gone back to her Aunt Jean's house in Prahan, where she lived alone. She stood in the shower until the water ran cold, scrubbed herself until her skin was raw. Now that she had decided to keep the baby, she was terrified it wouldn't survive. Two weeks later, when she woke up nauseous, her breasts still tender, she dared to hope. Staring at herself in the mirror with fresh eyes, she noticed how dark her nipples were, placed a hand on her still flat belly and imagined she felt the flutter of a heartbeat. A quiet, expectant joy that the bean had survived the violence following his conception after a loveless, drunken coupling. Tori whispered to the bean, determined its life would begin not with its conception but the day she chose motherhood, the day she started to make decisions about her body and her life. Her child's life would be filled with love.

Tori stared at herself in the mirror, at jutting collarbones and hips, hollow cheeks. She was determined not to let him get under her skin.

She hurried to the shop with barely a minute before opening, grateful there were no early customers waiting at the door.

Tori panicked when she heard the door jingle, relieved when she realised it was Indigo. 'You're early.'

'Morning. I had a few ideas and wanted to rearrange a few things if you agree.'

'Be my guest. You seem to have a knack for it.'

A shadow passed the door, a male silhouette, his outline hazy through the stained glass. Tori paled and shot behind the counter, pretending to look at something behind the velvet curtain of the change room. The bell gave its characteristic jingle. A throaty male voice asked about a piece of jewellery in the window.

Tori breathed through the tight gap in her throat. She had to get a grip. She made a show of sorting out some dresses that needed to be re-hung while Indigo talked him over to a more expensive piece before ringing it up.

After he left, Indigo turned to Tori. 'What the fuck was that about?'

Tori kept hanging dresses, didn't look at Indigo. 'Nothing.'

'Bullshit. You shot into the back like a bloody human cannonball.'

The dress Tori was holding slithered off the hanger and formed a puddle at her feet. She would have to tell Indigo sooner or later. The bastard might just come into the shop. 'Leo's dad rang me the other day. He wants contact with his son.'

'Did the two of you separate on bad terms?'

Tori's mouth went dry, and the churn of nausea started. It had been a long time since she had been punched by that overwhelming sense of panic. She forced her breath to slow, clenched and unclenched her toes.

Her muscles softened while her heart eased its drumming in her chest.

Tori shrugged. 'Just a casual shag.'

'So, why now? What does he want?'

'That's just it. I don't know why he is suddenly all keen to see his son.'

'What do you want?'

'I just want him to go away. To leave us alone. I haven't told Leo yet.'

Indigo gave a low whistle, leant back on the counter, folded her arms. 'If he comes in here looking for trouble, he'll find it.' She paused. 'I think you need to tell Leo though.'

Tori turned away. The words evaporated whenever she tried to breach the topic with Leo. Only last week, he dropped a casual comment. 'Will I get to see my father one day?'

'I have no idea where he is. No idea how to get in touch.'

Only now that wasn't true anymore. He was right here, breathing down their necks. Tori glanced over at Indigo who was busying herself moving furniture. She seemed so solid and sure of herself. It was a relief she knew about Leo's father. Somehow, it made Tori feel safer.

13

KATE was driving back to the clinic when her phone rang. She pulled over.

'Hello?'

'It's Bea.'

There was an edge of hysteria to her voice.

Kate pressed the phone to her ear. 'Where are you? Are you alright?'

'I really just rang to say thanks for everything.'

Her voice cracked.

It felt like someone had pressed something cold against Kate's skin. A gut feeling that things were not right. 'Where are you, Bea?'

'I'm leaving. I rang to say goodbye.'

'Wait, Bea. Let me help you. I'll arrange some support. Just hang tight, tell me where you are.'

Kate was talking too fast. Yet not fast enough. She was speaking to a dial tone.

She meant to ask about Artemis. That cat stared at her from the posters around the school, outside Vincent's, at the White's Hill Woolworths.

She floored it to the clinic, rang the afternoon patients and apologised, explaining there was an emergency. She left a message that she would reschedule their appointments. Then she rang the police and reported the call. Finally, she rang Dorothy's Place. The woman at the other end was brusque and promised to document Kate's concerns.

Kate knew it was foolish but drove to Bea's house, heart pounding. Fifteen minutes later she pulled up outside an ordinary timbered home with an old car parked on what might once have been a front lawn. The shutters were half down and looked like threatening, lidded eyes. Kate shivered and wondered what she had expected to find.

She parked outside, patted her pocket to check her phone was there. Jake's threat, *Butt out, bitch,* echoed in her ears.

She looked up and down the empty street and pushed open the gate. It creaked and she jumped, glancing over her shoulder before making her way up the cement path cracked open by grasses and weeds.

Then Kate saw the front door and screamed. She backed away, nearly tripped, righted herself and ran.

Kate bent over at the gate, doubled over, and vomited. She retched and retched until there was only green bile and mucus.

The shocking image of Artemis crucified on the door seared into her brain. She shuddered afresh, tried to block out the legs outstretched, a nail through each paw, head lolling glassy eyed. And then the bloodied knife jammed in splintered timber above. She retched again, her throat raw. Wiping her mouth with her sleeve, Kate fumbled with the gate. Her dress caught and ripped. She was shaking like a leaf. That was when she saw her.

An older woman standing distraught near the letterbox, bent forward, like she was walking into a stiff breeze. Kate reached out and touched her arm. It was bony beneath the threadbare cardigan. When Kate glanced down, she saw the woman's apron and shoes had blood splats on them, saw her lips move, her voice a croak. 'I thought he'd left.'

Kate nodded, couldn't find the words to explain Jake had been in prison and was only recently released. The woman leant on the letterbox, tugged her cardigan around herself. 'I heard her scream, rang the police, went over and saw…'

She faltered, helpless. 'It was too late.'

Kate realised she still had her hand on the woman's bony arm, then felt it slide away as the woman crumpled to the pavement. Kate slid down beside her, could taste the scent of blood in her nostrils. The woman rocked back and forth, her head in her hands.

'She loved that cat…'

The words were lost as she started to weep, huge gulping sobs that racked her body. Kate moved closer, feeling numb, the hard concrete of the pavement digging into her hips. She whispered, 'Did you see what happened to Bea?'

The woman looked up, hazel eyes filled with tears that slid down the creviced landscape of her cheeks. 'She left maybe an hour ago. Drove off carrying just her handbag. I called out, but she just kept moving like a ghost. She didn't respond.'

The strain of Kate's heart made her breastbone ache. She helped the woman to stand, keeping a firm hold of her gnarled hand.

'I'm Kate.'

She fumbled in her bag, handed the woman her card.

'Peg.' She slipped the card into the pocket of her apron.

Kate noticed a dusting of flour between dried spots of blood and thought she might vomit again. She looked away. 'Call me if you need anything. Let me know if Bea comes back or if you hear from her.'

Kate called the police, nearly choking as she reported the incident. She called Dorothy's Place, an unreality to the words. Finally, she texted Georgie.

Please take the cat posters down. Don't ask.

She drove home.

14

KATE longed to talk to Ryan when she got home, but he had his first gig in a few of hours and was such a mix of anxiety and nervous excitement, she couldn't bring herself to tell him. The minute she walked in the door he was edging to go and barely noticed her.

'Wish me luck, beautiful.'

He dropped a kiss on her cheek, didn't even notice the vile smell of fear and vomit in his eagerness to be off.

'And don't wait up. I'll be very late.'

She lay awake for hours and wished she had a sleeping tablet. Ryan crept in at two in the morning, his clothes reeking of stale beer and greasy food. When he finally crawled into bed wearing just his jocks, she lay very still, pretending to be asleep, not interested in listening to a blow-by-blow account of the gig.

In the morning, Kate sat at the dining table with a half-eaten yoghurt in front of her, surrounded by piles of sheet music, unopened mail, and a game of Cluedo, abandoned before the final revelation. The place was a tangled mess of loose ends, chores, and unfinished business.

Noah and Edie spooned cereal into their mouths, the only sound the clink of spoons against bowls and the scuff of Noah's feet swinging back and forth against the leg of his chair. Kate frowned at the time. Ten minutes before they needed to leave. It was Ryan's turn to do the drop-off today. He finally emerged, his hair towelled dry, the top of his tee shirt wet, his eyes dark-rimmed from lack of sleep.

She stood and discarded the yoghurt. Ryan hugged her from behind, put his chin on her head. She stayed stiff and didn't respond.

'I wish you'd been there. It went so well. The audience loved it. In fact, we've been invited to play some gigs up the Queensland coast, a short tour. I'll be away for just over three weeks.'

His voice sounded so calm and normal that the words took a moment to sink in. 'Three whole weeks? How am I meant to manage everything, and work, on my own?'

She slipped under his arm and snapped at the kids. 'Pack your lunches and get your shoes on. We have to leave in a few minutes.'

They left their bowls on the bench, midst splats of milk and a trail of flakes.

'Sorry, Kate, but it is such an opportunity. The break we've been working so hard for. The usual support band couldn't make the tour. Their lead guitarist fractured his arm, so they invited us to step up. You know how hard I've worked and how I've dreamed about this.'

The day closed in on Kate. If they didn't leave now, it would be a rush. She slid past Ryan without letting any part of her touch him then reached for her bag and phone. It pinged. She glanced at the screen and dropped it like a hot potato back into her bag. Daryl wanted something. Someone was always wanting something from her. It seemed like a month since she sat at that café with him. Was it really only yesterday? The pulses in her fingers buzzed.

Ryan called after her. 'How about I take the kids today?'

'Well, as it is your turn, I'd appreciate it.' Her voice sounded cold.

She took another look at the disarray on the table, emblematic of their shambolic life then burrowed in her bag for the car keys. When she found them and tried to leave, Ryan blocked her way. He crossed his arms, and they faced each other across the grubby quiet between the kitchen and dining area. Ryan's hair was damp, tousled. She stared at the faded Amnesty tee shirt she thought she discarded years ago.

Noah and Edie paused, their satchels on their backs. Noah clutched one scuffed shoe and Kate wondered what had happened to the second one.

Ryan frowned. 'Are you alright?'

She ducked past him. 'No, I'm not all right.' She thought she might start crying if she hung around another minute.

'Hey, it's no big deal. I'll be back in three weeks. The kids will be fine in afterschool care.'

There was no point even trying to talk about Artemis or Bea. No point mentioning that Noah had football training, that Edie and Noah hated afterschool care and that she was fully booked and relied on Ryan to help. 'Excuse me, I really have to go.'

Ryan watched her, his arms still crossed. She thought he was about to say something else. Instead, he bent down to look for Noah's second shoe. Her gaze paused on Ryan's butt while he reached under the lounge.

She wanted to call out good-bye to the kids, but no longer trusted herself to hold it together and left, pulling the door shut quietly behind her. It was only once she was sitting in the Corolla that tears poured down her cheeks. While she backed out, she had to block visions of Artemis, the blood-spattered porch, and Peg's bony arm sliding from her grasp.

Both hands tight on the steering wheel, she headed towards work while The Waif's song, *London Still,* filled the car with reminiscence and sadness, a reminder of the evening she first met Ryan.

A couple of friends invited her to the Byron Bay Blues Fest. They drove up in a battered Kombi van. Tori had left uni and moved to Melbourne. Shelley left uni after she got engaged to Daryl. Kate felt alone, lonely, and jumped at the chance to get away and forget about her study for a few days.

On the first evening, she decided to head off for a swim by herself, to immerse herself in the ocean and decompress. She lay on her back in the silky water, arms and legs outstretched, the gentle swell of waves making her feel weightless. When she felt cold and walked out to get her towel, she saw him. A lean bloke with scruffy brown hair and brown eyes. He had lost something and was scouring the sand with his foot.

'You, okay?' she asked.

He looked up with that now familiar lopsided smile and her heart flipped like a tossed coin.

'My keys. I left them with my towel. Now I've lost them.'

It was dusk, there was little chance of finding them, but she knelt and swept the sand with her hands.

Incredibly, her fingers contacted metal and like magic pulled a set of keys attached to a guitar shaped key ring out of the sand. It felt like fate.

'Fan-bloody-tastic.'

His relief was palpable.

'Hey, let me get you a drink.'

She was still dripping sea water, the hibiscus bikini she bought the day before clinging to her. 'Dressed like this?'

He draped his towel around her, gave her a playful rub on her back and arms.

'Sure, this is Byron. Everyone wears beach gear all the time.'

The sun melted into the sea, and they sat, talked, and drank then shared a plate of barramundi and chips and talked some more. It seemed the most natural thing in the world to let him take her to his tent.

She remembered bracing herself, but they lay next to each other for ages, talking, then not talking. They listened to The Waif's live concert float over them. He lay on his back, his arms crossed behind his head and hummed to *London Still.* Then he leant over and kissed her neck, her jaw, and her mouth. Her heart swelled, her skin prickled with sand and desire. She parted her lips against the pressure of his and tasted the salty warmth of his tongue on her own. He stopped and checked in with her, 'You alright?'

She responded by slipping off her bikini top and reaching her arms around his neck. She let him run his finger down her cheek, across her lips, around her erect nipple. He paused, one hand cupping her breast, and she thought for a terrible moment he had changed his mind.

He turned away, reached in his bag and slipped on some protection. When the tip of his tongue nestled in the fleshy top of her ear she moaned, pulled him towards her and wrapped her bare legs around him.

After the Easter weekend she learned that he lived not that far from her, studied music at The Con and they became inseparable. They moved into a one-bedroom flat in West End and she went to all his gigs. While she worked as a waitress, he supported himself with his music, playing at pubs and bars on the weekends and of course with the band.

She avoided discussing her own childhood and only once mentioned that dramatic stormy night her mother pushed her into the car, to leave and start afresh. A decision that lasted one week. Kate was at high school when her father died unexpectedly, and she deliberately attended classes instead of the funeral despite her mother's pleas.

Ryan's family embraced her. She adored his chaotic, noisy brothers. There was a rude intimacy when sharing a tent while on the road. She joined the Murphy clan on the festival circuit whenever university allowed and spent nights sweating under a canvas in the heat or pressed close to Ryan in a shared sleeping bag in the cold. He insisted she complete her degree, never pressed her with uncomfortable questions about her own past.

Their coming together seemed seamless, inevitable. It never occurred to Ryan to make any public declarations about his feelings and she eventually let go of a romantic dream of wearing a white dress barefoot on a beach, vowing to love him forever. The two of them fitted perfectly into the shape of each other's lives. Kate with her big ambitions tempered by Ryan and his dreams. She would work and he would put his music on hold, stay at home when the kids were little. They would be a modern, happy family, secure and living in a nice house in the suburbs, everything she longed for growing up. It had been perfect except that, somehow, they had lost their way, and it wasn't anymore.

When Kate pulled up at work, she was crying. She pulled out a tissue, blew her nose. Her phone pinged. Daryl again.

I need to see you. Please.

15

THE kitchen table was strewn with fabric, beads, and thread. Tori was doing the finishing touches on a winter dress and had to complete it, even if it meant staying up all night. It was being picked up early in the morning.

The thing was, she didn't mind; she loved her work, her shop, The Treasure Chest, and the deadline of getting a piece ready. Sometimes she pinched herself that this was all hers. It was proof that even during the bleakest times in life, opportunities presented themselves.

It all seemed so long ago now. When she got that phone call from Aunt Jean just over twelve years ago, the call that changed everything.

'Victoria?'

Aunt Jean's voice, sounding weepy.

'Is everything alright?'

'Uncle Raymond died.'

Tori felt the unravelling of a knot she didn't realise was there. Release and relief.

Uncertain how her aunt felt, she didn't say anything, just let Jean talk.

'It was sudden. A heart attack. One minute he was watching the news, drinking a whisky and when I called him for dinner, he was gone.'

'I'll drive down, give you a hand with things.'

'Would you?'

Tori packed up her small car and started the long drive to Melbourne that day. She arrived thirty-six hours later and held Aunt Jean close.

The funeral was a brief bleak affair. It felt good to support Jean through it all. Neither of them mentioned Raymond after he was buried. Tori helped clear out his things. His clothes, the office, and his favourite lounge chair, until it was like he had never been there at all.

'You don't want to hang around with an old woman like me. Go back to Brisbane, to your friends, your new life.'

'There's nowhere I'd rather be. You're my family. I can go to uni anytime.'

And Tori really meant it. It was Jean who brought Tori home after her parents were killed in a head on. Jean who scrimped together enough money to enable Tori to leave, move interstate and study at university. Now, Tori was uncertain she wanted to finish her degree. She felt untethered and found a job at a local boutique that not only sold beautiful pieces but did alterations. Working there, she discovered a talent for fixing up dresses, working with fabric, bringing the beauty out in an old garment. It motivated her to sign up and do a dressmaking course.

Three months later, Aunt Jean had a stroke. She survived for three days while Tori sat beside her in the hospital, squeezing the veined hand with its papery skin. A second funeral, only this time Tori was the one who needed support and there was nobody. Tori was completely alone, now the owner of a house in Prahan.

When she learnt she was pregnant, she sold the house and rang Kate.

'Do you think I could stay with you for a while? Just till I find my feet and a place to live.'

'Of course. Are you coming back to uni?'

'Nah, I've changed my mind. I'll tell you when I get back to Brisbane.'

She placed her hand over her abdomen protectively. 'And can I ask you to please call me Tori from now on?'

A new name, a fresh start. Her new life.

Leo was absorbed playing a game on his iPad, the McDonald's wrappers still on the coffee table, evidence of her capitulation on the way home. Tori knew she would need the evening to finish last minute stitching and was so absorbed in her work that she was only half aware of the tap on the door. The masculine voice caught her off guard. She jabbed herself with a needle and just managed to stop the drop of red staining the dress.

'Hi, Leo. Is your mum home?'

Leo was wearing his old track pants with the stain on the front. The ones she had urged him to discard.

'Mum, it's Mr Brady.'

What the fuck was he doing here?

Daryl stepped inside. The air around Leo vibrated with energy and excitement.

'Mum, Mr Brady started coaching our team. It's pretty cool learning with one of the greats.'

Tori crossed her arms, wondering why Leo had not mentioned it before.

Daryl looked past Leo, scanned the living area, and locked onto Tori. Her first thought was to sweep the McDonald's refuse off the table, to plead that she usually fed Leo organic, fresh food, like it was a call from social services. She hated the way she behaved like her single parenting was constantly under the microscope.

Daryl fixed her with a gaze, one eyebrow raised. She pulled her thoughts into line while he stood all casual, leaning against the doorframe, his chest filling a blue Tommy Hilfiger shirt. He must have doubled in size since those university days. His voice was a confident drawl. 'Shelley mentioned you left university and didn't go back. She found your shop online and showed me.'

'Did you drop around at nine o'clock in the evening to tell me that?'

He shrugged. 'Each of the coaches has been given a couple of corporate box tickets to the game tomorrow night. We've been asked to select our most promising player to take along. I thought I'd just pop in and see if Leo was interested.'

His gaze wandered down to Leo. 'I should have called but I was driving past. The Wild Dogs are playing.'

Leo stood wide-eyed, quivering like a puppy with a bone dangled in front of its nose. Tori stood, arms crossed. She resented being put on the spot like this. Leo piped up. 'I didn't know you knew Mr Brady?'

There was awe in his voice. Before Tori could respond, Daryl took a step closer and put a hand on Leo's shoulder. 'Your mum and I were at the University of Queensland together with Kate and Shelley. We go way back.'

Leo looked up at Tori, question marks in his eyes. Before she could put Daryl in his place, he continued, 'This fellow has the potential to be a great player. I've been watching him train and play over the past few weeks. I always have my eye out for an upcoming star.'

Tori wanted to scream, *get your hands off my son*. She shot daggers at Daryl with her eyes. 'Do you make a habit of dropping around at the boys' homes in the evening?'

Daryl let go of Leo and took a step closer to her. 'Only the promising players. I like to give them a leg up and nurture them.'

Tori looked away. There was no way she was letting Leo go to a football game with Daryl Brady. He hadn't changed one bit. If anything, his newfound notoriety had expanded his ego even further.

He raised an eyebrow. 'So, what do you say?'

Tori could feel Leo watching them, wished he would go to his room and leave her alone with Daryl while she told him to piss off.

'I promise I'll bring him back safe and sound.'

Tori gritted her teeth, determined to let Daryl know what she thought of him. She frowned at Leo, pointed a finger to his door. 'I want you to go to your room.'

'Mum!'

Leo was about to say more. She shut him up with a look.
'NOW.'

Her heart tripped when she saw the shock in Leo's eyes when he stumbled to his room.

She took a step closer to Daryl. Her chest hurt with the dull thud of anger. She kept her voice low, not wanting Leo to hear them. 'How dare you come around and assume you can just take Leo out for an evening.'

Daryl stood stock still in front of her. 'Don't tell me you won't let Leo see a game of footy because I was pissed and behaving like an idiot the last time you saw me. Jesus, that was so long ago. Do you have any bloody idea what pressure I was under? My career was about to take off and I was excited as hell, shit scared. Loosen up. Give Leo a chance to be a boy and have a bit of fun.'

Tori looked away, pulses thudding all over her body. She hated the way Daryl made his poor behaviour sound so fucking reasonable. Just when she worried that he wouldn't leave he turned and headed for the door. Before pulling it shut behind him, he added, 'Give it some thought. Don't let your opinion of me get in the way of an opportunity for Leo.'

After he left, Tori locked the door and stood with her back against it, breathing hard. When she calmed down, she went to Leo's room and opened the door a fraction. 'Leo?'

She pushed the door open, hating how Daryl reminded her of a time in her life she preferred to forget.

Leo stared at her, his voice trembling. 'I want to go. It would be so cool. We've never been to the Gabba to a live game.'

Tori didn't meet his eyes. She could easily have taken him to a game. If only she had taken more interest in Leo's football. The truth was, she thought it was a passing phase and never imagined he would become so passionate about the bloody game.

'Why can't I go?'

'You don't even know the man.'

'He's been my coach for a couple of weeks now. Anyway,

everyone knows Mr Brady.'

His voice had gone up a notch. 'And you went to uni with him.'

There was accusation in his tone. She wanted to tell Leo what Daryl had been like, that all the glossy stories about him and his football career did not erase his past. Somehow, being able to kick an oval pigskin around gave you the licence to be a shit and all was forgiven.

'I said, no.'

'I hate you! Get out of my room.'

Shocked, she stumbled backwards and he slammed the door in her face.

Tori stared at his closed door and pushed away the tears that threatened to spill.

✦

Leo had asked to try Australian Rules when the local club advertised after school training sessions with all sorts of gimmicks thrown in. A cap, drink bottle, Wild Dog pencil box and family tickets to a game – which to her shame, they never used – all in that rust-coloured sports bag, embossed with a golden dingo standing on a dune like the Lion King. Leo carried it around like a badge of honour. Turned out he was a natural and was moved up the ranks until he was asked to help with the younger kids. Now that he was twelve, he umpired the little ones and got paid a small allowance.

If only she had taken more interest. She never imagined her Leo to be a sportsman. She had envisioned having a son who was creative and never considered for one moment he might prefer to play Australian Rules football. The truth was, she thought if she ignored it, he would move on. Now that Indigo was around, Tori would go along on Saturdays, watch Leo play more often. His words, *I hate you*, felt like he had hurled stones at her.

She tapped on his door. 'Leo?'

There was no response. She opened it a crack. He was lying in the dark, staring at the solar system stuck on the ceiling.

'I'll get Indigo to do the shop in the morning, come and watch you play.'

He shifted on the bed, didn't speak.

'And Leo. I might try and get tickets to the game myself. Let me see what I can do.'

He sat bolt upright. 'Really?'

He looked so happy again. The sweet warmth of relief swept through her.

'If you want to play tomorrow, I insist you get some sleep.'

Leo leapt off the bed and bounced into the bathroom, humming. She heard water hit the basin, the sound of him cleaning his teeth.

'Night, Mum.'

He even grinned at her before he went to bed without a whimper of protest.

Tori went online and managed to get two tickets to the game, then was up till past midnight finishing the dress. She folded it carefully, layered it between crinkly tissue, then slid it into one of her brown paper bags with its black Treasure Chest logo and string handles, ready for Indigo to give to the customer when the shop opened.

16

IT was a couple of days after Daryl's last text and Kate was having a long shower. She washed her hair and watched the suds gurgle down the plughole. She worried about Daryl. Why had he come to her of all people? Now she carried his secret around in her head and it felt like a grenade was lodged in there. How would she face Shelley again? And yet, Daryl was right, he would be crucified if a journalist writing for some smutty magazine got wind of an affair. It would destroy not only Daryl but also Shelley.

Kate switched the water off and reached for her towel, the steam fogging up the mirror. She felt trapped. He had come to her desperate for help and she had agreed to hear him out. The only way to make this whole disaster right was to use her skills as a professional to get him to confess to Shelley. It was up to Kate to make him realise how much better it was for Shelley to hear the truth from him. These things had a way of being unearthed and it would be a tragedy if Shelley learnt the truth via a headline.

Kate sat on the edge of the bathtub and let her mind wander back to her days with Daryl. Most people didn't realise how tough his childhood had been. She wondered if he had confided in Shelley. It was one of the things Kate had found attractive about him. His vulnerability and how it mirrored her own.

It was at the end of their first week together when he confided to her. They had been lying naked, skin glistening after summer sex, his leg hooked over hers, his head resting in his hand staring at her.

'My mum left when I was ten. Went to see a friend in Melbourne and never came back.'

The scent of frangipani drifted through the window and the old Queenslander creaked and popped in the heat.

'That's so awful. Did you ever see her again?'

'Maybe five years later. I was waiting with Dad at the departure gate at the airport. He was heading on one of his sales trips and dragged me along. I saw her with another man, holding hands. She didn't see me. She looked so bloody happy and boarded her flight just before Dad came back with his newspapers. I wonder if she even missed me. I never told Dad, but I think he knew.'

Kate pulled him close and longed to smooth away his grief.

'Dad came home with his girlfriends all the time. I could hear them in the room next to me. They never stayed around long.'

Daryl rested his head between her breasts and made her hot and uncomfortable, but she stroked his hair, stayed very still, and waited for him to continue.

'Nothing I did was good enough for Dad. He was always disappointed in my grades at school and thought football was a waste of time. He never came to watch me play.'

He lay there for a while, then bit her breast, made her cry out. Her instinct was to push him away and tell him he'd hurt her. Then she thought about that sad, lost boy, longing for his father's approval. She bit back her response and let the incident go. She didn't want to overreact.

The bruise came out the next day. It throbbed and changed from red to deep purple then faded to yellow and green a couple of weeks later. She thought of her own frightened, angry childhood and how it complemented his. His motherless, hers fatherless.

Kate reluctantly shook away her memories and wrapped herself in the towel. The mirror was still foggy, but she could see a blurry image of her face. She blow-dried out the kinks in her hair before pulling it up into a ponytail.

Was she really doing the right thing? It was too late to back out now. She would just have to keep a firm boundary around their friendship and convince him to talk with Shelley. Today, she had agreed to see him at the clinic in her lunch hour. Not as a client, of course. As a friend. One who needed a shoulder to lean on, someone to talk to. A quiet suburban café in another suburb would have been preferable, but she was heavily booked and didn't want to go somewhere local in case it was misinterpreted. *Football hero seen having lunch with local psychologist.* Kate gave her head a shake. She was being paranoid.

Kate looked at herself in her bra and undies and sucked her tummy in. She turned side on and decided to leave her hair out for a change. Next, she rummaged through her make up and found concealer, used it to make her lightly freckled skin look airbrushed. Finally, she added a subtle, pink lipstick.

It took a lot of time choosing what to wear and she settled for a blue belted dress. It was a firmer fit than she remembered but flattering. She bought it years ago for a job interview, and it was perfect for today's mission. With her heels, she looked professional, yet feminine. She reassured herself with a final glance in the mirror. The skirt made a soft swish, swish sound when she walked. It was important to look and feel professional when dealing with Daryl. It would make it easier to call the shots if needed.

She half hoped Ryan might comment favourably, but it was unlikely. He was oblivious to what she was wearing. On one of their early dates, she had bought a new dress hoping to impress him. When he didn't say anything, she pressed him. *What do you think of my outfit?* He had pulled her close, pressed his hand over her heart and stared into her eyes. *You always look gorgeous to me, it's what's inside that I'm in love with.* The thing about Ryan was, he really meant it. It was not some corny line he used to get into your pants.

Ryan's response to her childhood had been to draw her into the chaotic, happy Murphy clan where she was adopted as their own. It opened her eyes to what family could be. The playful teasing banter of people around you who loved you enough to let you see their flaws, who were exasperating yet capable of making you ache with the joy of unconditional acceptance.

Edie was poised with the Sultana Bran and two bowls. 'You look nice, Mummy.'

Kate smiled, felt a rush of warmth for her daughter, bent down and gave her a kiss on top of her unruly head. 'What do you want in your lunch?'

'No cheese, it goes yucky.'

Kate pulled her phone out of her bag. 'Here, why don't you and Noah have tuckshop today. What should I order?'

Edie's eyes widened at this unexpected treat. She wanted tacos and a strawberry milk. When Kate tapped it in without protest, she added a chocolate chip biscuit.

Tonight, Kate vowed, she would sit down with Ryan and talk, prepare a nice meal and explain how his endless rehearsals were taking their toll on her work, on the family, and that going away to tour was not realistic with a young family. Ryan was fumbling through the pile of music books on one of the dining room chairs. He seemed agitated.

'Have you lost something?'

'The schedule for the trip. I had it on the table. I was reading it last night.'

Kate sighed. 'The one I pinned to the fridge?'

He strode over and snatched it off. 'Please, don't touch my music stuff. It might look disorganised, but I know exactly where everything is.'

He picked up his satchel, looked ready to leave then stopped. 'Sorry, I'm a bit uptight right now. Everything's happening so fast and there's so much to get sorted.'

He leant in and gave her a peck on the cheek. 'See you this evening.' He winked and his face crinkled into that familiar grin of his. 'And, I have a surprise for you.'

The angry knot inside Kate loosened. She felt herself smile and wondered what sort of romantic surprise he had planned.

✢

After dropping the kids off, Kate hurried to the clinic and worked her way through the morning's patient list. At lunchtime, she retreated to her tiny kitchen, desperate for a coffee. The high-pitched squeal of the kettle faded away and Kate pulled out the plunger and heard the door. He was early. She smoothed her dress, licked her lips and the sickly gloss of Rose Dahlia pink stuck to her tongue. 'Daryl, come in.'

He smelt of shaving cream and wore a crisp white shirt with golden cufflinks. His dark crinkled hair was cropped close to his head and flecked with grey. Why was it, Kate wondered, that grey made a man look distinguished but a woman tired and old?

He seemed larger today, loose-limbed and relaxed.

'I just boiled the kettle. How about a coffee?'

'Sounds great.'

'Black with one?' God, the things you remembered about people. Maybe he no longer had his coffee the same way. His scent filled her nostrils and for a moment she felt dizzy. She walked to the kitchen and rinsed out the black residue in the coffee pot, pouring away the cold slosh of coffee and sediment. Brown, dark swirls that disappeared down the sink, the dark clots disintegrating under the pressure from the tap. He stood at the door, arms folded, and watched her. Kate focused on measuring a heaped tablespoon of coffee into the glass pot and realised her hand was trembling. She poured boiling water over and fitted the plunger into the top before applying gentle pressure.

'Great rooms you have here.'

Instead of responding, she chose a dark blue mug with a gold rim for him, placed it next to her floral cup, and poured two coffees. She added a teaspoon of sugar to his and stirred, watching the crystals dissolve. There was a reason you were advised not to see your friends as clients. Even old ones you had not seen for over a decade.

'How about we chat in my consulting room?'

Kate handed him his coffee, careful not to touch him, and led the way. She motioned to a chair and pushed her own back to create a bigger space between them.

He sat with one arm stretched over the back of the chair, his knees slightly apart, the crease in his trousers perfect. His shoes were black and very shiny. 'Well, who would have thought I'd ever be sitting in a room like this. You know, I always thought it was a bit of mumbo jumbo.'

Kate opened her mouth to counter his comment and remind him she was seeing him as an old friend, then changed her mind.

He held his coffee aloft, drank some then reached over and put it on her desk. 'I'm so glad I found you. I wasn't sure how to sort this shit out.'

He lifted one hand in the air, palm out, then let it drop and leant closer to Kate. 'You know Shelley and the kids are everything to me, but sometimes I feel like I can't trust her anymore.'

The casual challenge in his tone made Kate feel both defensive towards Shelley and curious about the marriage. 'When you feel like that, it can help to reflect back on the happy times, you know, the early days when you first met, and things were uncomplicated.'

He dropped his gaze, put his elbows on his knees and locked his hands together so his forearms shaped a triangle. The silence between them stretched until Kate intervened.

'Try and think back to the last time when you were really happy together.'

Daryl shifted in the seat again, his coffee getting cold.

'How about when Melody was born? Or the twins?'

He dropped his head and stared at the floor, clenching then unclenching his right hand. 'What do you know?'

'Nothing, I met your three kids for the first time at school drop-off and had a quick catch-up with Shelley over coffee.'

He banged his fist on the armrest, startling Kate. 'Shelley needed an emergency caesarean for the twins and after that she lost it, couldn't get it all together. Things went downhill after they were born.'

Kate clutched her coffee with both hands, reminding herself this was not a consultation but a chat with an old friend.

'That must have been really tough, for both of you.'

Daryl looked at the door, his voice low. 'I wasn't there.'

He sat up and crossed his legs. 'I was still playing football. I had no choice. The team came before family.'

He uncrossed his legs and leant back against the chair. 'I didn't know she would go early. It was all over by the time I got there.'

He looked past Kate. 'She cried all the time, nothing I did was right.'

'I'm so sorry.'

'She wanted to breastfeed the two of them, but it was too much. I went and bought tins of formula, and she cried again.'

He thrummed his fingers on the armrests. 'I was working long hours and wanted to be a good husband and a good dad.'

He raised his hands in a helpless gesture. 'She stopped communicating with me. I had no bloody idea what to do.'

Kate recalled those blurry first weeks after having Noah. Ryan was home and played with Edie, while Kate sat on the deck breastfeeding, watching two hatted heads, one big, the other small, bent over the soil, spacing sunflower seeds. She remembered Edie's unadulterated joy when they germinated ten days later and the thrill when the stalks grew taller than her, their bowed heads crowded with black seeds haloed by yellow petals. It had been exhausting managing a toddler and a baby, even with a partner who was there and supportive. It must have been a nightmare for Shelley with two babies, a toddler, and alone.

'It must have been so difficult.'

'Yeah, it was pretty crappy. I remember thinking, I'm bloody tired, my wife doesn't notice me anymore, we never even have sex. Shit, this is the rest of my life.'

Kate wanted to berate him, *Have you any idea what having a baby does to your body, how tough it would have been for Shelley trying to look after these babies. Sleep-deprived and alone.* She remembered she wasn't meant to know about Shelley's post-natal depression and couldn't just ring her and reassure her that being a mother was challenging with one let alone two newborns and a toddler. She finished her coffee and longed to eat the chicken salad languishing in the fridge. Her lunch hour was rapidly coming to an end, and she knew she had to draw things to a close. It felt uncomfortably close to a counselling session.

She touched his knee and felt its contours beneath the fabric of his trousers. 'You two need professional help, marriage counselling. There's so much to unpick here.'

He brushed her off, stood up, took a step back. 'That's why I'm telling you. You're not going to talk, are you? You promised me. Imagine this in the papers. I'd be screwed.'

'Of course not. I won't breathe a word to anyone.'

When he left, Kate felt nauseous and wondered if it was from hunger or anxiety about Daryl. Somehow, she needed to convince him to get outside help. He had not even mentioned the affair today. The whole situation was a complicated mess. Talking to him had been a mistake.

⚘

The afternoon clinic ran a bit later than she expected. Kate took out her compact and topped up her lippy then ran a brush through her hair. She thought it might be fun to splash out and get a nice take-away meal from Ryan's favourite Thai place and talk about things. It filled her with hope when he texted her to say he was home early and had already picked the kids up from afterschool care.

When she pulled into the carport, she saw a pile of timbers stacked in the front. She frowned and wondered why the neighbours were cluttering their nature strip. Surely the endless renovations were finished. When she opened the door, she was welcomed with loud excited shrieks. 'Mummy's home.'

A floppy eared mutt, with a drool rimmed snout and pink tongue gambolled to the door. Ryan emerged, dishevelled. 'Surprise!'

Kate reeled and her good intentions evaporated. 'What the hell is going on?'

Ryan gave his stupid, lopsided smile. 'We got paid for the gig and I arranged for the place to be fenced.'

He waved vaguely towards the back. 'It should be finished in the next day or so.'

Kate stood very still, tried to process the unfolding of events in her own home.

'Mummy, we got a dog.' Noah stated the obvious while he tried to cuddle the squirming, black-splotched mutt that wriggled its backside, tail banging against the timber floor.

'How dare you get a dog behind my back.'

Kate's fury erupted. Edie and Noah sensed the change in mood and tried to haul the dog back to safer ground.

'Kate,' Ryan let his hand drop, slipped it into his pocket, 'we promised the kids a dog.'

'But not now. God, Ryan. You're about to head off for three weeks. I work. We discuss things like this.'

Ryan looked at her, his brown eyes filled with disappointment. 'There was a time when you would have been excited with the kids.'

'There was a time when you would have talked to me first.' She raised her voice. 'Who do you suppose is going to look after the dog once the novelty wears off?'

She turned and her heels punched the floor hard with every step until she reached her office and slammed the door. She sat at her desk, kicked her shoes off and dropped her head onto her arms, too spent to cry. Her childhood bear, Ted, stared down at her from the ledge near the window. He looked forlorn, one eye loose on a thread, his stuffing spilt from a ruptured seam.

How dare Ryan complicate their lives with a dog. She sat, exhausted, head on her arms, and ignored the clatter of dishes interspersed with excited hushed voices.

Ryan tapped, then let himself in without saying a word. He placed a bowl next to her elbow. Cheap pasta with a jar of sauce stirred through then sprinkled with parmesan. The smell of warm cheese made Kate wrinkle her nose. She didn't thank him or even glance his way, unwilling to concede.

A few hours later, when she eventually tiptoed into the bedroom and slid under the sheet, it was past midnight, and the household was asleep. She stayed on her side, curled over herself and wide awake.

17

SATURDAY morning the pale sun was squeezed between thick clouds and the suggestion of autumn chilled the air. Tori foraged for something warm to wear, thrilled how excited Leo was about the game tonight. She regretted she hadn't thought of buying tickets to a game as a treat or birthday gift before yesterday, when Daryl forced her hand.

Daryl had always had an overinflated ego. She had been surprised when Kate fell so hard for him. Tori would never have picked Kate as one of those women who ignored their friends and stopped going to other social events just because they were hitched up with a bloke. Kate had changed after Daryl dumped her for Shelley. Tori tried to talk about it, but Kate had been reticent and changed the subject, so Tori left things alone. Kate had probably worked out what a loser Daryl was, embarrassed to have fallen for his charms. It was a relief when Kate eventually hitched up with Ryan. Tonight would be fun, even if Tori didn't know the first thing about Australian Rules. She vowed to take Leo to games more often, to schedule more time where the two of them hung out and just had fun together. Next holidays, she would ask Indigo to manage The Treasure Chest and take Leo to the Sunshine Coast on a proper holiday. Over the last two years, life had been so busy with the business and establishing an online presence they had not gone away at all, not even for a weekend.

She slid her arms deep into her purple coat then added a red scarf, deciding she might as well be visible as it was the first time she would see Leo play a full game. Unlike school mornings, he was up with an hour to spare. He scoffed breakfast, dressed in his Wild Dog gear with everything ready in the special bag. He grinned, happy. Tori's heart melted.

Clusters of boys shivered in their football jerseys, and some started to kick a ball around. Tori felt out of place in this testosterone dominant playground and reminded herself that she was doing this for Leo. He was such an ardent fan and knew the names of all the Wild Dog players as well as their strengths and weaknesses. He spent hours kicking the ball around with the young team he helped to coach. Tori's teeth clenched when she thought of Daryl coaching Leo's team.

A straggly queue was lined up at the square concrete canteen where volunteers served drinks and a small selection of hot food. Tori toyed with the idea of a coffee but dismissed it. The crap they served at these canteens was just not worth the effort. She turned to Leo who had sprouted in the last year, spindly legged and big footed like a pup. He didn't seem to feel the cold in his flimsy jersey and shorts, his muscles flexed, raring to go. Some of the smaller boys looked up at him with something akin to awe. He high fived a couple of tiny players who came up just to say hello. It was strange to think of her boy having such a presence, a whole life apart from her that she knew little about. 'Would you like something from the canteen? A hot drink?'

'Not now, Mum. I always get myself a couple of potato scallops after the game.'

Tori was determined to get more involved and to inhabit this world where her son was so comfortable and happy. She would learn the fundamentals, so that it would be more than a blur of boys chasing an oval ball around the field.

Kate and Noah headed towards her with a black puppy straining on a leash. It must be new. Noah looked tiny in his oversized jersey, shorts flapping like loose sails around scrawny legs. He saw one of his friends and veered off. Kate was red-faced with cold, her arm stretched while the dog pulled at the leash, eager to explore.

'The dog seems like a handful.'

Kate rolled her eyes while Tori bent down and let the dog jump up and try to lick her.

'Another one of Ryan's hare-brained ideas. He just thought he'd get the kids a puppy before heading away on tour.'

Tori played with its ears and looked into its chocolate almond eyes. 'Well, you have to admit, it's pretty cute.'

'Just don't, Tori. I'm so bloody furious with him. Anyway, good to see you. I haven't seen you at the footy before.'

'I'm always at the shop. I usually drop Leo off, and he hangs around most of the day; plays, coaches, and helps out with stuff.'

'He's a bit of a star around here. The next Daryl Brady.'

'Jesus, I hope not.'

She looked at Kate shivering in a flimsy long sleeve shirt and jeans with sandals. Brisbane could catch you out in autumn with sudden unexpected cool days. 'You might have to come past the shop. I've got some great winter gear that I'm in the process of sorting. Would you like my scarf?'

Kate accepted the bulky cable knit and wrapped herself in it. The red was a burst of colour in the grey morning.

'I love it. I flew out the door in the last minute and forgot my jumper.'

The dog saw something and gave a sudden tug at the lead, nearly bowling Kate over. Tori laughed and watched Kate rein him in.

'You've got to admit, that fellow is very sweet. I bet the kids love him.'

'Hello there!'

Tori and Kate turned around. There was Indigo holding one of Vincent's coffees aloft. It smelt so good Tori went weak at the knees. 'Thanks, appreciate it.'

Indigo looked at Kate, apologetic. 'I should have brought you one too. I'll try and remember next time.'

'Anytime you are giving coffees away, keep me in mind.'

'Well, I'd better head back to the shop. Only ten minutes to opening.'

Tori warmed her hands around the coffee and inhaled the pungent scent escaping from the tiny hole at the top. It made her realise how exhausted she felt. 'Thanks for this. I really needed it. I left the dress on the counter. See you around lunchtime.'

Kate eyed the coffee with envy. 'You seem tired. Did you have a big night?'

'I guess you could call it that. I was up most of the night finishing off an urgent order for a customer.'

She sipped her coffee and huddled lower into her collar. 'And Daryl just bowled into my place last night with tickets to a football match. He wanted to take Leo to the game tonight and walked into the place like he had a goddamned bloody right to take my son out.'

Kate jigged from one foot to the other to warm up. 'Leo is a great player, and Daryl keeps his eyes peeled for potential.'

'He should have run it past me first. Given me the opportunity to say no. I was in an impossible situation yesterday with Leo standing there. I felt cornered.'

Kate rubbed her hands together inside a fold of the scarf. 'Daryl was just being enthusiastic. He means well.'

Tori disappeared further into her coat in the face of a brisk breeze. 'Football stardom does not give him the right to turn up on my doorstep and make me feel like a shit mother.'

A shrill whistle blew. The games started and they shifted closer to the action at the field where Leo's team was playing. Tori was grateful Kate didn't head off to watch Noah. She probably watched him play every week.

Kate's voice sounded muffled, her face buried inside the scarf. 'Daryl is making a real effort to become part of the community. Shelley and Daryl both are. Georgie sent me an excited text to tell me Shelley was coming along to the next music fest meeting.'

'Jesus, I might just give it a miss. Imagine if Daryl came along as well.'

'Don't be too harsh on him. He's just finding his feet here and trying to reconnect with old friends.'

Tori didn't bother to respond. Instead, she watched Leo, mesmerised. It was like she was seeing him for the first time. He ran along and bounced the egg-shaped ball a few times, other players in hot pursuit. She tried to reconcile this lean, muscular figure flying across the damp grass with the boy who slouched in his track pants and drank milk from a carton.

Tonight would be all about Leo. If he wanted to buy some Wild Dog bling, get himself a hot dog or a soft drink, fine. She always assumed Leo would be like her and clueless about sport. Now it was clear Aussie Rules was his passion, she would put aside her own lack of interest and support him.

Kate and Tori stood in silence for a while and didn't join the parents shouting encouragement and the occasional expletive from the sidelines. When Kate's phone pinged, she excused herself. 'Can you hold the pooch for a sec?'

Her thumbs punched a response, then she grabbed the lead back again, keeping it short.

The final whistle blew, and a scramble of boys converged into a single organism. They lifted and carried one of the players aloft on a tangle of muddied arms chanting a war cry, then tumbled in a pile of writhing bodies.

Kate waved to Noah who turned up grubby from another field before smiling at Tori. 'Hey, don't be too hard on Daryl. I suspect he is dealing with a lot, being injured and not able to play, then moving house.'

She blew a kiss. 'And don't forget, I'm here if you need a shoulder or a chat. Just call.'

Tori checked the time. Six hours until they caught the bus to the Gabba. With a bit of luck, Daryl would be safely in the corporate box and not notice Tori and Leo sitting amongst the riff raff in the stands.

18

AFTER football and lunch, Edie and Noah went outside into the newly fenced backyard and played with the dog while Kate reread Daryl's text in the privacy of her office. *It's been great talking to you. Can I see you Monday?* She hoped Tori hadn't seen it. Kate suspected Tori would not approve.

After rereading his message for the umpteenth time, Kate felt torn. What she needed to do was send him a text advising that it was all a mistake, that she should never have agreed to see him. Daryl should be discussing Shelley's post-natal depression, and his affair, with a marriage counsellor. It felt wrong knowing about Shelley's struggles and her husband's infidelity while feigning ignorance.

Kate longed to reach out to Shelley, to reassure her how common it was for women to feel depressed after having a baby, let alone twins, but knew that was impossible. She hovered over her phone, the sounds of yapping and children's laughter floating through the open window. She couldn't just dismiss him with a text. It was something she had to do face-to-face. Her thumbs tapped out a message. *Let's catch up first thing tomorrow morning at The Grindhouse Café.*

As soon as she heard her text whoosh, she felt a chill and imagined his large hands holding his phone while he scanned the message. Kate rang her first client and moved them to her lunch hour, apologising for the inconvenience.

There was a yelp and the glitch of the sliding door, followed by dog paws on timber and excited voices. Kate walked to the living area where Noah and Edie vied for the puppy's attention. Its black rump wriggled with enthusiasm. He was a shaggy, black splodge with a spring-loaded tail.

Edie sounded anxious. 'Please Mummy, can we keep him? I promise to feed him. Dad showed us how to pick up the poos.'

Kate was aware that both Noah and Edie were staring up at her waiting for a verdict. She recalled her own dog growing up. A brown Labrador cross, Bailey. One week after that unforgettable day, when Kate and Mum fled to Nan's place at Bribie, Mum went back after Dad pleaded and promised to change. A couple of weeks later, Nan drove all the way to Brisbane, something she never did. Kate remembered her at the door, holding a cardboard box that whimpered and wriggled. 'For you.'

Nan handed the carboard box to Kate. Mum invited Nan to stay but she didn't even come inside. She walked back to her car and drove straight back home. Nan didn't like Dad. She never said anything but made a point of avoiding him.

That night, Kate slept with the puppy warm inside the curve of her belly. He became her loyal companion, his rapid heartbeat pressed against hers in the wardrobe whenever she heard raised voices and the shatter of dishes against the wall.

Kate looked at the black, floppy-eared pooch who gazed at her and brought those warm safe feelings rushing back. The pressure of three sets of eyes willed her to say yes. She nodded assent, feeling suddenly emotional. 'He really is a cuddly black bear.'

Kate leant forward and picked him up and he tried to lick her face. 'But I'm setting a few ground rules. You guys have to look after the puppy even when it grows up and you don't feel like it.'

Edie and Noah screamed, came over and hugged her on both sides while the pup squirmed in her arms. Kate nearly toppled over and realised with a pang that it had been a while since the two of them had been this happy and in agreement about something.

✢

Monday morning dawned and butterflies whirled in Kate's tummy when she remembered she was seeing Daryl again today. She kept wanting to run things past Ryan, remind him to drop the kids off and pick them up, then realised he wasn't there. The house seemed different, filled with empty Ryan-shaped spaces. The kids were more subdued without their dad around. He sent daily messages filled with emojis. *Miss you. Sad face.*

After Kate stepped out of the shower and selected a straight skirt and soft, silky blouse that billowed up from her wrists, she called out to Edie and Noah, but they were already up and dressed. There was the sound of kibble being poured into Bear's bowl and excited chatter from the living room.

Bear was meant to sleep in the laundry. They had gone to Pet Barn and bought a soft basket, dog toys, and bags of treats. The night after Ryan left, Bear had found his way into the bedroom, wriggled next to Kate, and found that warm hollow between her pulled up legs and belly. Half asleep, Kate tucked herself around him, finding comfort in his softness and willingness to cuddle up. Now she missed him if he wasn't there and promised herself that she would train him to sleep in the basket after Ryan returned.

Kate put Edie and Noah's satchels into the boot, slammed it shut and got ready to back out of the drive when her phone pinged. She frowned at the message. Bloody Daryl had cancelled. It had better be a one-off. She really had gone out of her way to accommodate him.

'Is it Dad?'

Edie's hopeful voice.

'Sorry, Edie. He would have been up very late with the band performing. I suspect he's asleep. Promise we'll Facetime him tonight.'

Kate pulled into a park and saw Tori standing beside Georgie who looked like she was crying. Edie and Noah ran off, their satchels bouncing on their backs.

Cautious, Kate raised an eyebrow to Tori who stood thin-lipped, one arm over Georgie's shoulder. Tori kept her voice low. 'It's Shelley and Daryl's kid, Melody. She's making Gaby's life hell.'

Georgie's shoulders were shaking. 'Poor Gaby. Mark gave her an

Apple watch for her birthday. He wanted to get her something grown-up and special. We told her not to bring it to school, but she slipped it into her pocket without us knowing. I asked her to go and get it when her aunty came over, just to show her, and Gaby burst into tears. She'd been too scared to tell us because she did the wrong thing and took it to school.'

Staggered that Mark had bought his ten-year-old an Apple watch in the first place, Kate asked, 'So, she lost it?'

Tori replied. 'Far worse than that. Melody grabbed it off her and taunted her by pocketing it. Gaby was too scared to tell anyone because of the no electronic devices policy. Then after school, Melody stood near the drain on that rainy arvo and just dropped it in and watched it wash away.'

Georgie started weeping afresh. 'It's so awful. Why would she do that? I haven't told Mark, please don't tell him.'

Kate stood shocked and tried to imagine the scenario. No wonder Gaby had kept quiet.

The school bell rang shrill across their conversation and a stream of black, grey, and gold funnelled to the assembly area. A gleaming four-wheel drive screamed up to the curb and stopped. Shelley jumped out, bracelets glinting, her soft crème knitted top the perfect complement to her jeans. Kate, Tori, and Georgie stood in the stillness of the recently vacated school grounds and watched her get the kids out of the car before waving them off. In the awkward silence that followed, Georgie mumbled a goodbye and hurried away. Tori greeted Shelley then turned to head back to The Treasure Chest.

Kate remembered Daryl had cancelled their chat this morning. On impulse she turned to Shelley. 'How about a coffee before I head to work?'

✦

Vincent's was a buzz of activity with take-away food and meals flying out the hatch and the smell of cooked breakfasts and warm pastry scenting the air. The reputation of the place had spread, and it was pumping. Their drinks arrived, and Kate wrapped her hands around the steaming mug, the quiet between them punctuated by the clink of spoons and cups rattling in saucers.

Shelley spoke first. 'One day we should all head out and watch Ryan and his band play. I'd love to get to know him. Being married to a musician must be so romantic.'

Kate clenched her jaw. 'Not too sure about romantic. You need your partner to be around for romance.'

'Sounds like being married to a footballer. He's away half the time too.'

The conversation was veering towards dangerous territory. 'Ryan has his moments. He's great with the kids.'

One of the waiters poured them water from a glass carafe. The breakfast crowd thinned and was replaced by mothers wheeling huge prams. Shelley pulled her chair in to let one of them past. Kate took a risk. 'How is Melody settling in?'

Shelley paused. 'Why do you ask?'

'It's tough changing schools mid-year. I know Edie would be very upset.'

Shelley lowered her voice. 'Melody is going through a stage. She gets so angry and blames me for the move. I really don't know what to do.'

She toyed with one of the daisies and plucked off some petals. 'I feel awful after what happened. Guilty, when it was nothing really.'

Shelley glanced over her shoulder. 'I was working on reception at a local medical clinic, just three days a week. They had a party to celebrate the clinic's thirtieth year. It was so much fun. I arranged a babysitter for the first time. All the staff went to a local pub for drinks and dinner. I drank a couple of cocktails and some wine and became a bit silly. One of the doctors danced with me and just then, Daryl walked in.'

Shelley stared at the table. 'He apparently went home, wanted to know where I was. He came to get me and saw me dancing cheek to cheek with this bloke.'

She looked up at Kate, her eyes teary. 'It was all a bit of fun.

Nothing happened.'

Kate reached over and put her hand over Shelley's just as she continued. 'Daryl read it all wrong. He thought I was cheating on him, called me a slut, and forced me to resign. Between that and Daryl's injuries, things have been a bit tense.'

'Oh, Shelley. I'm so sorry.'

Kate's stomach tensed.

'Melody just thinks if I hadn't gone out that night, we'd still be in the old place.'

Then Shelley grabbed Kate's hand between hers. 'Has there been trouble at the school?'

'Not really.' Kate stared at a drop of water sliding slowly down the side of her glass. 'Actually, yes. Melody and Gaby are having issues and Georgie is upset.'

Shelley nodded. Her coffee cup was still half full. She stood up and the chair grated. 'Thanks for telling me.'

Driving to work, Kate wondered if she should have said more. It seemed Shelley was not surprised about Melody. Kate went through the conversation in her head and worried she'd overstepped. Had she betrayed Daryl? Shelley? Kate really needed to talk to him and urge him to see a psychologist. Maybe she could arrange for the two of them to have marriage counselling. Keeping who told her what in her head was proving to be a challenge. It started to slide together in her head and blur.

The coffee burnt holes in her gut, and she felt a headache starting to pound her forehead. When she arrived at the clinic, she nearly dropped her keys. An enormous bouquet wilted on the doorstep next to a bottle of Penfold's Shiraz. For one crazy moment, she thought it was from Ryan and her breath caught.

She bent down to pick up the small card. The note was brief. *Sorry I had to cancel our brekky date.* Of course, it wasn't Ryan. He never bought her flowers.

She picked up the bouquet and unlocked the door. When she reached for the wine, her heart banged like a jackhammer in her chest.

19

TORI sat in the car daydreaming about the game at the Gabba. Leo had been so happy. She bought him an overpriced Wild Dog scarf and joined in when he stood shouting in excitement. The Dogs lost, but it barely dampened his enthusiasm. She was careful to listen properly when he raked over every detail of the game on the bus home.

The phone interrupted her thoughts. It was Georgie reminding them of the music fest meeting this evening. Lots of smiling emojis and her usual cheerful text. *Looking forward to a great production this year!!* Damn. Tori had forgotten. She wondered if Shelley would be there and if the bullying had been addressed. Dropping her phone into her bag, Tori walked into The Treasure Chest and thought she might ask Indigo to keep an eye on Leo this evening.

Tori was surprised to find she was the first to arrive at the school hall. She turned on the lights and pulled out chairs in the small backstage room where the three of them usually met.

'Oh my god. Am I late?'

Georgie sounded flustered. She always arrived at least fifteen minutes early. 'Kate dropped Edie and Noah around to Mark. She's right behind me. Sorry you had to wait.'

'No worries. I'm early. Indigo offered to take Leo to the new burger place, so I came straight here.'

Just then Kate hurried in, coat flapping open and scarf flying. 'Made it. And thanks for letting me drop the kids off.'

Georgie waved one hand in dismissal. 'Completely fine. Knowing Mark, he'll order Uber Eats and sit them in front of a movie while he works.'

She slid into a chair, reached into her leather briefcase, and pulled out a laptop, while Kate sat down with a sigh. Georgie logged on. 'We might just wait a few more minutes. Shelley promised to come and help.'

Tori looked over at Kate and gave a small shrug. 'So has this thing with Gaby and Melody been sorted then?'

'Oh yes.'

Georgie blushed and looked away. 'I just decided to deal with the whole thing myself and rang Daryl. I told him how devastated Gaby was and an hour later he was at mine with a brand-new Apple watch.' She placed a rose-tipped finger to her lips 'Not a word to Mark though.'

Tori was about to ask how Gaby was when Georgie turned away, indicating the topic was closed. 'I keep forgetting to ask, Kate, did you find that cat, Arthur.'

Kate balled her hand. 'Artemis.' She thumped the table, startling Tori and Georgie. 'Nothing changes. I've been working at Dorothy's Place for years and it makes not one iota of difference. Artemis was murdered.'

Georgie's hand went to her mouth. 'Who would murder a cat?'

Kate's face looked bloodless in the harsh fluorescent light. Tori stood to get her a glass of water when she heard a loud voice and froze.

'Follow the light and presto, here they are.' Daryl filled the doorway, half his features indistinct in the darkness of the unlit school hall. He gave Shelley a little push and she stumbled, righted herself and tottered over in sharp, pointy heels. Tori slumped back into her chair just as Kate stood and pulled out a chair for Shelley, without looking her in the eye.

'Daryl! Shelley! What a wonderful surprise to see both of you here.' Georgie greeted them with enthusiasm and started to stand, but Daryl lifted a hand to stop her. He bent down and kissed each of her cheeks before pulling up a chair next to Shelley. He was carrying a small esky and put it on the table. Tori shifted away and crossed her arms tightly across her chest. Kate looked startled, like an animal caught in headlights.

Daryl reached in and pulled out five champagne flutes, followed by a bottle of Bollinger. With a deft hand, he nudged the cork to the lip where it exploded on a stream of effervescence and dented the noticeboard pinned with upcoming events.

Georgie's laugh was shrill. 'Oh, how delicious. I adore champagne.'

Daryl tipped the first flute and poured. 'We want to celebrate living amongst old friends.'

A brief shadow crossed Georgie's brow until he handed her the first glass. 'And new ones.'

Tori declined with a shake of her head. Shelley sat curled like a comma and didn't touch hers.

Daryl raised his delicate flute. It looked insubstantial in his large hand. One squeeze and it would be crushed to splinters. Tori tightened the grip around herself and gritted her teeth, willing Georgie to get on with things. She cast a worried look over Kate who stared at the table. Daryl raised his glass with a flourish. 'Cheers, ladies.'

To Tori's relief, Georgie bent her head towards the agenda on her computer. Her voice fizzed and light bounced off her nails, her earrings and the champagne in her glass.

'I thought we might have a raffle this year. Get lots of baskets and fill them with donated goodies and vouchers from local businesses.'

Daryl leant back in his chair balanced on two legs. 'How about I donate a signed football?'

Georgie clapped her hands, brought them both to her mouth. 'That would be amazing. Just imagine how many tickets we'll sell.'

She leant over her computer, her fingers flying over the keys. 'Can I put you in charge of the raffle then, Shelley?'

While she was typing, Daryl's chair crashed back down on four legs and he leant towards Tori, so close she could smell the soap on his skin. 'That Leo is really something. A natural on the field.'

He reached for the Bollinger, tipped the final glass, poured until it frothed over the edge. 'Go on, enjoy one glass. A special treat on me.' He gave a suggestive wink that made her gut churn, and she looked away.

'I said, no thanks.'

To her relief, he sat back in his chair, shifted it closer to Shelley. Tori made a point of pushing the glass away and ignored the questions in Kate's eyes and unnatural pallor in her cheeks.

Daryl tapped the table with his three middle fingers 'I could probably wrangle VIP tickets to the final. A corporate box. Add that to your raffle.'

He scanned their faces again, eyes wide. 'Only if you think people would be interested.'

Tori watched him edge towards Shelley and place his possessive arm around her shoulders. The bubbles in her flute had escaped, leaving the champagne still like a pond.

Georgie's voice was shrill, 'You're such an asset to our school. We would love to raffle the football and tickets.'

Tori cut across. 'Look, I need to go. Do you have any jobs lined up for me?'

Georgie looked over at Tori then consulted her screen. 'Could you design a programme please? This year's theme is Starry, Starry Night.' Then she turned to Kate. 'And maybe I could get you and Ryan to line the kids up before each number and get them on stage in an orderly fashion.'

Soon afterwards, Georgie called the meeting closed, gathered her things, and lifted a hand in farewell. Daryl repacked the esky, made a point of taking Shelley's arm and pulled her close. He grinned at Kate and Tori. 'Just like the good old days.'

Daryl and Shelley walked to the door and were swallowed by the darkness.

Tori avoided Kate's eyes while in silence they stacked the chairs, wiped the table with paper towels, then locked up. Just before they went their separate ways, Tori put her hand on Kate's shoulder. 'Is everything okay?'

Kate shook her head.

'Do you want to tell me about it?'

'There's nothing to tell.'

Tori gave Kate's shoulder a squeeze. 'I'm here if you want to talk.'

Tori shoved her hands in her pockets and watched Kate get into her car and drive off. Even after she had disappeared around the corner, Tori stayed, unease fluttering beneath her rib cage like trapped moths trying to escape.

20

WHEN she got home, Kate walked across the road and picked up Noah and Edie who complained about not seeing the end of whatever movie Mark had set up for them. Gaby sat glued to the screen, wearing her spanking new Apple watch, while Fran was nowhere to be seen.

'Thanks, Mark. You're a lifesaver.'

He looked up from his laptop, his tie loosened, shirt unbuttoned. 'No worries. Say hi to Ryan.'

Kate turned and dragged her two out, thinking, *I would if he was home*. It felt like a year since he left.

'Can I watch the last bit at home?'

'No, Edie. It's time for teeth and bed.'

'I wish Dad was home.'

'Well, he isn't.'

Noah looked exhausted, his lids drooping. Kate picked him up. He felt heavier than usual with his head lolling over her shoulder. At home, she undressed him on the bed, made a feeble effort to clean his teeth, then collapsed into the lounge. She picked up the remote and started surfing mindlessly.

Then she froze at a news report. A woman had jumped from a high rise on the Gold Coast and died shortly afterwards. It was Bea. Pictures of her alive and smiling came up on the TV. There was one where she was holding Artemis. Kate looked away, a hard lump in her throat. She remembered that final tearful call and wished she had done more.

100

The reporter mentioned Bea had not been to work for a few days which was uncharacteristic and spoke about her family who lived in Perth. There was no mention of Jake or Artemis. The story shifted to an interview with a psychologist about mental health and suicide. Kate balled her fist and wanted to shout, *he murdered her,* before pointing the remote and turning the news off.

The phone rang and Kate answered without looking.

'Kate Simpson?'

She sat bolt upright.

'Speaking.'

It was her former supervisor from Dorothy's Place. 'Have you seen the news?'

Kate found herself unable to speak.

'Your client, Bea.'

Kate's heart plunged, she felt cold all over, clutched the phone harder, the images of Bea scrolling through her mind.

'I'm really sorry to tell you, but I thought it was better to hear it from me before seeing the news report.'

There was an uncomfortable pause.

'She jumped from a high rise.'

Kate nodded, forgetting her supervisor couldn't see her.

'I just wanted to let you know. You rang a few times about her.'

Kate choked. 'Yes, yes, I did. Thanks for ringing.'

She buried her head into the cushions and wept. There was a wet nose, a whimper, and Bear's paws reached up on the lounge. His tongue licked her hand and her cheek.

She picked him up, nuzzled his black fur, felt his warmth against her skin, the reassuring beat of his heart where her arm held him tight.

'Oh, Bear,' she moaned rubbing her hands over his belly. The thought of finding him dead like Artemis set her off again and she wept fresh tears while Bear pressed close, licking the salty wetness off her arms and hands.

Kate stared out the sliding doors, searched for stars, but dark oily clouds blanketed the sky and snuffed out their shimmering.

✠

The next morning, Kate felt numb. Moving through the motions of showering and getting the kids up felt like walking through a dense fog. While Noah sat scruffy haired, uniform askew, eating cereal, and Edie spooned Milo off her milk, the phone rang. Kate startled and her favourite coffee cup slipped out of her grasp and smashed to the floor. Breathless, she responded, 'Hello?'

'Morning, Beautiful.'

'Ryan, it's you.'

'Now, who else would be ringing you at seven in the morning? Should I be worried?'

There was a teasing edge to his voice. Kate felt a twinge. 'I expected you to ring last night. I stayed up.' It sounded like an accusation.

'It was a big night. The crowd in Townsville loved our gig. We played an encore, stayed on and had a few drinks. Sorry, it just got too late.'

Bear stood at Kate's feet. She crouched amongst the shattered pieces of her favourite mug, fondled his ears, and waited for the right moment to pour her heart out to Ryan, tell him about Bea, about Artemis and Melody.

'God, Kate. You would have loved it. Wish you were here. Are the kids there? Can I say hi?'

Edie and Noah were standing right in front of her, expectant. Noah had a milk moustache. Edie had a smudge of Milo on her school shirt. Kate switched the phone to speaker.

'Hello, Dad!'

They bubbled with excitement and tried to talk at the same time. While they chattered, Kate pulled out the dustpan, swept up the broken pieces of ceramic. It was the mug Ryan had bought her that week they met in Byron. Seeing it shattered filled her with dread like it was some sort of premonition. She had moved into his tent, but he'd only had one mug. They found a shop in town, and he invited her to choose a mug she liked. She selected one patterned with sunflowers.

It still felt special, something that echoed the life she imagined she might live, and she used it every day.

She poured the pieces into the bin.

'Mum, Dad wants to say good-bye.'

She switched speaker off. 'Ryan?'

'Hey, beautiful. There are some gorgeous places along the coast. We'll plan a road trip up here one day soon. You'd love it. The kids would too. How's Bear?'

Kate felt tearful and longed for him to be right here in the kitchen, holding her close, asking her how she was, before making her a coffee. When she saw a piece of her sunflower mug she missed sweeping up, her eyes filled with tears.

'Just fine. Bear is just fine.'

As if to confirm what she said, he gave a small yelp and wagged his tail. Kate bit back a sob. 'Sorry, Ryan. Gotta go. The kids need to be at school early for music.'

After she dropped the kids outside the hall for music rehearsal, Kate had time to kill before work. She decided to head to Carindale and get herself a mug to replace her precious sunflowers. Something to distract her from the awfulness of everything and the sadness that threatened to drown her. She pulled into the largely empty multi-storey carpark. Inside, staff were setting up, pulling covers off cabinets and rolling up shutters to boutique shops. Kate headed for Target, the only store open. They were bound to have something.

All the aisles had been rearranged. Kate searched for kitchenware, frustrated that what should have been a straightforward task was time-consuming and difficult.

'Kate! What a lovely surprise. What are you doing here?'

Her heart skipped a beat or two. *What was Daryl doing in Target?* Her face suddenly felt red hot. 'Just getting myself a new coffee mug, mine broke.'

Somehow, the thought of the shattered sunflowers on her kitchen floor made something inside Kate disintegrate and she started to cry. Without missing a beat, Daryl dumped his items on the nearest shelf, enveloped her, stroked her hair. 'Hey, what did I say? Are you alright?'

She pulled away, frightened how good it felt to have strong arms around her and to allow herself to cry. 'Sorry. It's been an awful couple of days.'

'I can see that. How about a coffee. My treat?'

She hesitated. 'I'm not sure that's a good idea. Anyway, I have to work soon.'

'A quick one. Just till you're feeling better.'

They sat on a bench with coffees, Kate careful to ensure no part of her leg was close to his. The rising hum of the morning surrounded them. Daryl took a sip from his cardboard cup.

'That must have been a special mug.'

'Yeah. It was a gift and reminded me of happy days.'

He looked at her, one eyebrow raised.

Tears hovered just below the surface. Kate willed herself to hold it together in front of him. Her mind wandered to Shelley dancing with her doctor, and she wondered what Ryan would say if he saw Kate in Daryl's arms in the aisles of a department store with Taylor Swift lyrics playing in the background.

'Sorry about back there. I just have a lot on right now and feel a bit overwhelmed by things.'

'Just glad I saw you. You looked like you needed a hug. I was hoping to get some prizes for the boys in the Wild Pups team I'm coaching. You know, player of the week, best sportsmanship… just to keep them committed.' He laughed. 'To keep their eye on the ball.'

Kate wanted to reassure him that while he was coaching the team, he was guaranteed one hundred percent attendance. Not only by the boys, but by the parents, many of whom were star-struck. She drained her coffee and stood up. 'I really need to get to work.'

'Are you sure you're alright? You seem a bit fragile.'

'Just tired. It was nothing.'

She dropped her cup into a nearby bin. 'By the way, the flowers were gorgeous. Thanks. You didn't have to do that.'

He came over and stood a fraction too close. Kate felt her face heat up and stepped back when his hand reached towards her neck. Instinctively she jerked away, just as his finger lifted the silver star pendant she was wearing. It snapped and suddenly Daryl was holding it aloft between two fingers.

'God, I'm so sorry, I didn't mean to break it.'

He stared at it, recognition in his eyes. 'I remember this. You were wearing it the last time we were together, before you stopped talking to me.'

The memories from that day crowded her head like white noise and she put her hands up, pressed her palms on her temples. 'I really have to go. Just keep it.'

She hurried back to the car, eager to get away, leaving the past glinting between his fingers.

21

TORI had felt the lump in the shower a few weeks ago then shelved it after seeing her doctor. It had taken a week to book in the scan and she'd cancelled once as a customer needed a dress finished urgently. It was just so busy with Indigo starting, the online orders at The Treasure Chest multiplying and now the threat of Leo's father hovering. Dr Chong had been efficient and asked all sorts of probing questions about Tori's family history, how much she drank, whether she smoked, and how long she had breastfed Leo. Tori made a promise to herself to start a bit of self-care. Cut back on the alcohol, put more effort into eating well, exercising, getting enough sleep; all those impossible things that felt incompatible with running a business and raising Leo.

The moment her phone rang and the doctor advised her she needed to make a follow up appointment, she knew. Dr Chong, who looked like she had graduated a couple of months ago, was kind, but it didn't lessen the shock.

'I'm sorry, Tori. I'll refer you to a surgeon, get you seen this week.'

Later that afternoon, Tori burst into tears when Indigo walked into the store and called out, 'How are things?'

Indigo dropped the bundle of new clothes she was bringing inside to sort and swung the closed sign around on the door. She came down and embraced Tori.

'Hey, what's going on? Has that man come back to stake a claim on Leo?'

Tori wept afresh, the soft brush of Indigo's skin against her own undid her. It reminded her of those blissful days when she drove up from Melbourne and lived with Kate. The two of them often hugged at the end of a long day, when Kate had looming deadlines and Tori was studying towards her Diploma in Fashion and Textiles while her belly bloomed.

Tori's words escaped like an exhalation. 'Breast cancer.'

She pushed her face into Indigo's shoulder, inhaled her eucalypt scent and longed to reach back into the past and change things, live a better life.

Indigo held her and asked no more questions. Tori succumbed to the warmth of another body pressed against hers. She was aware of the curve of Indigo's neck, the gentle pressure of her hand in the small of her back. Eventually, her thoughts quietened. Indigo still held her close, used one hand to brush hair from Tori's tear-stained face.

Indigo stepped back, keeping her hands on Tori's shoulders. 'I'm sorry.'

There was a stillness, a silence where neither of them needed words. Indigo let go and stood with her arms loose by her sides. 'Why don't I set up the back room. Stay here while you get whatever treatment you need. I could help with Leo.'

Tori's brow creased. 'Are you sure? The room is tiny.'

'I could sleep in before heading to work next door. Win, win.'

'I appreciate it. Thanks.'

Somehow, the thought of Indigo being close filled Tori with a warm peace.

✦

On the two afternoons Leo did football training, Tori half-thought of going along and keeping an eye on him while Daryl was involved with the coaching. These were Indigo's afternoons off, and she had already taken on so much more than Tori expected.

An older woman shuffled up to the counter with a soft, green scarf and brooch. Tori remembered to smile, rang up the items, took care to wrap them in matching green tissue, and handed the bag over.

Just then Leo walked into the shop, dirt-covered and dishevelled. Something was wrong, he usually went around the back of the unit, let himself in and did his homework while she finished up at The Treasure Chest.

She ignored the customer scanning the shop for help and hurried over to Leo. 'What's up?'

Leo wouldn't look her in the eye. He rubbed the scuffed toe of his footy boots on the floor. His socks were around his ankles, the laces undone. Several late customers were milling around the racks. An elderly gentleman inspected the maple chest. Tori wondered if she could fob them off and talk to Leo alone. For a moment, she wondered if Leo knew about the cancer, but that was impossible. Only Indigo knew. Tori planned to tell Leo herself, to keep her voice upbeat. After all, Dr Chong had been guarded but positive and given her an optimistic chance of doing well. This was what she wanted to convey to Leo. *You know me, I'm too tough to let the cancer win.*

He let his satchel drop to the floor with a thud and shoved his hands in his pockets. 'Mr Brady offered me a place in a two-week footy camp. A scholarship so it won't cost you anything. It's during the next holidays for selected players only.'

Tori had to turn her head so he wouldn't see the anger in her face. How dare Daryl ask Leo before running it past her first.

'He's only been your coach for a few weeks. You barely know him. How can you go away with him for two weeks?'

'It's Mr Brady. Everyone knows him. He said he would talk to you. I really want to go.'

Leo sounded defensive, like his future happiness depended on Tori's goodwill.

'I planned to go away ourselves in the holidays. A week at the beach. Just you and me.'

Tori had been planning it and checked a few places on the Sunshine Coast online, wanting to surprise Leo. For the second time, she turned her face away and hoped her voice would not betray her. 'How about you head inside. I'll see you in half an hour or so.'

Leo snatched up his satchel, turned and left without saying a word. Tori noticed the older gentleman had left. There was still someone shifting through the coat rack near the front. Then Kate stepped around with a grey woollen cape and green belted jacket draped over one arm.

'Tori, how are you? Leo didn't seem himself.'

Shrugging, Tori held herself together. 'He's growing up. I guess we can't agree on everything.'

Her voice had a quaver. Kate lowered her voice. 'Something's up, isn't it?'

Tori looked away not wanting Kate to see her on the brink of tears. 'I'm scared of losing Leo.'

Kate dumped the two items on the counter and gave Tori a hug. 'He's just going through the normal stages of growing up and asserting his independence. That boy is devoted to you.'

Tori let herself soften in Kate's arms, the second time she had dissolved against someone within an hour.' Tori didn't recognise this new fragile, vulnerable woman inhabiting her body. She pulled away. 'I'm having a patch. I'll survive.'

The jingle indicated another couple of customers, and she handed Kate her two items. 'Here, why don't you try them on?'

Kate disappeared into the changeroom while Tori forced the ends of her lips upwards, scanned The Treasure Chest, and went back to the task of serving her customers.

Tori imagined talking to Kate about it all. They used to talk about everything during those months they shared a bedsit at West End. Tori slept on the futon, covered the Laminex table with fabrics, dress patterns drawn on butcher's paper, and coloured thread, while Kate hunched over the tiny desk in her room swotting away. While careful with her inheritance, Tori insisted on paying the bills, went to the Saturday markets and bought fresh produce, advising it was because she was looking after the baby developing in her belly.

When Tori's waters broke, Kate had been more anxious than Tori and missed the turn-off to the Mater Mother's in her flustered state. It would have been humorous if Tori had not been so terrified. The pain was so much more intense than Tori imagined. She sweated, breathed, and panted for twelve hours, refusing drugs or an epidural. The labour was a test of her mettle, a forging of Tori, the woman. When Leo finally lay sticky on her abdomen, his cry piercing, she fell in love for the first time, overwhelmed that an episode of unwelcome coupling could end with such perfection. Nothing prepared her for the arrival of that perfect little boy with dark eyes, tufts of black hair, and curled fingers that gripped hers. The gasp of pain when his mouth latched onto her nipple, the way his fist pushed against her when he suckled, filled her with a desire to be there for him, keep him safe, keep him for herself.

Kate wandered out of the change room and held up one of the items. 'This one, thanks.'

Tori emerged from her thoughts. 'So, the cape?'

'I think so. It's always so hard to choose.'

'How about I give it to you for half price.'

'Oh, I can't accept that.'

'Of course, you can. Now, no arguments.'

The cash register gave a metallic ping when the change drawer opened. Tori missed that sound when customers used their phones and plastic to pay. She wrapped the cape in tissue and slid it into her signature brown bag aware of all the things she hadn't told Kate muddying the space between them.

Tori handed Kate her purchase over the counter, wishing herself back in the safe space of the past.

✣

The door jingled again. Tori's heart sank. It was a couple of minutes to closing time. Maybe she would tell the new customer to come back tomorrow. Daryl strolled in and came up close. Tori's throat closed.

'A great boutique you've got here. Shelley talks about it all the time.'

He let his eyes wander around the store. Tori gritted her teeth, her anger about the football camp still fresh. 'How dare you invite Leo to a camp without asking me first. I had plans for the holidays and wanted to surprise him.'

He put his hands up in surrender. 'Hey, chill. I just mentioned it, and suggested he ask you if he can go.'

She crossed her arms, but Daryl ignored her body language and ran his hand along the maple sideboard.

'I was wondering if Shelley was here earlier this afternoon.'

Tori lost her footing, thrown by his change of topic, and wondered why he wanted to know.

The truth was, Shelley came in often. She ran her fingers down fabrics, gazed with longing at some of the items, but never bought anything. Today she lingered over the jewellery cabinet and fondled the antique, amber pendant in there. Tori had reached over and slipped it around Shelley's neck. 'It's Baltic amber. See the insect trapped inside?'

Tori fastened the clasp. It was one of her favourite pieces. 'Amber is a fossil resin, formed forty-five million years ago. It's quite incredible. Pine trees formed a sticky resin sap that dripped and oozed down the trunk and branches trapping insects along the way. Eventually, the sap hardened and became fossilised.'

Shelley felt the smooth, honey-coloured stone. 'Poor thing, trapped inside forever.'

Tori wondered about Shelley and what had happened between her and Kate. They were close buddies until Daryl started dating Kate, and then it all fell apart.

'You should buy it. It really suits you.'

Shelley blushed, slipped the necklace off, held it for another moment then shook her head. 'No. Thanks anyway.'

Another customer called Tori for help. She didn't see Shelley leave.

Tori shrugged, watched the way Daryl's fingers slid over the edge of the maple. 'Not sure to be honest, it's been flat out today.'

Daryl's fingers continued to glide over the polished timber without looking at her. 'Don't deny Leo opportunities because of me.'

He turned and walked over, stood a fraction too close, and Tori stepped out of reach. 'It's past closing time. If you would excuse me, I need to lock up.'

He leant against the jewellery counter, reached in and pulled out the amber pendant, holding it up to the light. Tori held her breath. Maybe Shelley had mentioned it to him, and he was planning to buy it and surprise her.

'I know you girls hang out together. Please keep an eye on Shelley. She's taken the move hard.'

Tori forced herself to take slow breaths, willing him to go, when he dropped the pendant back into its velvet casing in the cabinet. 'Shelley is a great girl, but not fierce and independent like you. She needs someone to look after her.'

He leant towards Tori.

She stared him down and remembered her phone was under the counter, out of reach. Just when she thought she might make a grab for it, he sighed and headed towards the door. He put one hand on the handle then stopped. 'See you around.'

He walked out and pulled the door shut behind him.

22

KATE picked Edie and Noah up from afterschool care and tossed their satchels into the boot. She reached up to touch her star pendant and remembered it was gone. She blushed to think about Daryl and how he had held her this morning.

'Mum, can we have fish fingers for dinner?'

'Why not.'

To be honest, the thought of preparing anything for dinner was exhausting. Since Ryan was on his jaunt up the coast, everything at home had deteriorated. Washing was piled up to be folded, the dishwasher waiting to be emptied with another stack of dirty dishes waiting on the sink.

'When is Dad home?'

Noah's little voice sounded sad.

'Not too long now.'

The truth was, she wasn't sure. He meant to tell her a few days ago once he confirmed whether the final gig in Caloundra was going ahead. Kate's mood plunged. She revved up the driveway and swore under her breath when she heard the back of the car grind on the gutter. Bear started barking.

'Now I need you both to have a shower, get into your PJs and come out to the kitchen.'

When Edie opened her mouth to complain, Kate gave her the *don't start* glare. She ferreted in their satchels, tossed dirty lunchboxes in the sink, and cursed Ryan under her breath. When she heard the shower water running, she sighed with relief, pulled out the bag from The Treasure Chest and reached into the tissue paper. It rustled with the thrill of a purchase and the promise of transformation without effort. She draped it over herself, feeling the soft warmth of cashmere wool against her skin and imagined it was Ryan's arms around her. The unbidden image of Artemis crucified and hanging bloodied on the door filled her consciousness and her legs suddenly felt weak. She sank into the lounge, crumpled inside the soft shell of her cape. Head in her hands, she felt the warm rush of tears. She longed to tell someone and share her grief and sense of failure. That final phone call from Bea, *I just wanted to say goodbye,* echoed in her ears.

On impulse, Kate texted Georgie, hoping she was not wearing out her welcome. *Could I leave the kids with you for an hour or so? Something's come up.* Less than a minute later, Georgie responded. *Sure. Bring them over. I've made spag bol. Hug emoji, smiley face.*

I owe you. Three hug emojis, three heart emojis.

Half an hour later, Kate reached into the bottom of the pantry and pulled out the bottle of wine Daryl had gifted her. She would take it over to Tori. It was the perfect opportunity to drink it while Ryan was away. Somehow, sharing it with Ryan felt wrong. Kate would check in with Tori and tell her about Bea and Artemis while whinging about Ryan not being around when she needed him the most. Tori would understand. They used to talk all the time when Tori was pregnant with Leo and sharing the tiny flat.

Kate teared up again just as she pulled over and found a park near The Treasure Chest. She reached to grab the shiraz, ready to step out of the car, but stopped short. Daryl emerged from the shop, scanned the street, and seemed to look directly at her. She sank lower into her seat. He jumped into his four-wheel drive, did a U-turn, and disappeared. What on earth was he doing here? He didn't seem a vintage gear kind of bloke and the shop normally closed half an hour ago. Kate rested her head on the steering wheel feeling very alone.

She tried to text Ryan. *Hello? R U there?*

Deafening silence.

Kate sat in her car in the darkness gripping the bottle of red. She nearly dropped it when her phone lit up. She just needed to hear Ryan's voice, to feel reassured.

Just checking you are all right. You seemed very upset this morning.

She stiffened. Was it really only this morning she had wept in Daryl's arms? It felt like a year ago. Her fingers hovered over the phone, wondering where he was. It made her shiver to think she watched him walk out of Tori's shop a few minutes ago. She dropped her phone into her bag and decided not to respond. Her hand moved to the passenger seat. When she touched the cool, curved glass of the shiraz, she wavered. There was no harm in thanking him, he was being a gentleman after all.

Her thoughts in turmoil, Kate pulled out from her park and drove past the midweek crowd milling down Martha Street. Couples holding hands, heads bent together in conversations over wine in the restaurants. She drove up the hill along Martha Street and headed onto Boundary Road, the city twinkling below. She continued up the hill until she left the light behind and turned off at White's Hill Reserve. The weight of grief and loneliness pressed down on her. She pulled out her phone again and, fingers trembling, texted back. *Thanks for the hug. I needed it.*

The minute she pressed send and heard her message whoosh across the empty night, she regretted it. Three dots indicated an incoming message, and her stomach knotted. *Are you free to talk?*

Kate hesitated again. *Yes.*

'Hello?'

His voice was warm inside the car while she sat in the darkness and gazed into the night. She found herself unable to respond.

'Are you there?'

'Yes.' Her voice was wobbly again.

'You sound upset again.'

Kate started crying, unable to control the tears that ran down her face. Then she saw a figure walking towards her in the darkness and froze, huddling down into her cape, ready to drive away.

'I thought it was you down in Martha Street.'

Her phone lit up just as Daryl's face peered into the driver's window. His mouth moved as the message came up on her screen.

'I was worried about you and followed you up here.'

She wound down the window, her heart beating wildly against her sternum.

He reached in and handed her a large, masculine hanky, then glanced down at the shiraz she was clutching. 'Nice drop.'

She blushed. He winked.

'Hang on a minute.'

He disappeared and, looking in her rear vision, she made out the shape of the four-wheel drive parked some distance behind her. A few moments later, he returned with a couple of acrylic picnic goblets. He let himself into the passenger side, reached over for the bottle and poured two glasses.

'Cheers to friendship.'

The dull clink of plastic on plastic.

23

KATE tossed and turned all night, relieved she had scheduled a day off to get her paperwork and invoices up to date. Sitting up at White's Hill with Daryl two weeks earlier felt like a strange dream. After a few mouthfuls of wine, she had felt a welcome calm, the dark a cocoon that encouraged revelation.

My client jumped from a balcony.

I want to give Leo opportunities. Tori doesn't trust me.

Their inside voices spoken aloud. When she lay in bed at night and alone it made Kate uneasy and vulnerable. She reminded herself she had done nothing wrong. They had taken great care not to touch one another, even when he handed her a glass of shiraz. They were friends, supporting each other. That was all. Whenever her phone vibrated, Kate panicked, unsure of what she would say to Daryl, but to her immense relief, he didn't contact her.

When Kate finally fell asleep, morning streamed through the blinds, and it was time to get ready and do the school drop off. Her mouth was dry. Her head throbbed with fatigue.

Noah and Edie were up and eating cereal. Bear gambolled around Kate's legs and nearly tripped her up. 'Has the dog been fed?'

He looked up at her, his shaggy face hopeful, but Edie nodded, her mouth full.

Kate's phone buzzed. She jumped.

It was Ryan.

'Morning, Beautiful.'

'Dad!'

Edie and Noah left their cereal to grow soggy and crowded around the phone. Kate was grateful their excitement compensated for her own lack of enthusiasm.

'Have you been practising for the concert? I can't wait to see it.'

'Miss Nightingale is letting me play the song I wrote, *A Star Lights the Way*.'

'Edie, I'm so proud. Can't wait to see you up on stage.'

Noah pushed forward and tried to get Edie out of the way. 'I'm in the orchestra. We're playing three songs.'

'What a pro. I'm so proud.'

Noah puffed his chest out and smiled at Kate. 'And Mum's helping backstage. Miss Nightingale said *your mum is a rockstar. We can't do these concerts without people like your mum helping*.'

'Miss Nightingale is a wise woman. Your mum is my shining star.'

Kate was aware of an uncomfortable heaviness in her head.

'And there's going to be food. Hot dogs and pizza.'

'And wine for the grown-ups,' added Edie.

'Sounds amazing. Now, can I speak to Mum, please?'

Kate hugged herself, reluctant to look at Ryan properly.

'I'm coming back the day before the school's music fest. We won't be playing in Caloundra.'

'Thanks for letting me know.' Her voice sounded tight.

'You okay?' His face fuzzed for a moment, froze, then came back into focus.

'Fine, thanks. It's been busy.'

'Hey, I appreciate your support with my music, I really do. Thanks for holding the fort. We'll have to celebrate when I get back.'

'Ryan, we have to go. I need drop the kids at school.'

He blew them all a kiss. Edie pretended to catch hers. 'Love you, Dad.'

The phone went black.

✦

Half an hour later, Kate pulled up at the school and helped the kids get their stuff out of the car. Today was the rehearsal for the music fest and the boot was piled with Edie's glockenspiel, her guitar and Noah's cello. Edie loved her guitar, had spent hours practising her own song. *Murphy genes,* Ryan often said. When he was home, he jammed with Edie, pretending they were on the stage with an adoring crowd screaming for encores. Kate eased satchels onto backs and watched them lug their instruments to the hall in readiness for the rehearsal.

When Kate finally sat at the desk in her home office, the phone rang. She glanced at the number. What did Georgie want? Kate's voice was abrupt. 'Hello?'

Georgie sounded relieved. 'Are you at work? Noah mentioned you were at home today. Miss Nightingale wants to run through the entire program, and we need someone to direct the kids onto stage, so the transitions are smooth and quick. One of the staff is away and we are a bit desperate. Can you come?'

Kate's mood plunged and she squeezed her eyes shut. She gave her blank screen a longing glance and spent another five minutes sitting at her desk appreciating the rare quiet solitude of being home alone with Bear. She owed Georgie. Reluctantly, she shooed Bear outside, nearly wrenched the screen door off its sill when it got stuck, locked up, and made her way back to the school.

Kate stood behind the hall with a series of lists, detailing the order of seating on stage for each item. She caught sight of Noah who was thrilled to see her. Her face crinkled into a warm smile and forgave him for telling Georgie she was home. When she lifted her hand and waved, she hoped it would not embarrass him, but he gave an enthusiastic one back. 'That's my mum!'

Giggles followed. Kate forgot how kids could make your insides warm and soft as toasted marshmallow.

Children chattered in loud whispers, interspersed with excited giggles and shrieks. Georgie poked her bobbed head around and raised a finger to her mouth. Kate clapped her hands. A single beat followed by three in rapid succession. The kids repeated the same series of claps, and the excited chatter ceased like someone had turned off a switch.

In a soft voice, she called out a list of names and the relevant children formed a neat line. The rest of the rehearsal went without a hitch and during the final performance, Tori arrived with bundles of programmes and handed them over to Miss Nightingale.

Kate wondered if she could slip away unnoticed and spend the rest of her day in blissful quiet with Bear nudging her feet when Tori looked up, mouthed, 'Finished?'

The thought of Daryl's disclosure prickled Kate's conscience. She exited the stage and joined Tori, then flicked through one of the programmes. 'These look great, really professional.'

Tori tensed next to her. Kate looked up and saw Daryl enter the back of the hall. He walked up to Georgie and started chatting. She glowed, her hands gesticulating as she laughed at something he had said. Soon afterward, Daryl started carrying stacked chairs and setting them up. Kate looked away, determined not to catch his eye, afraid she might betray them and their shared confidences.

'Jesus, let's get out of here.'

Kate nodded and followed Tori onto the oval.

The bell for lunch was shrill and the children all ran to their respective classrooms.

'Fancy a bite to eat? I want to talk about a couple of things.'

Tori looked at her hopefully. Kate longed to head home and curl up on the lounge with her computer. She bit her lip and attempted to muster enthusiasm. 'Why not?'

Tori punched her on the shoulder. 'Let's head to The Battered Fishwife and get fish and chips.'

'Perfect. I'll meet you on Riding Road.'

❖

The smells from the fish and chipper were divine. They joined the line and soon were sitting on benches holding cardboard boxes greasy with crispy, fat chips and melt-in-the-mouth, lightly battered fish pieces. Tori toyed with her food, dunked a chip into tartar sauce and took a half-hearted bite.

'I want to talk to you about Daryl.'

Kate stopped, her chip poised mid-air. Had Tori spotted the two of them and come to a false conclusion? Kate scrambled in her head to assemble explanations to reassure Tori and herself.

'I know the two of you were an item back in the day, that something happened, and you broke up. It's none of my business, but I thought you might have insights into Daryl.'

Part of Kate's poised chip broke off and fell to the pavement, while anxiety twisted her insides into a tight knot. A noisy miner tipped its head, made a stab at the chip, then, unsuccessful, flew out of reach.

Tori stared at the cracked bitumen. 'Daryl is bad news. He came into the shop a couple of weeks ago and pestered me to let Leo head off on a bloody football camp. For two whole weeks.'

Kate nearly choked on a chip and threw out another piece to lure the miner back. Tori raised her voice. 'His behaviour is totally inappropriate. He wanted to know if Shelley had been there. It made me so uncomfortable.'

The miner hopped a little closer, tentative, one eye on the broken chip.

Kate was aware of the rise and fall of her chest, while the sound of Tori's strained voice filled her ears.

'Shelley comes in most days.' Tori's brow creased. 'It's odd. She never buys anything, just looks around and touches things with this longing. Even when I ask if she is looking for something special and offer to discount an item, she leaves empty-handed.'

'There's no rules about looking. I thought you enjoyed customers just browsing and enjoying the ambiance of The Treasure Chest.'

Tori took a few bites of her battered fish and crossed her legs. The miner aborted its second attempt to snare a chip and flew to the back of a nearby chair, its eyes beady.

'She's looking for something and whatever that is, it won't be found in my shop.'

Tori put her fish and chips down and wiped her fingers on a

napkin. 'Anyway, I gave Daryl the short shift and told him I had no idea if Shelley had dropped in as I'd been flat out all day. He moved into my personal space and pressured me to let Leo attend this football camp.'

Kate watched the bird's expectant posture. 'He thinks Leo is a great player and wants to offer him opportunities. Don't be too hard on him.'

'Don't tell me you're defending him. No offense, but I never liked him, even back at uni. Full of bullshit and a false sense of entitlement because he was good at football.'

'The bloke is having a tough time. He's being forced to retire because of injuries and is trying hard to fit into the community.'

Tori snorted. 'There is no way I am letting that man take Leo anywhere.'

Kate looked away, hoping her emotions had not spilt onto her face. Tori did not know the half of it. Kate didn't want to hear any more and started to wrap up the remainder of her meal. Tori grabbed her arm with greater urgency this time. 'There's one more thing. Would you promise to look after Leo if something happens to me? I want to rewrite my will, make you and Ryan his guardians.'

Kate spun around, stared at Tori. 'Of course, we'd be honoured. That's a bit out of the blue. What prompted this?'

Kate stared down at her phone and noticed the time. 'I'm so sorry, Tori. I just noticed the time and really need to go. Edie has her music lesson. Let's go out for lunch very soon, discuss it properly and sort out the paperwork.'

Tori looked poised to say something else when the miner took his opportunity and swooped down to pick up the chip, finally victorious. Tori clammed up, the remainder of her meal cold and limp beside her. Kate put her hand on Tori's shoulder. 'Shelley is struggling to settle in, and Daryl is adjusting to life as a retired footballer. They are both having a hard time.'

She hurried to her car, felt her phone vibrate and read the message. *Thank you for a beautiful evening. XXX*

She broke into a sweat. Why did he send that two weeks later? She reached into her bag and touched the photo of the two of them from their uni days before driving off, hands moist on the steering wheel.

24

24

TORI sat a while longer then tossed her nearly full takeaway container into the bin, angry for no discernible reason. Talking to Kate usually made her feel relieved and better about things. Tori drove home the long way, wanting to see the afternoon sun speckle the river and watch the CityCats ferry passengers to their destinations. There was something reassuring about the rhythms of the city. The sun dipped behind a cloud and Tori indicated and headed back to The Treasure Chest to help Indigo get ready for tomorrow.

When she pulled into the drive, the now familiar black four-wheel drive was parked outside. Furious, she ran to the door, wondering if Leo was all right. He was meant to be at football training tonight. When she fumbled with the key, she realised the door was unlocked and sweat beaded on her hairline. She kicked the door open, and two faces looked up.

'What the hell are you doing in my home?'

Daryl put his arm up in surrender. 'Leo left his mouthguard at home. I offered to drive him to pick it up.'

Leo's eyes were wide with fear.

'Mum, why didn't you tell me?'

He turned his face away from her, his voice trembling. 'I was looking for my mouth guard and found this.'

He waved the report above his head. The one with the words *spiculated with calcification, suspicious for malignancy* typed in the conclusion. How did Leo even know what the word malignancy meant?

Tori's mouth went dry. He took a step towards her, still holding the paper. 'Mr Brady was here when I found the report.'

Tori's nails bit into her palms and she prayed her legs would hold her up. She had planned to sit him down tonight and mention the breast cancer over dinner. Without knowing how she got there, she found herself sitting on the lounge with Daryl handing her a glass of water. Her hand shook when she snatched it and took a sip. There was a knock at the door. Would this god-awful day never end?

Daryl went to get the door and Indigo stepped in. She raised an eyebrow at Tori who shrugged. Leo made a sobbing sound and stood at a distance from his Mum. Daryl slipped away and some of the tension drained from the room.

Indigo absorbed the scene. 'Have I come at a bad time? I was thinking of moving my stuff in this evening.'

'No, it's the perfect time. Just give me a few minutes with Leo first.'

Indigo nodded and pulled the door closed, leaving them alone.

'Are you going to die, Mum?'

Tori reached her arms out to Leo. He slid away.

'No, Leo. I'm going to the hospital and the doctors will sort things out. I'll be home before you know it. Promise.'

'You didn't tell me.'

'I only just found out a short time ago myself. I wanted to tell you this evening.'

He sat, elbows on his knees, head held in his hands. He started crying. 'I'm scared. I don't want you to go.'

Tori wriggled closer, enveloped him in her arms and held him tight to herself. 'Me too, Leo. It's okay to be scared.'

Leo loosened from her grasp and ran to his room. Tori stayed very still on the lounge and willed Leo to come back out. A minute later he came with a shoebox. He tipped it up onto the coffee table and out tumbled at least twenty origami treasure chests, just like the one he had made for her but in different colours.

'I saw the ad for the footy camp and really wanted to go. I thought

I'd make these, that you could sell them at the shop, and I could pay for it myself. Then Mr Brady offered me the scholarship. He said it wouldn't cost me anything. I'm sorry I upset you.'

'Oh, Leo. Why didn't you just ask me?'

'I thought you would say no, that if I saved up my own money, you might let me go.'

'I'm so sorry, Leo.'

'Mum, it's okay. If I pay for myself and don't use the scholarship, can I go? I'll make lots of chests and do all my jobs.'

He looked so young and helpless standing there. 'Is that why you got sick? Because of me making you upset. I won't go if you don't want me to.'

'Leo, it is absolutely nothing to do with you. I promise. Let's talk about the football camp again later.'

He buried himself in her arms, his body racked with sobs. Tori hugged him so tightly that she could feel every one of his ribs pressed into hers. She stared at the colourful pile of treasure chests and wept with him.

⚴

An hour or so later, Indigo returned with her small duffle bag, a bottle of red, and her favourite pottery mug. Watching her unpack felt like the most natural thing in the world. Leo disappeared and Tori heard the shower water running.

'I appreciate you coming over. Sorry the room is so small.'

'I don't need much space.'

Indigo dumped her bag, came back out. 'How about I make us a cuppa?'

Tori reached for a tissue, blew her nose, used her sleeve to wipe the tears from her cheeks. 'Let me do that, I know where everything is.'

'How about you just chill tonight. I'll find what I need or ask.'

Tori watched Indigo pull down the kettle, measure leaves, and wrestle the red knitted tea cosy over the spout of the pot. Placing it all on a tray, she poured, adding milk and two sugars to Tori's. It felt intimate, someone remembering details like that.

They sipped in companionable silence. Tori stared out the window onto a cobalt sky getting darker by the minute. They didn't turn the lights on, just sat in the growing dimness. Tori clutched her mug, whispered, 'What if I don't make it? I'm not sure I can go through with it all.'

Indigo stopped what she was doing and sat down close, her presence a solid wall of warmth. 'How about we just focus on today. Let's get through this evening. One thing, one day at a time, huh?'

Tori put her mug down, pulled her legs up to her chest and wrapped her arms around them. She whispered, 'What about Leo?'

'He's a top kid. This will rattle him, but I reckon he'll do just fine.'

Indigo spoke in a low, reassuring voice, 'I've ordered some curries that should arrive any minute. Let's keep everything easy.'

Tori kept her arms tight around her knees and stared straight ahead. 'You ever done stuff you are ashamed about?'

Indigo leaned in close, her breath soft on Tori's neck. A gust of wind shifted the silhouetted branches outside. 'Too many things to keep track of.'

Tears found their way down Tori's cheeks. 'I can't help thinking that if I'd looked after myself better and shown my body more respect, I'd be okay.'

Indigo's hand was firm on her shoulder. 'Life can sure dish up some shit. To be honest, I'm not sure I want to be around forever, never letting go a bit. I prefer to take my chances, drink a bit too much, and eat crap sometimes.'

She lessened her grip but did not let go. 'How about I pour us both a shiraz? If you want, I've a joint we can share after Leo's asleep. No pressure.'

Tori looked up, her face tear stained. 'Yeah, that would be great. Take the edge off things. It's been a while.'

Indigo bent down and their foreheads touched. Indigo's lips brushed Tori's so briefly she wondered if it really happened. She touched the spot with her finger and tried to hold the memory of it in place when the doorbell announced the arrival of dinner.

Indigo clattered around the kitchen looking for bowls and cutlery. 'Let's have dinner,' she said, just as Leo emerged smelling of shampoo, his hair damp.

25

THE following morning Kate cut sandwiches for the kids' lunches, while her mind whirred through her catch up with Tori, wondering what was going on. She jammed the slices of bread together and cut them into triangles, butter and vegemite oozing out. Tori hadn't been her usual self and seemed to have lost weight. Had Kate missed something? The minute Ryan came back, she would mention the will to him and arrange for Tori to come around so they could talk properly.

Noah thrust a crumpled note into Kate's hand. 'Can I go to Underwater World?'

Her phone pinged and she jumped. It was Miss Nightingale. Something about the music fest next week. There was never a moment's peace. Kate pushed concerns about Tori aside and filled out Noah's form. She scribbled her signature at the end and the phone rang again. This time it was Ryan.

'Morning, Beautiful.'

'Well, hello.'

She regretted the irritation in her voice.

'I'm home next week, only a few more sleeps.'

'Good for you.'

'Are you sure you're okay? You sound stressed. Why not cut back a bit, take a bit of time off?'

She glanced over at the bills and wondered if she should sit down and fiddle with the mortgage calculator.

'I can't, Ryan. Those inconvenient bills just keep coming. The car needs a service, and Noah needs new footy boots.'

'Dad!'

Edie appeared with toothpaste on her chin. Noah climbed onto a bar stool and crawled onto the bench and waved at Ryan's smudgy face on the phone. Bear, not wanting to be left out of the action, barked. Kate rolled her eyes and left the kids to chat, coaxing Bear out the back. Before jiggling the sliding door shut, she bent down and buried her face into his black fur, absorbing the unconditional love that quivered from his feathered tail up along his spine.

Noah's bottom was in the air, his elbows on the bench, head in his hands. Edie knelt precariously on a stool. Both were eager to tell their dad everything.

'Time for school, kids.'

'Dad wants a word.' Edie nudged the phone towards her.

'Kate, you worry too much. I'll be home soon. Try and relax a bit and let go of stuff.'

She pushed her exasperation down. 'See you soon, we really have to head off.'

He blew her a kiss. She made no effort to catch it.

✢

The minute Kate parked outside the school, Shelley walked past, shepherding the twins ahead of her. Kate watched Shelley scan the cars then check her phone looking flustered. Without looking Kate's way, Shelley grabbed one twin in each hand and walked through the gates.

When Georgie hurried past with her two girls, Kate ducked her head down, pretending to fumble in her handbag on the floor, hoping Georgie wouldn't notice her. Kate didn't feel like getting caught up in a conversation about the music fest. When she peered out the window, Georgie was flapping her hands about, talking to another mother. With a sigh of relief, Kate turned to Edie and Noah. 'Okay, get your bags out. Don't forget afterschool care.'

Noah scrambled out of the car, but Edie stayed looking stricken.

'I forgot my hat. Can we go home and get it?'

Kate's heart dropped like a stone. She really needed a coffee this morning. 'I'm afraid you'll have to sit under cover at lunchtime instead of playing with your friends. Next time, you won't forget.'

Edie's bottom lip dropped. 'Dad would go back.'

Ryan would, even if it meant being late to work, not that he had his job at Soul Sounds anymore. Kate swallowed her irritation. 'Sorry, Edie, but I need to get to work. Maybe next time leave it on the hook in the hallway and then you won't forget it. It's not the first time.'

Kate swung past Vincent's, keen to get herself a proper brew, when she spotted Shelley walking towards her, her sharp heels sinking in the grass. When she saw Kate, she looked around again. She whispered, 'Can you spare a minute?'

Kate did a quick calculation. Her first client was straightforward and didn't need any prep. 'Is something up? You don't look yourself.'

'Do you mind if we go inside?'

'Sure.'

They sat in one of the corners. Shelley fiddled with the sugars, then reached over and grabbed Kate's forearm. 'I just can't seem to get myself together since moving.'

Shelley softened her grip and let go. Her blue eyes were moist. Kate could see tiny black dots of mascara on individual lashes. Their coffees arrived.

Shelley looked away and started to roll her wedding ring round and round her finger.

'Daryl loves the kids, I know that. He says he loves me too, but he can go from zero to one hundred in a second, gets irritated by the tiniest things.'

'Is he hurting you?'

'He never hits me, but he gets so angry. It got worse after, you know, the incident I mentioned.'

Kate reached over to touch Shelley's hand. It remained passive under hers. 'Are you sure you're okay?'

'He's always very sorry afterwards. And the thing is, sometimes everything is great, and we have fun. When I told him how I just can't do this anymore, he broke down. Then he got angry and said I never remember the good times, only the bad times.'

Shelley's fingers trembled, and she pulled away from Kate. 'I really don't know what to do. Imagine the media if I left him. Hounding after me for gossip and dirt about my marriage.'

'Have you thought about booking in to see someone?'

'I mentioned it and he teared up. He didn't want someone telling him how to live his life. Then he held me weeping and said that every woman he ever loved has left him.'

Kate felt a stab and remembered Daryl's whispered confidences in the sultry heat of sex and summer. *My mum left when I was ten. Went to see a friend in Melbourne and never came back.* She bit the inside of her cheek when she thought about her own silence after the miscarriage.

Then Shelley sat upright again.

'I thought maybe I could see you, not just as a friend, but as a professional. I want to ask you for advice, for help.'

Her words tumbled out. 'I realise that you don't see friends, but I know and trust you. And Daryl does too. I could see you without him getting suspicious, thinking I was divulging dirt to a stranger. I'd pay, I'm not expecting a freebie.'

She hung her head again. 'The thing is, I'm terrified of being alone. I admire Tori. Running that business, raising Leo by herself, but I'm not sure I could do it. I just don't know what to do.'

Kate squirmed in her chair and let her gaze flitter away from Shelley. Diners around them were chatting and laughing. The clink of cutlery on plates sounded loud. The blood drained from Kate's face. 'I'm sorry. I'm always here for you as a friend, but I can't see you for counselling.'

Kate fished her phone out of her bag. 'Let me text you a few names. Psychologists who I know who will be happy to help you and provide confidential counselling.'

Shelley turned away, shoulders shaking. 'Of course. I shouldn't have asked. I'm so sorry.'

Kate's heart went numb. She longed to reach out, but Shelley stumbled away without even saying good-bye.

Kate pulled out into traffic and drove to work. When her phone pinged, she held her breath somehow knowing who it would be before she read the message. *I really need to talk. How about breakfast one morning?*

Sitting in the carpark outside her clinic, a chill rippled down her spine.

26

THE phone call from the hospital took Tori by surprise. The surgeon could fit her in tomorrow.

'I'm not ready,' she panicked.

Indigo leant in the doorway, watched Tori pack. 'You'll never be ready. Let's get this over and done with. And don't worry about anything. I'll manage the shop and pick Leo up from school.'

Tori looked up from her bag, eyes wide. 'That older bloke is going to pick up the maple sideboard. He's arranged a trailer. And there's a couple of dresses ready to go under the shelf, all wrapped with names tagged on the front.'

'I know, Tori. I'll manage. I promise.'

'And Leo has footy training on Monday and Wednesday. Please keep an eye on things. Don't let that coach, Daryl Brady, talk him into anything.'

'God no. With me here, he won't dare.'

They stepped outside. Tori locked up and handed Indigo the key. A sports bag slung over one shoulder, she was headed over to Indigo's minivan, when she saw Georgie running over from The Treasure Chest.

'What's up? I wanted to get some pieces for a period wedding I'm organising.'

She glanced at Tori. Her eyes dropped when they moved to Indigo. 'Something's wrong, isn't it?'

'Yeah, you could say that. I'm having a bit of breast lopped off.

It's all pretty sudden.'

'Oh God, Tori. I'm so sorry. Let me know if there is anything I can do. I mean it.'

Tori gave her a nod. 'Thanks.'

Indigo opened the slide door of the minivan and hoisted Tori's bag inside. They drove to the Mater Hospital.

❖

Tori woke up to the smell of antiseptic, the sound of beeping and the presence of a blue clad figure scribbling notes. There was a hand on her wrist, the inflation of a cuff on her arm and a thick bandage on her chest.

She was outside herself looking in, observing herself from some other place. She marvelled how simple it was to leave your body behind. Maybe she could just float away and never return to her corporeal form. Then she remembered Leo and panicked. She focussed on pulling herself together, forced herself back to her discomfort and tried to sit up. The dizziness and nausea were overwhelming. Plastic tubing snaked from her arm, tied her to the bed and kept her away from her son.

'You're awake. How do you feel?'

Tori realised the blue clad figure was speaking to her. The chilled air goosed her skin. She fought the urge to rip off the constrictive dressing, wrench out the tubing and walk away. Her body remained uncooperative and heavy on the bed. 'I need to get home. As soon as possible.'

The blue figure responded, 'The surgery went well. Someone will take you up to your room in a little while.'

Tori realised she must have fallen asleep. She awoke in another room, the pillow firm and high, the sheet tight across her body. She heard hushed voices and forced herself to concentrate. It was important to get home and back to Leo.

Another woman with a stethoscope around her neck placed a cool hand on Tori's. 'We'll discharge you before long. Just give yourself some time to recuperate. We'll have the pathology early tomorrow.'

It was the surgeon, Dr Bronwen Philip. She was kind in a reserved, professional way and scrolled through screens next to the bed, brow creased. 'Any pain?'

To be honest, Tori had never felt so disconnected from her body. This felt worse than those days when she had drunk too much. At least then her body punished her and let her know how awful she felt. She almost wanted some pain just to remind herself she was still alive. She shook her head, hopeful that not having pain would get her home sooner.

A young nurse hurried in, wrapped the cuff around Tori's arm again and checked the monitor with its saw-toothed and wavy lines. Here I am, Tori wanted to shout. I'm alive, you don't need that machine to check my vitals. Dr Philip spoke to the nurse. Why did people behave like she was not here? A fresh wave of anxiety threatened to send the monitor into overdrive. Her lips tingled, her breathing shallow and painful. She took slow breaths and allowed the anxiety to subside.

Tori caught drifts of the conversation between the nurse and Dr Philip. They were not talking about her anymore. Her breathing went back to a steady, normal rhythm and her heart rate visibly slowed down. Those white pills hypnotised her brain and old memories wafted in her semiconscious like floating dandelion seeds, each carrying a promise.

Tori slipped into her past. Suddenly every detail from a lifetime ago scrolled vivid in her mind. Scene by scene unfolded behind her lids. How old had she been? Seventeen?

She found herself back in the changerooms where she watched Elspeth's skirt drop to her feet and stared at the dark tufts of hair under her arms when she pulled her top off. One snap released Elspeth's breasts from the captivity of a bra. They looked fleshy and soft. The nipples were surprisingly dark. Elspeth caught her watching and Victoria (no one called her Tori back then) turned away. Her pulse was too fast. She wriggled into her speedos, let her fingers run over her own flat chest and imagined running them down Elspeth's curves. The whistle was shrill and called them all to the edge of the pool.

That night, Victoria imagined Elspeth's rounded curves in the dark of her bedroom and touched herself. In the weeks that followed, she avoided being near Elspeth, mortified that somehow, she would know.

It was during Tori's final year at school, now with her own clutch of pubes and modest breasts, that Donna joined the friendship group. Donna, olive skinned and lightly muscled from all the sport she played. She always trailed the scent of perspiration, her armpits damp from her latest exertion. Victoria started to stay behind after school to watch Donna play basketball and volleyball. She was lithe and fluid, aggressively competitive. Her legs were long and lean, the skin smooth, shaved. Victoria recalled stealing her uncle's razor and shaving the hairs off her own legs, running fingers down the smooth fresh-mowed skin. She struggled with the contour of her armpits; a few lacy hairs eluded her.

One afternoon, after school, Tori watched Donna shoot a record number of goals in a basketball game. Donna had come off the court, skin glowing. Tori waited for her and handed her a towel. Donna sat next to her on one of the bleachers, one damp thigh close. She leant forward to take off her trainers and Tori had a view of her sports bra through the armhole of a soaked white tank. Her mouth was dry when she asked, 'What about a milkshake?'

'Sounds great. Let me scrub up and get changed.'

The two of them sat for a while until the courts were quiet then headed for the lockers near the change rooms. There were unspoken currents in their friendship, things just out of reach and below the surface.

Victoria planned to wait while Donna showered and changed. Then right there, behind the lockers, they embraced, Donna's sweaty body pressed against hers, her contours firm. Victoria remembered the feel of Donna's moist skin, the sweet musk taste of her tongue.

A bleep, bleep sucked Tori out of the soft cocoon of her memories. She pressed her eyes shut and longed to return to her memories, wondering if getting more of the white pills would help.

'Sorry, love. Just checking your blood pressure.'

Another nurse, an older one this time. The cuff tightened around her arm and a thermometer pressed against her forehead. The nurse lifted the sheet, prodded the dressing and checked the drain.

'All looking good.'

Tori lay wide awake, stared at the ceiling and tried to imagine herself back in the locker room, her breasts fresh, perfectly formed and intact.

<h1 style="text-align:center">27</h1>

DOROTHY'S Place rang to let Kate know that Bea's funeral would be at the Kate Mary Chapel in Bowen Hills. 'Did you know Bea was from Perth? Her mother, Lena, and brother, Filip, are flying over,' her supervisor said.

Kate rescheduled her clients and ensured she had the full day off.

She wore her black dress, boots, and grey cape, matching the sullen mood of the curdled sky. Bea had shrugged when asked about friends and family. 'They're in Perth. I don't see much of them since my brother had a falling out with Jake.'

And now, for the first time, Kate would meet the people who knew and loved Bea. Kate bit her lip and winced as an image of Artemis' glassy staring eyes flashed in her mind. She shivered and pulled her cape tight around herself as she headed for the car.

It was so dark when she arrived at the chapel, it felt like evening. Gracious stairs swept up to the grand entrance and led to the green carpeted chapel, the initials K.S. patterned into the weave. Someone turned a harsh light on and Kate blinked as her eyes adjusted. The stained-glass windows softened the fluorescence and lent a reverence to this space that felt too large for the small number gathered today. Kate hesitated, uncertain whether her coming would be welcomed.

They must be Lena and Filip. Another unwelcome image of Artemis hanging bloodied. A quick scan confirmed Peg was not amongst the few who mourned the loss of Bea, and Kate regretted not inviting her along, if only to stand alongside someone who had witnessed what Jake was capable of. People spoke in hushed clusters and avoided each other's eyes.

An older lady in a burgundy skirt with hair pulled into a silvery bun fumbled in her handbag and pulled out an embroidered hanky. When she dropped it, a lean, suited fellow bent like a hinge, picked it up and handed it to her before placing a hand under her elbow and guiding her inside. Kate grabbed one of the small packets of tissues placed at the entrance and forced herself to go inside and take a seat.

It was hard to hear anything. The soft music piped through speakers was drowned by rolling thunder and the lashing fury of one of Brisbane's fierce, brief storms. Kate stared at the white coffin. It seemed so small and incapable of containing the hopes and dreams of Bea, a young woman whose life had been stolen from her. Kate had the crazy thought that Artemis should be inside too, forever safe, curled beside her mistress. Kate stifled a sob and squeezed a tissue in one hand as Filip took his place at the front to read his sister's eulogy. A montage of photographs flashed past on the screen and just as he finished speaking, there was a sudden quiet, the storm over.

Kate hesitated, then joined the small cluster of mourners in the adjoining lounge. On impulse she took a second copy of the funeral programme for Peg and folded the picture of a younger, laughing Bea into her handbag. Celine Dion's *Fly* was piped into the function room and Kate longed to believe that Bea was present in some way but felt only an aching sense of futile loss and emptiness. Jake was not mentioned and for that Kate was grateful. She wondered how many here knew the truth or whether Bea's shame ensured her silence leaving Jake free to inflict himself on a new victim.

Lena stood pressing her scrunched hanky to her nose, her skirt and blouse uncreased and not a single tendril escaping the pins holding her hair in place. Kate approached her, wondering how much she knew. 'Hello, I'm Kate. I was Bea's psychologist.' She hesitated, remembering Bea had not been in regular contact with her family. 'I was devastated when I learned that Bea was no longer with us.'

Filip joined them, handed his mother a cup of tea and offered his hand in greeting. 'Filip, Bea's baby brother.'

Lena's voice quivered together with the surface of her tea. 'Thank you for coming. Bea didn't tell us much about her life here.'

Lena placed her teacup on one of the small tables and reached into her bag. 'She loved cats. This was her latest.' Lena scrolled on her phone and showed Kate a picture of Artemis.

Kate blinked away tears. 'Artemis,' she croaked.

'You knew her?' Lena's hand trembled. 'We want to take her home with us. I know Bea would want her looked after properly.'

Kate shook her head, choking back tears. 'I'm sorry, Artemis died.'

Lena sagged. 'Bea never said anything.'

Filip steadied his mother, kept his hand on her arm. 'We lost my sister when she met Jake. He insisted she move to Brisbane even though she had a great job and lots of friends in Perth. When I suggested she go over for a holiday first, Jake was furious and told me their relationship was none of my business. The only thing where Bea stood her ground was taking Artemis. She adored her cat.'

Kate nodded, remembering that wild night when Bea came to her for help, terrified her furry friend was missing. 'I know.'

'Bea left Perth and slowly stopped making contact. The only time she came home for Christmas was after he left her. We learnt later he was in prison. Did you know?'

Kate looked at the floor, her mind sullied with blood splats, blank staring eyes and matted fur. 'She came to me for help after Jake was let out of prison.'

Filip balled his hands and lowered his voice. 'He killed her, you know. He took away her will to live.'

Kate nodded, unable to speak. A couple of young women approached. 'Hello. You must be Bea's mum. We worked with Bea.'

Kate excused herself and stumbled out into rain-washed sunshine. It was too bright. She slipped dark sunglasses on and hurried to her car where she scrolled through her phone and looked at that first photo of Artemis Bea sent her. Kate touched the pink nose with one finger. 'I hope you find each other.'

Kate longed to talk to someone, to loosen the twisted anger and grief tight inside. She drove past The Treasure Chest to check in on Tori and hoped they might slip next door to Vincent's, to share lunch and confidences. She might even casually mention the will and check Tori was all right.

When Kate pulled up, she frowned at the closed sign dangled in the door. The clouds had dispersed, and a gust of wind blew a scatter of leaves along the path. She crossed her arms under the cape, its wool soft and warm, puzzled. At lunchtime the place was always busy with customers fingering the fabrics, shuffling through racks of clothes, admiring the restored pieces, and inevitably grabbing a few items to purchase. A twinge of anxiety fluttered Kate's heart. On impulse she dialled Georgie. She always knew what was going on.

'Hi. The Treasure Chest is closed.'

'Tori headed to the Mater for her surgery today.'

'Surgery?'

'So, you didn't know either. She was diagnosed with breast cancer; they fitted her surgery in a couple of days early.'

'Breast cancer,' whispered Kate.

Everything clicked into place.

Kate drove to the hospital. Visiting hours started just as Kate arrived. She hoped to be the first there. She found her way to the ward and paused when she saw a nurse speaking to Leo in the corridor. 'Your mum is awake and okay.'

Leo disappeared into the room and Kate pulled back, wanting to give him a few moments alone with his mum.

Ten minutes later, Kate peered inside, cautious about intruding. Leo stood pale and wide-eyed near the bed near where a woman with a stethoscope typed notes into the computer on wheels. When Tori spoke, Kate was relieved she sounded normal. 'I feel great, Leo. Don't you worry, I'll be home soon.'

'Tori,' Kate wanted to apologise, and offer her support when

Georgie arrived, low heels tapping, a clutch of glossy magazines, tucked under one arm. Her nails were shellacked pink, her lips a perfect match. 'How did it go?'

The woman with a stethoscope around her neck answered. 'Well, we are waiting for the histology, but the surgery went well.' She smiled at Tori. 'I might leave you alone with your visitors.'

They crowded around the bed. Tori sat up, her hospital gown loosened, exposing a wad of bandage on the left side, her arms thin, like brittle twigs. Tubing snaked out from the bandage, more tubing connected Tori to a bag of fluid. Kate imagined the cancer scooped out like a firm yolk, leaving a white, perfect hole behind, and willed the surgeon to have removed all of it. The other possibilities were too dreadful to contemplate.

Indigo joined them, bringing fresh clothes, which she folded into the drawers beside the bed. She placed a tiny origami treasure chest on the top. 'I thought you might enjoy this beautifully made little piece.'

Leo blushed. Tori picked it up. 'How did you know? I was going to ask you to bring it for me. I can't believe I left it behind.'

She showed the others how the lid opened and held it up to be admired.

Indigo looked thoughtful, one hand on her chin. 'I reckon we could sell them for a decent price. A little something special for people to take home. We'd display them near the counter. I can see them flying out the door.'

Leo's eyes darted from Indigo to Tori just as Shelley hurried in, breathless, holding a basket of fresh fruit. 'I hope you don't mind me coming. I went to The Treasure Chest, saw it was closed and rang Georgie.'

'It's lovely of you to come. The Treasure Chest will be open again before you know it.'

Shelley saw the little chest and her hand flew to her mouth. 'Oh, that is just divine. Could I get one of those? Are they for sale?'

⚜

After Kate left the ward and headed to the carpark, she felt her phone vibrate. It was Georgie inviting them all to meet at her place to discuss how they could support Tori after her discharge. Kate bit her lip. Why hadn't she thought to arrange that?

When Kate pulled up and saw Ryan's car in the driveway, she hesitated, uncertain whether to be pleased or not that he was home a day early.

'Kate, it's so good to see you.' He came out and enveloped her in his arms. 'I have so much to tell you.'

Her embrace was lukewarm, unable to muster enthusiasm for his trip in the wake of the day's events. She disengaged herself and walked inside where Noah and Edie were enjoying a glass of milk and smartie biscuits Ryan must have brought home for them.

'Dad's home,' announced Noah rather unnecessarily, his mouth full of crumbs.

Kate dropped her bag on the bench and ignored Bear who was leaping up and down in the hope of a pat. 'Tori had surgery for her breast cancer today. I've just come back from the hospital.'

All the joyful energy was sucked out of the room while three sets of eyes stared at her. Bear, sensing the flattening of the mood, dropped one of his drool-soaked toys on her boot and pushed her ankle with his wet nose.

'God, Kate. Why didn't you tell me?'

'I only found out myself today.'

'What can we do to help?'

'A few of us are heading to Georgie's to work out what we can do. If you manage the kids, I'll put you down to help at the shop or with school drop-off for Leo.'

She headed to the bathroom, keen for a long, hot shower. Ryan called after her. 'Let me know what I can do.'

She nearly tripped on his bag dumped at the bedroom door with dirty washing spilling across the floor. Kicking it aside with one foot, she bit back what she wanted to say and replied, 'Thanks.'

28

EVEN though Kate had known Georgie for years and regularly dropped in wearing old jeans, it felt important to present well this evening. Kate chose a sombre, grey woollen dress and added a red scarf and lipstick. Ryan, of course, didn't comment, did not notice she had changed.

'See you, Kate. And let Georgie know I'm happy to help.'

He barely has time for his own family thought Kate as she walked across the road, rang Georgie's doorbell, and listened to it reverberate through the house.

'Come in, Kate. Can I get you a coffee? Tea?'

Kate hoped for a glass of wine but nodded yes to tea and marvelled at the immaculate surfaces devoid of the debris that seemed to sprout on every bare bit of bench or table at home. She sat down at the polished dark timber table and admired the two candelabra in the centre when the bell rang again. 'I'll get it,' she called out to Georgie.

Kate was startled to see Daryl looming behind Shelley. Without looking at him, she stepped aside to let them in. 'Come in, Georgie is making tea and coffee.'

Without removing his hand from Shelley's waist, Daryl bent down and gave Kate a chaste kiss on each cheek, the scent of him intoxicating. With a tremble in her voice, she waved them to the dining room. 'Have a seat.'

Georgie emerged from the kitchen with a tray. She set out the teapot and cups. When she noticed Daryl, she startled, her voice became light, girlish. 'And look who has come along to help.'

He put his hands behind his head, leaned back. 'So, who do I have to kiss to get a drink around here?'

Georgie went pink and waved one hand about while she ran through the options. 'Red? White? Beer? We have a small cellar if you want to choose something.'

She poked her head down the hallway, 'Mark, could you sort out drinks, please? The Bradys are here.'

Kate brushed away her annoyance. 'A chardy please.'

Daryl winked at her. She pretended not to see.

He added. 'Let's make that two.'

Mark appeared a few minutes later with a few beers, and a Penfold's 2017 Chardonnay. He pulled out glasses and poured, then sidled up to Daryl and started to discuss last weekend's game. Daryl draped one arm over the back of Shelley's chair as he held his glass to the light. 'A classy drop.'

Mark's chest swelled. 'More than happy to show you the cellar, mate. We had it custom designed so I could build up a serious collection.'

Daryl gave his glass a swirl. 'I might just take you up on that.'

He tipped his glass towards Georgie whose cheeks sported two distinct red dots.

'Cheers.'

'Let's get started, shall we?' She flipped open her laptop, ready to make some notes. 'I thought maybe we could work out pick-ups and drop-offs for Leo, a roster of meals, and a bit of help in the shop.'

The doorbell's distinctive sound reverberated through the house. Mark stood up this time and a few minutes later escorted Indigo to the table.

Georgie gave a nervous laugh, her voice unnatural. 'How about a drink?'

Indigo held up her hand. 'Just water thanks.'

Georgie headed to the kitchen. They heard the fridge click, then she came back with a jug of iced water and a tray of glasses. She picked up exactly where she left off. 'We were just discussing Leo and getting him to and from school.'

Daryl shrugged. 'He can come and stay with us. I'll do school drop-offs and, of course, take him to football training.'

Indigo stared him down, arms crossed. 'Leo's sorted.'

Georgie faltered but kept a pink smile painted on her lips. 'Are you sure? We all have kids at the school.'

Indigo shifted her stare to Georgie. 'I said, it's sorted.'

Georgie disappeared behind the screen again. 'Meals?'

Daryl nudged Shelley who sat very still, her wine untouched. He half raised a hand. 'How about we feed the boy after training and on Saturday.'

Indigo kept her arms crossed. Moisture slid down the sides of her glass and she ignored the strategically placed coasters. 'Don't worry about meals, I have it in hand. I'm staying there for now.'

Kate felt Georgie cross then uncross her legs and watched the small ring form around the base of Indigo's glass. She waited for Georgie to slip a coaster under it the way she usually did. Shelley fiddled with the teaspoon resting on her saucer. It dropped with a clatter, and they all jumped. Without looking up, Shelley spoke, 'I'd love to help out in the shop.' She knotted her hands together, looked over at Indigo. 'If that suits you.'

Daryl laughed. 'Well, I'll have to hide the credit cards. Money is not your strong suit.'

Shelley looked down into her lap.

Indigo looked over at her. 'Help in the shop would be great. Come around tomorrow and I'll give you a briefing and show you where stuff is.' She stood up, picked up her glass and drank it in one long swig then put it down in a new spot, creating a fresh ring on the table. She pushed her chair back in. 'I'm heading back to the hospital to pick up Leo.'

When Georgie made to stand, Indigo held up a hand. 'I'll let myself out.'

A moment later there was a firm thud and Georgie picked up a napkin and wiped away the two water stains before she sat down again and cleared her throat. 'More wine anyone?'

Kate offered to help on Saturday mornings and advised Ryan would be happy to help also. The remainder of the evening was stilted. Not even the wine smoothed the jagged edges.

By the time Kate walked across the road home, she felt light-headed. The moon was a nursery rhyme sliver in a black sky shimmering with stars. Soft yellow light filtered through broken blinds at home. Just before she reached the gate, her phone vibrated, no doubt Ryan wondering why she was taking so long. Kate glanced at the screen. *I booked our breakfast catch-up for Monday at Stone's Throw. I need to talk. X D*

Kate froze, abruptly stone sober. She shivered to think of him sending that text when five minutes earlier he had sat opposite her with Shelley tucked under his arm. Tomorrow, Kate vowed to tell him she couldn't see him alone like this anymore, that he needed to see someone professionally.

Her hand felt sweaty when she opened her front door and called out. 'Hello, I'm home.'

29

TORI was surprised how anxious she felt about going home after looking forward to her discharge from the minute she was admitted. Now she worried how she would manage. She touched the dressing where the cancer had been, wondered how they would know it was all gone.

Running the washer over herself she was shocked at how thin she was. Her hip bones protruded, her ribs a cage over her heart. She slipped into a shirt and pulled on her jeans wanting to drag out the inevitable moment of departure. Somehow, she imagined it was the antiseptic walls of the hospital with all its science and expertise holding the cancer at bay.

The thought of Indigo staying in the box room and looking after Leo made Tori anxious in a completely different way. It was important for Leo that things went back to normal as soon as possible. She was barely dressed, her hair still wet, when Indigo arrived.

'Hey, all packed and ready to head home?'

'I guess so. I have an appointment with the radiation oncologist early next week.'

Indigo picked up Tori's small, overnight bag and gathered all the cards scribbled with good wishes. Many were customers from the shop, their messages heartfelt and cheerful. *You got this, girl. Your shop makes me smile. You are an inspiration.*

'Your friends are all very keen to help. Georgie arranged a meeting and has rostered them to work shifts at the shop. I figured you might want a bit of privacy, so I told them I was managing with Leo and meals.'

'I'm not sure I want anyone nosing around The Treasure Chest either. I think we'll cope without help. I'll be fine in a few days.'

'Well, let's just take it a day at a time. Right now, I suspect you'll be doing Shelley a favour getting out of the house a couple of days a week and once you don't need her, just let her know. Sometimes it's good to let people feel they are being helpful.' Indigo paused. 'And no being bloody polite either. You just tell everyone to fuck off if you want time to yourself.'

Did that include Indigo? wondered Tori to herself.

Tori's heart sank when she saw Kate and Georgie waiting outside when she arrived home. The pressure of Indigo's fingers on her arm felt firm, but the minute Indigo let go Tori felt untethered, like she might collapse. She grabbed the side table near the door. Georgie rushed up and gave her a huge hug. 'God, it's so good to have you out of hospital. Such a relief.'

The knot of anxiety inside Tori dissolved and she gave herself up to warm spontaneity, overwhelmed with warmth and gratitude towards these friends. 'Thanks, Georgie-girl.'

Kate looked drab and tired, clutching her Tupperware. 'I made you some of my raspberry melting moments.'

'Thanks, I love those biscuits you make. It reminds me of old times.'

Georgie barely waited for her to finish speaking. 'I made a few things too. Soup, a casserole, and a flan. I've put them in the fridge. I know you said not to worry, but I thought it would make life easier. Just while Tori finds her feet again. There's nothing like a homecooked meal to make you feel better.'

Indigo nodded thanks.

Tori sank into the lounge, overwhelmed by fatigue. 'Great, Georgie-girl. I appreciate it.'

There was another tentative knock, and Georgie almost ran to the door. 'Shelley, it's so lovely to see you. Come in, come in. Yes, we're all here and Tori's home.'

Shelley clutched a bottle of St Hugo's 2014 Cabernet Sauvignon. 'You probably can't drink, but Daryl needed me, so I just ran out of time to make something.'

Tori hugged the quality bottle to herself, unable to recall if Dr Philip mentioned anything about alcohol. It was the one thing she really longed for. 'That is perfect, Shelley. I really mean it.'

Shelley's shoulders relaxed and she gave one of those smiles where her eyes sparkled and her whole face lit up. Tori gave her a friendly punch on the shoulder then held the bottle at arm's length and admired the label with everyone peering over her shoulder. Shelley's phone pinged.

'Gotta go, I'm afraid. Enjoy the wine.'

She hurried out the door, followed by Indigo. 'Just picking Leo up. Home soon.'

Georgie blew Tori a kiss as she followed Indigo. 'Just ring if you need anything.'

Kate gave Tori a hug. 'I'd better head off as well.'

After the flurry of goodbyes, there was blessed quiet. Tori closed her eyes and absorbed the simple joy of being home without beeping machines and regular checks on her vitals. She must have drifted off when she heard a shuffle at the door. 'Mum?'

Leo hurled himself at her and buried his face in her shoulder. She breathed him in, not wanting to let him go. 'I'm going to be alright. I need to keep seeing the doctors a bit longer but it's all going to work out.'

He pulled away and looked over at Indigo, who stood waiting at the door with Leo's bag hanging loose off one shoulder.

Tori gave Leo a little push. 'You go get changed and I'll get you a snack.'

The afternoon dissolved into evening. Leo was in his room doing homework and Indigo was next door at The Treasure Chest. Having Indigo stay over made the place feel different, even though she didn't have a lot of stuff. The casual way her things were scattered around the unit; a jacket, the book she was reading, her mug. It made her seem present even when she wasn't there. Having Indigo so close all the time bothered Tori in ways she found hard to define, like an itch that got worse if it was scratched.

In the evening, she watched while Indigo chopped vegetables in the kitchen. Batons of carrots, strips of red capsicum, florets of broccoli and purple shredded cabbage. Lucinda Williams played on low volume and the sound rippled under Tori's skin. When Indigo pressed the knob on the rice cooker, its click sounded louder than usual and Tori startled. She inhaled the earthy, warm scent of toasting cashews and realised she was ravenous in a way she couldn't remember being. The bandage hugged her chest, and she visualised a hollow space where the cancer had been. She allowed herself the freedom to be and observe life without taking control of things. The pain medications blurred the evening into a collage of sound, light, and sensations. Leo called out, 'What's for dinner?'

Indigo tossed a rainbow of vegies into the air then caught them in the wok with a deft hand. She called out, 'If you don't come and set up now, nothing.'

Leo's door burst open. He appeared in his stained track pants. 'Looks good.'

The thought of doing anything exhausted Tori. Instead, she watched mesmerised at Indigo's fluid movements, the way her forearm flexed when she lifted the pan, the soft way she padded around in socked feet. Tori listened to the clatter of bowls, the clink of cutlery while Leo set up. Tori felt herself sucked into the slipstream of activity filling her small home and marvelled how she had never noticed how comforting it was to sit back and do nothing.

Indigo didn't speak and for that Tori was grateful. When everything was ready, Indigo served a scoop of rice in each red pottery bowl and stirred coconut milk and cashews into the wok. They sat around the wooden table, the flickering soft light of a candle casting shadows around the room and blurring the edge of things. Leo watched her with wariness, the realisation his mum was no longer invincible, her mortality suddenly a possibility. She wanted to say something but bit back the platitudes that rose to her lips. *I'll be fine, don't worry. I'll beat this thing.*

Soon the only sounds were the scrape of cutlery against pottery bowls, the heartrending echoes of Gurrumul Yunupingu soft in the background, the clink of glasses. Leo finished first and stood, scraping his chair on the timber floor. 'Thanks.'

He rinsed his bowl in the sink, excused himself and disappeared to his room to recalibrate. Indigo curled up on the lounge with a book and a glass of wine.

The evening felt thick with uncertainties. Outside sounds filtered into Tori's awareness. The distant clatter of a train, the drip of water down a broken gutter, and distant laughter from Vincent's. She tried to read but the words jumped around the page, refusing to stay in straight lines.

Instead, her mind drifted back to the day she first found the run-down shop on the corner with its quirky shaped unit at the back. A couple of days later, she took Kate to have a look, then without telling anyone, took a risk and bought it.

Kate and Ryan had bought an old place in the same area, a draughty old Queenslander oozing charm. Not long after, Kate met Georgie and the three of them hitched along together. When Georgie first saw Tori's place she cautioned her about overcommitting, worried the place needed extensive renovations. Tori ignored the advice and sank her inheritance into the dilapidated building, determined to preserve as much of the original as possible.

They all chipped in. Ryan and Mark helped with some of the repairs, Kate did a lot of the painting, and Georgie donated a couple of beds, chairs, and kitchenware. 'We're redecorating and don't need any of it,' she reassured Tori.

Tori provided chilled bottles of Mateus Rose while Georgie assembled picnic baskets of homemade quiches, baguettes, and salads for the weekend work parties. In the warm evenings, they sat on fold-out chairs and drank wine out of plastic tumblers, Leo playing in the sawdust, the remains of dinner scattered on the floor. Tori's dream to open her own vintage store really brought all of them together.

What if she didn't make it? Tori worried Leo would not be allowed to live with Kate and Ryan and that his home, The Treasure Chest would disappear, lost to the greedy bulldozers of development. She was the only one standing between Leo and this world she had built up from nothing.

Brakes squealed outside, the sound shocking Tori back into the present. She became aware of her pulse racing. The room looked fuzzy and distorted. The thought of leaving Leo behind made it hard to suck air into her lungs. Leo needed her and it was up to her to get on with things and ensure she was well to see him grow up and become independent. She had to do this alone, not like some bloody invalid dependent on the charity of her friends.

She stood, lost her balance, and bumped the coffee table. A vase wobbled then crashed to the floor, the stillness violated.

Indigo's voice sounded like it came from some place far away. 'You okay?'

'No, I'm not fuckin' okay.'

Tori was ashamed to find her face wet with tears. Pain tore across her chest and ripped through her body like a fire through a parched landscape. Angry, she kicked her chair and swore when the timber impacted her toe. Indigo moved with stealth, gathered the plates and placed them in the sink. She picked up the vase, now cracked, and set it back on the coffee table. 'Do you want to talk about it?'

Her voice was low. The music had ceased.

'What's there to bloody talk about?' Tori sat down, her face in her hands. 'I seem to have angered the fuckin' good luck gods. Just when life gives me a break, I'm cut off at the knees, writing my epitaph.'

Indigo didn't say anything for a long time. The candle continued to flicker and cast shadows around the room. One lamp glowed from the small side table. 'You are a long way from dead. Plenty of grunt left from what I can see.'

Tori kept her head low, clasped in her hands, rocked to and fro.

Indigo pulled a stool closer to Tori until their heads were nearly touching. Her skin gave off a warmth, made the hairs on Tori's arm stand up. She turned away, refused to look at Indigo, and made a superhuman effort to keep her voice steady, enunciating each word with equal emphasis. 'I'm alright now. I've changed my mind about help. I want you to leave.'

Indigo moved around the room and picked up her scattered things, placed them in her duffle sitting near the door. 'See you tomorrow. Usual time?'

Tori didn't trust herself to speak. She nodded.

30

IT was Monday morning and Kate got up early, tiptoed through the silence of the sleeping household. She'd laid out her clothes the night before, settled on a simple white blouse with a pretty lace collar and a blue skirt with a slit up the side, square heeled courts. Feminine without allure. She wrote a note to Ryan, reminding him to drop the kids off, let Bear out, and grab some groceries for dinner. When he came up behind her and she smelt the faint scent of her coconut shampoo she felt an unreasonable anger towards him.

'This is an early start. Is something up?' He bent towards her and glanced at the note.

Kate hoped her face was not as red as it felt. 'Just a meeting. I've left a list.'

Her lips straightened into a flat line. 'And please don't use my special coconut shampoo. It was a treat I bought myself.'

Before he could say anything, she blew him a kiss, picked up her handbag and left him in the dark light of early morning. He stood and watched her leave, his hair tousled, a hole in his pyjama top near his right shoulder.

The day was crisp, the grey cloud giving way to blue skies. Kate could just make out the steel vertebrae of the city's high-rises and the skeleton of the Story Bridge as she drove south. When she turned onto Old Cleveland Road, the traffic was still light. She would arrive in plenty of time. She had toyed with changing the venue; Stones Corner was a bit too close to home, but then reassured herself there was nothing wrong with meeting a friend for breakfast.

A queue of patrons scrolled on phones and waited outside for takeaway coffees. Kate glanced at her reflection in the glass, smoothed her blouse and fiddled with her hair. She had ten minutes to spare, so she picked up a couple of menus and headed to the tiny courtyard to find a spot to sit.

'Jesus, it's good to see you, Kate. You look great.'

She jumped back and pressed the menus against her chest.

'Daryl, I was just about to nab us an outside table.'

Did it sound like she was babbling?

He came up beside her, brushed against her elbow and she shivered. He seemed taller today, sleek in his white shirt and dark pants, his male scent a tang in her nostrils.

'Perfect. Here let me.'

He grabbed the menus from her and gestured for her to go ahead. He pulled a chair out at a small table in the sunshine. 'Do have a seat.' He sat opposite her, their feet nearly touching.

Before she said anything, he beckoned a waitress who looked over wide-eyed, recognising him, and hurried across. He put his fingers to his lips, winked and she giggled.

'One strong black and a long black with one, thanks.'

Black with one. A piece of knowledge impregnated in Kate's mind.

The waitress brought out two coffees and Kate's hand quivered as she lifted it to her lips, allowed the first sip to percolate through her body.

It brought back memories of that first morning after she stayed overnight at his place. She stood in his neat kitchen wearing nothing but one of his football tees that only just covered her butt. He had come up behind her, his breath soft on her neck, one hand over hers while she measured coffee into his percolator. Then he had lifted the tee and pressed himself against her and whispered, *black with one please,* one hand sliding up to her breasts.

Kate swallowed hard, put her coffee back on the table and left her hands wrapped around the mug. Daryl ordered two scrambled eggs on sourdough. She had her eye on the granola but let it go. Suddenly, he leant forward, blue eyes gleaming. 'I'm taking Shelley away. Just the two of us for a week to Port Douglas.'

Jealousy made Kate's voice sharp. 'Are you telling me that is what you wanted to talk about?'

His knee bumped hers. 'I'll make it really special. No expenses spared. I've even arranged a surprise. Bungy jumping in the rainforest near Cairns.'

He pulled a glossy brochure from his pocket. Kate scanned the white sand, palms, glistening pools, and softly lit restaurants.

His knee continued to touch hers. 'What do you think?'

'Not the bungy jumping.'

She recalled climbing Bald Rock at Girraween with Shelley one weekend when they were at uni. They had aborted when Shelley confessed to a fear of heights as she trembled pale-faced halfway up the rock face.

'She'll love it. The whole idea is to challenge yourself, get the begeezers scared out of you. It's the best tower in the world with spectacular views of the rainforest and the Coral Sea. Anyway, I'll be there with her.'

'It wouldn't be Shelley's thing.' Kate fiddled with her teaspoon. 'Have you talked to her about things yet?'

'No. I want it to be a surprise.'

'I meant the affair.'

He gave a dismissive wave of his hand. 'I'm sorting it. She doesn't need to know.'

He was forced to lean back when their meals arrived. Kate toyed with the egg, refusing to look at him.

He forked food, wiped his mouth with his napkin, and drummed fingers on the table. 'Now, I know you girls talk. Has she said anything to you about us?'

The light on the table shifted when a cloud drifted overhead. She thought of her chat with Shelley and knew she would never tell Daryl.

He put his fork down. 'You know, what she says is true. We've been having a tough time since the move with my career in fucking tatters. Did she tell you what she did?'

He stared at Kate. She refused to meet his gaze. He leant forward. 'Shelley broke my heart.'

Kate was aware of her pulse in her ears. 'The two of you need proper professional help, relationship counselling.'

There was an uneasy gap in conversation. A fly landed on her food, and she brushed it away. It landed again and flailed in dissolving egg. 'You should tell her about the affair. The truth has a way of coming out and believe me it is better she hears it from you.'

'I love that about you, Kate. Your high moral standards, your loyalty. That bloke of yours is a lucky man.'

The glossy brochure sat on the corner of the table. Kate stared at the enticing pictures. God what she would give to spend a week at a resort like that. Nothing to do but relax, enjoy a glass of wine and sex in the middle of the day.

Suddenly, Daryl's face was close to hers and she noticed a tiny nick where he must have cut himself shaving. The last time she had been at a resort was with Daryl and she had fallen pregnant.

'What do you think of the resort?'

Kate blushed and hoped he couldn't read her thoughts. He didn't wait for her answer.

'Once it's just Shelley and me, things will work out.'

He pushed his chair back and threw his napkin onto the table. His silhouette shaded the table and Kate realised afresh how much space he occupied.

'I always feel better after talking to you, Kate. Time's flying. I gotta go. And I'll get this, my treat.'

He left the brochure on the table. Kate whirled the final mouthful of cold coffee in her mug and drank it.

The fly was still struggling, trapped inside congealed scrambled egg. She cursed when she realised she had forgotten to tell Daryl they could not meet up like this again.

31

THE following morning, Tori heard the creak of Leo's bed, drawers opening and shutting, the thump of something on the floor. She glanced at the time and wondered why he was up so early. Head still blurry, she recalled her dismissal of Indigo last night and was filled with remorse. She curled around herself again until Leo's door banged. Tori leapt up, determined to get him breakfast. Bare feet chilly on the floor, she hurried out, her eyes still sticky with sleep.

'Morning, Leo. Let me get you some brekky before you head off.'

'I'm good. Indigo's picking me up. She said she'd get me a milkshake and muffin at Coorparoo Square.' He gave her a quick hug. 'See ya.' He headed to the door, his satchel hooked over one shoulder.

She called after him, 'Don't forget the music fest tonight. Have you got everything?'

'Yep.'

The screen door banged shut behind him.

Tori made herself toast, ignoring the acid fingers reaching up her gullet. She stirred some instant coffee into boiling water and tossed down the white pills for pain. She tried to read the brochure about breast cancer survivors and tossed it aside. Time crawled past.

After a long shower, Tori picked through her clothes and chose a loose, colourful shirt that skimmed over her scarred, uneven chest before pulling a comb through her hair.

It was ten minutes before opening and Tori saw the minivan pull up outside. She waited another ten minutes then walked down the

160

gravel drive and peered into the front window. Indigo was polishing the locked glass counter that housed the vintage jewellery. Relief made Tori weak-kneed, and she gave herself a moment to catch her breath.

'Morning.'

Indigo looked up. 'I thought you were meant to be taking it easy for a few weeks.'

'Nah, I just want to get back to normal. Put it behind me and get on with my life.'

'I'm not sure it works like that. You've a better chance at getting back to things if you give yourself a breather and let your body recover.'

'I'm terrified if I let go, I'll lose everything I've worked so hard for.'

Indigo dropped the cloth she was using. 'Yeah, I can imagine. Look, I'm not an expert, but why not trust your body for a moment? Give it time to heal properly after the surgery. We've all got your back.'

Indigo stood lean and invincible. Tori stared at the floor.

'Sorry I was such a bitch last night.'

Indigo resumed polishing. 'It happens.'

Tori hesitated, kept her eyes on the grains in the floorboards. 'Could I interest you in the school music fest? Leo plays percussion with the band. It's probably not your thing…'

'Sure, I'd love to come.'

✛

Indigo arrived looking gorgeous wearing sleek pants with a black-collared green shirt. Her dark heeled boots made her appear taller. Tori worried about her loose, sky-blue shift and gold threaded shawl.

Indigo grinned 'Hard to believe you just had a wedge of boob lopped off.'

Tori rearranged her shawl. 'Not sure if I should take that as a compliment or not.'

Indigo glanced towards Leo's room. 'Is he ready?'

'He went early. Georgie offered to take him and dropped past an hour ago.'

161

They arrived in plenty of time. Georgie was flushed, busy setting things up on the stage. She saw them come in and gave a quick wave.

A young student guided them to their seats about midway down the auditorium. There was excited rustling and whispering behind the curtains, the sounds of things being moved around backstage. Tori nudged her way past other parents' legs and sat down with Indigo close behind. Tori relaxed and looked forward to the show, quietly pleased to have Indigo beside her. Then she saw him. Two rows up from them sat Daryl, his arm draped over Shelley. Melody sat hunched forward, her legs kicking the seat in front. The twins shared one chair, their heads bent together. The family looked close-knit tonight.

The lights dimmed. Daryl's head was swallowed by the dark and the ceiling was lit with hundreds of stars. There was an indrawing of breath. Tori softened and allowed the magic to take her thoughts to a happier place.

Miss Nightingale's voice sounded over the microphone, clear like a bell. 'I would like to welcome all families and friends to our starlit night of music. Please, sit back, relax, and if you can, try to catch a falling star and make a wish.'

There were loud oohhs and aahhs and some shuffling in chairs as children gazed up hopeful, willing one of the twinkling lights to fall their way.

'And our very first item is a solo guitar piece, *A Star Lights the Way*, written and performed by Edie Murphy.'

There was loud applause, and a Tinkerbell light danced across the ceiling. Tori had to squeeze her hands tight to stop herself trying to catch it herself. Just as the light darted behind the red velvet curtains, they opened with a swoosh and there sat Edie in a perfect circle of light with a backdrop of stars and a waxing moon that appeared to blend with the sky in the hall so that it seemed they were sitting outside under the black arc of a starlit sky.

Tori imagined Kate must be bursting with pride. There was a pause while Edie gathered herself inside the stillness – no one wriggled or moved. Into the magic space, her voice began slowly then filled the hall, clear and true between the strum and pluck of her guitar. The audience listened, transfixed.

The concert continued with each item punctuated by darting, shimmering lights accompanied by squeals and tiny shadow fingers reaching in vain.

When the lights came on, they felt too bright and people squinted, rubbing their eyes and waiting for dilated pupils to adjust. Tori whispered to Indigo, 'See you at the servery in a minute. I'm going to see if I can catch Kate and congratulate her on Edie's performance. Keep an eye out for Leo, would you?'

Tori squeezed along the row of seats and headed to backstage where Kate and Ryan were organising the performers. She weaved between the crush of parents making their way to the refreshments bar for drinks and snacks. Finally, she reached the stage. Just as she made to slip behind the curtain, she heard Kate's voice, raised and angry. 'It's a bit rich coming from you. You're hardly ever home.'

'You missed Edie's performance. She's been practising for weeks. How can you not make it for her very first solo? What sort of mother puts her work ahead of her daughter's first live performance?'

The fury in Ryan's voice made Tori curl up tight inside.

'Somebody has to work. I did not miss Edie's song deliberately. How dare you pull me up when you spend every waking moment with that band of yours, while I juggle everything, including the rehearsals for the fest. You haven't even been here.'

'I don't want to discuss your obsession with your career right now.'

Ryan sounded so cold. Tori turned away, not wanting to eavesdrop.

When she tried to slip back into the crowd, she nearly walked straight into Daryl who blocked the way. 'Hey, I thought I saw you disappear around here. I just wanted to congratulate you on Leo's performance.'

It was impossible to slide past him. She forced a smile. 'He is a talented musician.'

'By the way, is Kate there? That girl of hers really is something.'

'Kate is busy, she can't talk right now. They are packing up backstage.'

Tori blocked his way to the backstage area, certain Kate would not want her domestic disputes overheard by Daryl Brady.

Shelley sidled up behind Daryl. 'Wasn't it great? Leo did so well on the drums and Edie was amazing.'

Daryl put his arm around Shelley and pulled her close. 'This is such a great school with so many opportunities. Now that football is ending and I'll be home more, I'd really like a few more kids myself. Maybe try for a boy.'

Shelley blushed red.

'I keep telling Shelley it isn't too late.'

He squeezed her hard, just as Leo pushed through the crowd, smiling at Tori. Daryl released his hold on Shelley and thumped him on the back. 'You were great on the drums mate. How about you give your mum here a break and I get you something to eat?'

Tori opened her mouth, a closed fist in her chest. Leo looked between Daryl and Tori. 'Can I go with Mr Brady please? I'll see you after the raffle.'

Tori said through clenched teeth, 'Meet you right here at the end.'

Leo turned to go when Tori called out. 'Wait a minute.' She pulled her emergency fifty from her phone and handed it to him. She silenced Daryl with narrowed eyes. He put his arm around Leo's shoulder and the crowd parted, allowing them through.

When Shelley reached out and touched her arm, Tori pulled away.

'I'm really sorry. He talks about Leo non-stop. He is obsessed with him and treats him like the son he wishes he had.'

Tori stood fixed to the spot, still staring at the space where Daryl and Leo had been standing a moment earlier.

Shelley sounded strained. 'I'm sorry about, you know, your diagnosis…'

It sounded like the word *sorry* slipped from Shelley's lips often.

'Don't be sorry. It's hardly your fault. I'm doing just fine.'

32

WHEN the concert was over, Kate found herself alone backstage, Ryan's fury loud in her ears. She had completely forgotten to mark off her last two appointments today and then her final client arrived late and had complex issues that demanded time. Kate's belly grumbled and she realised she had only scoffed a coffee and a chocolate bar since breakfast. The smell of sausages and pizza wafted inside but the thought of encountering Ryan kept her out of sight tidying up.

She'd glimpsed Tori outside the backstage area and hoped she had not overheard their heated exchange. When Kate was certain the crowd had finally moved to the quadrangle and servery, she slipped outside. She scanned the excited children eating hot dogs and pizza slices, determined to avoid Ryan, already dreading his sullen, angry silence when they finally got home.

Daryl waved and she tensed. He had his arm around Shelley who looked gorgeous in a mini dress and high strappy sandals. She looked fragile, a sliver that fitted perfectly into his shadow. His promise of a trip away must have lured her to stay and give the marriage another chance. Guilt churned Kate's gut when she thought about the secrets she couldn't share with her friend.

It was a relief when the warning bell sounded indicating the raffle was about to be drawn. Everyone crowded back into the hall. The excitement was palpable. The prospect of winning a football signed by Daryl Brady or corporate box tickets to the finals had drawn a huge crowd. Georgie had printed out several additional batches of tickets and invited the media along.

Georgie ascended the steps to the stage and tapped the microphone. Chatter ceased abruptly. 'We now come to the next exciting part of the evening. The moment some of you have been waiting for. We wish to thank all our sponsors and supporters for their generosity.'

She read through a list of local businesses then paused for effect. 'This year, we are lucky enough to have someone special amongst us, a man who does not need an introduction, Daryl Brady.'

There was loud applause and Daryl stood, looked around at the crowd and waved. He loped up and stood next to Georgie who turned pink. Her voice had a quiver.

'We would like Daryl to do us the honour of drawing out the winners.'

Kate spotted Melody, sullen and standing at the back of the hall, and wondered how Daryl had addressed the bullying and whether Shelley ever learnt the truth of what had happened.

Names were being pulled out of the box and the crowd pressed forward in anticipation as winners were called to the front. Georgie made a big show of greeting them and handing them their prizes. She was enjoying her evening of limelight behind the microphone standing next to Daryl. 'And now we will finally learn who the lucky winners are of a couple of very special prizes.'

There was a collective intake of breath while Daryl rummaged amongst the tickets. He called out the name Hayley Johnson, one of the younger girls. She stood, pink cheeked, and walked up to receive the football. Daryl bent down so that he was eye level with her. A proud dad snapped photos of his pigtailed daughter with the local footy hero. There was a tenderness in the way Daryl's grey flecked head poised close to six-year-old Hayley's. The flash of hundreds of phones ensured people's social media feeds would be buzzing for the next week.

The finals tickets were won by the school's caretaker, Mr O'Sullivan, a crusty fellow who had worked at the school for longer than anyone could remember. A devout follower of Australian Rules Football who could only have dreamt of sitting in a corporate box. He was overcome and wept when Daryl handed him the envelope with the tickets. The evening exploded with white flashing lights while Mr O'Sullivan was captured for posterity with Daryl's arm around his wiry shoulders.

Finally, all the lights went off and Tinkerbell's light did a final dance through the press of people now standing for a better vantage point. Then there was a loud bang as a big star cracked open to the tune of *Catch a Falling Star* while hundreds of sweets rained down to squeals of delight.

Georgie's voice came over the speakers for a final time. 'Enjoy the party, see you all next year.'

Parents queued to have their pictures taken with Daryl and he obliged them for what felt like hours. He signed programs, bent down to speak to kids, fist bumped fathers, and kissed mothers on the cheek. Children went back out to the quadrangle and played while their parents stood around chatting.

The thudding music and conversations sounded discordant to Kate. She saw spots in front of her eyes and her stomach growled. If she didn't eat something soon, she would collapse. She spotted Ryan holding a stubby and deep in conversation with Mark. When a plate piled high with fried spring rolls sailed past, Kate pinched a couple and scoffed them down, her nerves jagged.

She sat down on the stone wall that closed off the quadrangle, one foot dangling like a loose end. Mark gave her a half wave and beckoned for her to join them. He always looked awkward wearing casual gear. His slight paunch and scrawny legs meant jeans never fitted properly. Kate reluctantly stood and walked over. Ryan wouldn't say anything while Mark was there.

'Great performance by your daughter. Did she write the song herself?'

Ryan's chest swelled a little. 'Yeah, she did actually.'

Mark gave his head a small shake and looked at Ryan as if seeing him properly for the first time. 'Well, it's in the genes, I guess. Georgie tells me The Spiked Echidna is delighted with your gigs.'

Kate helped herself to one of the mini pies on offer, hoping to plug the hole in her gut. Mark raised his voice to be heard over the background beat of music being piped through tinny speakers and the loud babble of conversations. 'I'll have to come along one Friday night and hear you boys play.'

A familiar figure headed towards them, and Kate's heart gathered pace. She willed Daryl not to come over and talk to her. Surely there were plenty of parents falling over themselves to chat to him and brush against his stardom. Mark paused. 'Mate, let me go and get you another beer.'

He reached for Ryan's empty stubby and turned to leave. Daryl made his way towards them. Kate turned to Ryan, anxious. 'I really have a headache. Can we go get the kids and head home?'

He turned to her, unsmiling, one hand in his pocket. 'You just don't get it do you? Today is about Edie and Noah. I promised them they could stay for as long as they wanted. Our daughter is a bit of a star tonight and I'm giving her the opportunity to shine. If you want to go, you head off.'

Kate recoiled before stepping up to defend herself. 'How dare you tell me I don't get it. Who do you think pays for those music lessons, ferries them to rehearsals, and keeps the whole bloody show afloat so you can mess around with your band? I was late once. You haven't even been here.'

She realised she was shouting. Mark stopped short, holding a couple of beers aloft. Kate sensed someone behind her and knew immediately who it was. She was furious at Ryan for upbraiding her in public.

Daryl's voice sliced through the tension. 'Is everything alright here? It's sounding a bit heated.'

Kate stepped sideways to avoid touching Daryl. He reached over to shake Ryan's hand, and she stared at Daryl's large hand clasped around Ryan's long fingers. Daryl raised an eyebrow at her. 'So, are you going to introduce us?'

Kate wiped one moist hand down her dress. 'Daryl, I'd like you to meet Ryan.'

Daryl, of course, needed no introduction after his performance during the raffle. 'Delighted to meet you. I believe that your girl was the one who did that opening solo. Very impressive. Quite the talent.'

Ryan crossed his arms, beer in one hand. He looked pleased by the compliment.

'Yeah, she's good. We are very proud of her. She's been practising hard and it paid off tonight.'

'I hear you're a bit of a talent yourself. Georgie mentioned you play at one of the local pubs on Friday nights.'

'We've been signed up at The Spiked Echidna. You know that place? The old pub that had a complete refurbish. It's not a bad spot for a drink, good meal. The acoustics are excellent too.'

Kate turned away, arms folded.

Mark raised his beer. 'Cheers. I was just suggesting a night out to listen to The Bloody Bluebloods play.'

Daryl looked past them and raised one finger. One of the older teenagers he coached appeared and handed him a beer. Daryl's eyebrow lifted a fraction. 'Thanks, mate.'

Kate noticed Ryan grimace. He loathed that kind of presumption, excused himself, wandered off into the crowd.

She looked up and saw Noah running towards her, his face alight. Suddenly, he missed his footing at the wall, tripped and fell in slow motion. Time paused while he was airborne, and Kate registered what was happening. All at once there was an almighty thud and Noah face-planted. He lay very still for a terrible moment, then blood oozed from his head. It happened so quickly that it took Kate a moment to reach him while other parents stood around in shock. She crouched beside his prone form and placed her face next to his. His arm was bent at a strange angle. When he shifted and started to cry, she crumpled with relief and stroked his head.

The loud chatter around them stopped abruptly and other

parents moved towards them. He was bleeding onto the concrete and soaking her dress. Someone handed her a bundle of paper napkins and she mopped Noah's face and put pressure on a laceration on his forehead. His lip was cut and swelling up, his knees grazed. Kate muttered thanks for the napkins and looked up expecting to see Ryan's face. She startled to see Daryl, a mere breath away. He placed his hand on her arm.

'Let's have a look at the damage.'

His head touched hers when he bent down to wipe away the blood and did a rapid check of Noah's pulse, abdomen, face, and limbs.

A parent brought over the first aid kit and placed it next to Daryl while he rang for an ambulance. She watched his neck muscles flex while he searched for items, knowing just what to do. He pulled out a clean bandage and staunched the bleeding, then activated and applied a cold pack before securing the arm with a splint.

His movements were calm and practised. It was a relief to let him take over. Finally, he wound a bandage around one of Noah's knees and applied a dressing to his forehead. It seemed like hours later that Ryan appeared, ashen faced when the drama was over. Daryl stepped aside and Kate found herself clutching Noah while Ryan stood superfluous to one side.

While Daryl wiped blood off his hands, he spoke to Ryan. 'All good, mate. No damage done that won't heal up.'

Without looking at Kate, Ryan turned to Daryl. 'Thanks for your help.'

The paramedics arrived and lifted Noah onto a stretcher while Kate watched, both hands up near her mouth.

Ryan turned away. 'I'll grab Edie. Keep in touch.'

Kate stood at the end of the stretcher and buried her face in Noah's matted hair. Daryl smiled at her and she felt herself dissolve.

33

THE morning after the concert, Tori woke up later than usual to the sounds of activity in the kitchen. In that twilight of waking up, she was confused. Then she remembered. After they came home from the post-concert celebrations, she retched and retched, so Indigo stayed overnight.

Tori half sat up and tested herself. She seemed fine. In the excitement of the evening, she had forgotten to take the anti-nausea medications. She reached for her robe, swayed and grabbed the dresser. Yep, she was definitely alright. She headed out to the kitchen where Indigo was poaching eggs while slicing an avocado. The kettle reached a crescendo and a couple of muffins leapt out of the toaster.

Indigo looked up. 'Morning.'

Tori pulled out a chair. It scraped across the floor.

'Hey, thanks for staying over. I appreciate it. I'm feeling fine now.'

Indigo was busy mashing avocado onto the muffins. She slid a couple of eggs on top with the metal spatula.

Indigo shouted out to Leo 'You ready? I've called Shelley to help in the shop and I'm taking you to football.'

Tori forgot it was Saturday and Australian Rules. The days just blurred past like changing landscapes from a fast-moving train. Indigo pushed down the plunger on the coffee, poured some into a pottery mug, and set it in front of Tori. 'Have that for starters. I might get some eggs going for us as well.'

Tori wrapped her hands around the mug and took a sip. She reached for the sugar and added a couple of heaped spoons.

'Thanks for all this. If you want the day off, just let me know. I can manage the shop today.'

Indigo plunged the toaster down, cracked more eggs into the pan and gave it a stir. 'Just chill. Things are under control for now. I'll let you know when we need another set of hands.'

Tori bristled. It was her business after all. She let the hot bolus of liquid move down her gullet, pressed out a couple of her pills and swallowed them.

'I appreciate it. I should be fine in a few days.'

The next couple of muffins popped and Indigo assembled breakfast as Leo emerged, dressed and ready to head out.

He scoffed his food, and noticed Tori give him a look. He muttered, 'Thanks, Indigo.'

He drained his milk in one long skull then fled to his bedroom to pack his things, leaving the detritus from breakfast behind. Tori was about to protest his poor manners when Indigo called out, 'Remember, Leo. You are on for washing up Sunday.'

A shadow loomed at the front window. Tori jumped and spilt coffee on the table.

A loud knock. Indigo turned off the gas, strode over and opened the door a sliver.

Tori heard Daryl's familiar voice. 'Hey, I know it's Ryan's turn to take the boys to footy today, so I thought I'd swing past, help out.'

'Thanks. We're sorted.'

'How about I bring him home?'

'We're sorted. Thanks anyway.'

The sound of the door closing. A pause.

The sound of boots crunching down the gravel.

Tori didn't realise she was holding her breath. She exhaled.

Leo came out. 'Who was that?'

Indigo put the milk back in the fridge. 'No one important. Now, I'm taking you to the football today. Just a warning. I know fuck-all about Australian Rules, so I'll be expecting a crash course.'

Tori opened her mouth to say something, closed it again.

'And don't spare me. I'll be asking stupid questions and might need stuff explained more than once. Be tough on me.'

Tori wondered if Indigo realised what she was in for. 'Thanks, Indigo. You're a bloody lifesaver.'

'Don't mention it. By the way, I let Shelley into The Treasure Chest a bit earlier. Georgie has taken all the girls to some dance class. Don't even think about taking over. I've never seen Shelley look so relaxed. You might think about putting her on the payroll for a couple of shifts a week.'

Tori listened to the unequal crunch of footsteps head towards Indigo's minivan, Leo's enthusiastic voice regaling Indigo with details about his favourite topic.

✢

Tori finished her coffee, poured herself another mug and picked at breakfast. She pushed through fatigue and steadied her thoughts with the methodical task of clearing up, the suds in the sink stinging the cannula wound. She wondered how Noah was and whether he had to stay in hospital overnight. Something was going on between Kate and Ryan, and Tori longed for things to be playful between them again.

Having Shelley in the shop felt uncomfortable. They had not been close at uni, even though the three of them had gone out to dinner, drinks, and movies together. They had done the usual things girlfriends do, but there were no shared confidences with Shelley the way Tori had with Kate.

Tori knew Shelley's growing up had been tough. Kate mentioned it one day in passing. How Shelley's dad gambled, drank too much and got angry. Once he had been so certain of a big win at the races, he emptied their bank account of hard-earned savings Shelley's mum had scrimped together over a few years to buy their own place, only to lose it all and a bit more in an afternoon at the TAB. Kate joked that all the pictures at Shelley's place were hung in weird places to hide the holes in the walls before the draughty fibro dump was inspected a couple of

173

times a year.

Shelley hadn't hidden the fact she never wanted to worry about money again. Tori still recalled the sultry summer evening years ago when the three of them stayed out late and found themselves in a pub in the Valley. Feet hooked around bar stools while drowning in humidity and cheap wine, the three of them talked. Shelley shared how she resented wearing second-hand tat and was too embarrassed to accept party invitations because she couldn't afford a gift. She cried when she told them she never attended school excursions, and they hugged her and agreed that a life retrieving coins that stopped the dresser wobbling for bus fares sucked. Tori always assumed it meant Shelley would finish her degree and become a high-flyer earning big dollars, not that she would marry Daryl Brady and live off the spoils of his earnings.

Tori let Indigo's suggestion mull in her head. The truth was, Tori didn't really want Shelley working at The Treasure Chest. It was the thought of Daryl having an excuse to drop in anytime that chilled her. She gathered the couple of outfits she'd finished just before her surgery. A customer would be coming around lunchtime to collect them. It jarred, the thought of Shelley just stepping in. She didn't know all the clients the way Tori did, had not earned her right to be stepping into the space Tori had created. Shelley hardly needed the income with Daryl earning big bucks.

'Morning, Shelley.'

Tori placed the wrapped items on the desk.

'Indigo told me to shoo you out if you dared come over.'

Shelley's blue eyes sparkled, and her blonde hair was soft and loose around her face. She seemed so happy and relaxed compared to usual. Tori remembered how Shelley had come in most days and fingered the fabrics with longing, without ever making a purchase. It made Tori impulsive despite her misgivings. 'I actually came over to offer you a business proposition.'

Tori leaned against the counter. 'How about you keep working for me, say three mornings a week and I pay you a wage? I don't feel good about you doing all this work in my store for nothing.'

Shelley's hand flew to her mouth. 'I would love that.'

She hugged Tori. The pressure on the healing wound made Tori wince. 'Well, let me draw something up and get back to you. It will give me more time to deal with the online sales that are really taking off.'

34

BY the time Kate and Noah got home from hospital, it was the next morning. Georgie had taken Edie home and offered to take her to dance classes in the morning so that Ryan could join Kate at the hospital while they waited for Noah to be assessed. In the loud, antiseptic chaos of casualty, they stood subdued, neither keen to talk about their earlier dispute.

It was midnight when Noah was wheeled into the theatre. Afterwards, the orthopaedic surgeon spoke to them. 'Noah has a fracture dislocation of his elbow. No damage to his blood vessels or nerves. We'll book him into my fracture clinic next week for review.'

Kate suggested Ryan head home while she stayed with Noah for the rest of the night. She watched him sleep, his hair sticky with old blood, a bruise blooming around his lips, sutures across his forehead, and a blue fibreglass cast in position. By seven o'clock, the ward round was over, and they were discharged home. Kate carried Noah to the car, his little body a deadweight in her arms. She sent Ryan a text. *See you soon.* She hesitated and added a single X.

When she pulled up, Ryan was waiting at the door. Without a word, he picked Noah up and carried him to bed. The scent of freshly brewed coffee lured Kate to the kitchen. She dumped her bag, suddenly realising how dishevelled and dirty she looked. She slumped into a stool and poured herself a coffee, just as Ryan appeared. 'Thanks for the coffee. It's just what I needed.'

'How is Noah?'

'Fine. We have a follow-up appointment next week.'

The gap in conversation stretched a bit too long.

Kate heard a whimper and saw Bear's nose clouding the glass. When Ryan went to let him in, the sliding door caught on the track the way it always did. He jiggled it open, and Bear barrelled in, rump quivering, then jumped all over her, wet tongue leaving drool on her clothes. Kate was embarrassed at how appreciative she was of Bear's affection. She bent down and fondled his ears then picked up her mug and headed for the lounge.

It was a relief to curl up on its stained cushions, pull her feet up under her bottom and let Bear sit with his muzzle in her lap. Ryan took a chance and followed her with his own coffee. He sat a small distance away from her on the lounge. 'Do you want anything to eat?'

She shook her head. He put his mug down on the coffee table cluttered with last weekend's colour supplement and frayed music books. Hopeful, Bear jumped down and stuck his nose over the rim, then withdrew, disappointed there was no food to snaffle.

Ryan shuffled closer to Kate on the couch. She pulled her knees up and wrapped her arms around them, not sure she was ready to talk right now.

Ryan leant forward. 'I'm worried about you. It's not like you, not turning up in time for Edie's show last night.'

Kate's legs slid out from under her, fresh anger blooming. 'How dare you take off for three weeks then come home and suggest I'm a slack mother.'

'I just want to know why were you so late when Edie was playing her first ever solo piece?'

'I was held up at work with a client who really needed me. The work that pays for Edie's music lessons.'

'It's not always about money you know.'

'It is when you never have any.'

Ryan moved closer without touching her. He crossed one leg over the other and gestured to the age-stained paint and warping timbers in their old Queenslander. 'We have everything we need. This great place, two top kids. We have each other.'

'We have a stack of bills to be paid. We need to fix things in the place and the kids need stuff all the time.'

She thought about the thousand jobs that needed doing around the house, the trips she wanted to take, the life she dreamed of living. 'I bust my gut, but we never get ahead.'

'I thought you loved your work. We arranged our lives around it. I put my music on hold so you could study and work.'

She stood and picked up her mug. 'You always avoid the issue. I do love my work, but I'm sick of scraping, scrimping, and watching every penny. We need a new kitchen, to update the bathroom, and the place desperately needs a coat of paint. I want to send the kids to a good school.'

Ryan stretched one arm along the back of the couch and looked up at her. 'And do you think that will make you happier?'

Kate thought about the careful way she budgeted and the extra hours she worked to get ahead. 'It's okay to have ambitions, to want things.'

'Not when they become more important than seeing your daughter's first solo performance.'

Kate walked to the kitchen and banged her Target mug on the sink. With caffeine fizzing in her veins, she was suddenly wide awake, nerves firing. She snatched up her handbag, unwilling to justify herself to Ryan for another minute. 'I'm heading out for a while.'

When she pulled the door shut, it gave a satisfying shudder.

✦

Kate decided to head to the clinic and write up her last couple of clients from yesterday. It always soothed her to sit at work, especially on a weekend when she was there alone and able to write up her consultations without interruption. Driving up the hill, the sun poured into the car, the sky a hard blue you could reach out and touch. She unclenched when she pulled up in the empty carpark and gazed at the city, a hazy silhouette in the distance. When Kate got out of the car and slung her handbag over her shoulder, she noticed something at the door and her insides tightened again. She hesitated then realised it was a huge plant. Waiting on the bottom step was an impressive potted orchid in a moss lined planter. She glanced around and wondered who had left it sitting there. The enormous cascade of deep pink petals opened like butterfly wings. The label peeked out from the spongy green and she pulled it out, brushed off the dirt. *Phalaenopsis.* It sounded vaguely sexual. There was a small dusky pink envelope. She slipped out the card. *Hope Noah is OK XX.*

Kate's pulses whooshed in her ears thinking about how calm and capable Daryl had been when he tended to Noah's injuries. Her breath caught when she remembered the way his head touched hers. She forced her thoughts away from yesterday and wondered whether to take the orchid home but decided against it. She shoved the key in the door and went inside. The pot weighed a ton. She built up a sweat edging it into the corner of the waiting room. The darker centres of the blooms reminded her of lips slightly parted. It seemed inappropriate for her clients, too loud amongst the muted shades of green she had deliberately chosen.

It would do for now.

35

TORI paced in her kitchen. It was too late to withdraw her offer now. The satisfaction of making Shelley so happy now morphed into dread. Having her working next door three days a week would be just the opening Daryl needed. He would abuse it in some way, to lure Leo to more bloody football gigs and make her life impossible. She stood near her window and gazed out into the intense blue sky. After working so hard to create a life for herself and Leo, it was all unravelling and there was not a thing she could do about it.

She collapsed into one of the chairs, pulled out her phone, and found Kate's number. Tori hesitated. Kate might still be asleep after last night. Who knew how long she had been in hospital with poor Noah or if she was still there. She didn't need to deal with Tori's problems as well.

The faint tingle of the bell sounded from the shop and the thought of Shelley smiling at customers, helping them choose the perfect outfit or ideal piece of furniture made her sweat again. She bent over her phone and opted to type a message to Kate. *Are you free? How is Noah?*

The response was immediate. *Noah fine, asleep. Faffing at work. See you in ten.*

Tori bit her lip and leaned into her anxiety. It was time to come clean and for Kate to learn what sort of person Tori really was.

It seemed like minutes later, Kate's silhouette waited at the door.

'Tori, good to see you.' Kate gave her a careful hug. 'You know,

180

I went to work, planned to write up yesterday's consults but I just couldn't focus.'

'God, I'm sorry. Is it Noah?'

'No, he's at home with Ryan asleep.' Kate's brow furrowed. 'It's other things. But don't you worry about that. How are you going?'

Tori's shoulders slumped. She moved over to the lounge. 'Awful. Come and sit down.' She curled her feet up underneath her and twisted the bottom of her long-sleeved tee in her hands.

Kate dumped her bag, shifted closer. 'Tori, what is it? Is there a problem after the surgery?'

Tori shook her head. 'It's nothing to do with the surgery.'

Kate sighed. 'Thank god for that.'

The crisp cool of the autumn day snuck under the door and Tori shivered. She reached for her long woollen cardigan at the back of the lounge, pulled it on and wrapped it tight around herself.

'It's about me.'

She felt Kate move closer followed by the pressure of an arm around her shoulder.

Tori stared at the coffee table. 'Do you remember when I left uni? My uncle died and I went back to Melbourne to help Aunt Jean who had been so kind to me.'

Talking about events from long ago was like walking barefoot on a pebbled path, each step a painful reminder of events archived in her memory.

'I think I told you that I went to live with Uncle Raymond and Aunt Jean after my folks were killed in a head-on?'

Tori licked her lips, the details of her past vivid and painful. 'Raymond was an unpredictable prick. He erupted at the slightest thing and Jean spent a lot of time placating him and making sure everything was just how he wanted. He never hit her, but he sucked the joy out of her life. If she went out to have lunch with friends, he grumbled and insisted she make him some lunch before leaving. When she made him breakfast, he complained his morning coffee was too hot, too cold, or too weak. When I started puberty, I was aware how he started to watch me. He'd slip past me, brush against my breasts, try to catch me when I was getting changed. He had these rules about not shutting my bedroom door, so I used to change in the toilet. One day, he put his hand on my thigh while my aunt served dinner. I think she knew something was not right but neither of us had the words to talk about it. Instead, she opened an account for me. She took in ironing and put the money aside. I counted the days before I finished school and could leave. I was too selfish to realise I'd be leaving Jean behind.'

Kate spoke softly. 'It was not selfish, it was self-preservation.'

Tori shook her head. 'One afternoon, Jean visited a friend in hospital. He was fucking waiting for me. I opened the door and there he was filling the frame. I knew right away I was in trouble.'

Kate nudged closer and her hand squeezed Tori's shoulder.

'He grabbed me, pulled me into his office and shoved me across the desk full of paperwork.'

Tori found it hard to breathe and closed her eyes. Details rushed back at her like a huge wave, images like a horror movie vivid behind her lids. She almost forgot Kate was close until she heard her whisper. 'Tori, I'm so sorry.'

Tori took some deep breaths before she continued. 'My school uniform was hitched up around my waist and the thought that ran through my head was not *I gotta get the fuck out of here*, but *the bastard can see my knickers*.'

Tori turned, eyes wide, and looked at Kate 'I should have fought hard, struggled more, kicked him where it hurt. I just froze.'

Tori shivered and goosebumps prickled her skin. Kate let her arm drop and took Tori's hands and held them in her own. 'You were a kid; it wasn't your fault.'

Tori's hand clenched inside Kate's, and she pushed through, determined to finish. 'He held me down with one hand and I heard him unzip. I thought he was going to kill me and still didn't dare move.'

Tori broke away from Kate and leant forwards, her face in her hands. She rocked back and forth. 'He pushed his hard penis into my face. It smelt of urine. I turned away from him and he slapped me hard on the cheek, forced himself into my mouth. I gagged and nearly vomited. Then he ripped off my kickers, forced my legs apart and I nearly died from the pain. I cried out and he covered my mouth with his sweaty palm.'

Tori stopped rocking and stared up at Kate, her eyes wide, her cheeks damp. 'Instead of fighting, I stared at a damp patch on the walls and willed it to end. I let him rape me.'

Kate hugged Tori but she stayed rigid and unresponsive.

'Afterwards, I managed to slither from under him. He fell back into his chair, laughing, his pants around his ankles. I just remember his dick floppy against his pale thigh. It reminded me of a dead fish. I walked out, went to my room, shut the door, and shoved a couple of chairs in front.'

Tori paused and softened against Kate again. 'I never told Jean, but I think she suspected. I marked the days till I finished and made sure I was never home alone with him again. I worked at the local newsagency, saved up and bought an old Datsun 120Y. I used it to drive up here. I didn't care what I studied, I just wanted an excuse to leave.'

Tori realised Kate was still holding her upper arms, tears on her cheeks. 'Oh, Tori. That is just awful. Really awful. You do know it was not your fault.'

'I barely kept in touch with Jean afterwards. I sent a couple of postcards and brief letters. I just wanted to put Melbourne out of my mind. I feel so guilty about that. She deserved better.'

'You were a teenager. She should have protected you. I can totally understand what you did. Don't blame yourself.'

Kate was still holding her, the two of them facing each other on the couch. Tori pulled away first. 'I might just make a pot of tea and pull out some of those beautiful melting moments you made.'

Neither of them spoke while the kettle boiled and Tori moved around pulling out cups and saucers, sugar, milk, and biscuits. She poured the milk into a pretty creamer, laid out biscuits on a floral printed dish with petal-shaped edges. Kate helped carry everything over and they sat down.

Tori poured. She knew just how Kate liked hers and handed her a dainty teacup balanced on a delicate saucer. 'Just like real ladies. Although, I'm far from being a real lady.'

Kate leant over, rattled the crockery as she set it on the table. 'Please, don't say that. It was not your fault.'

Tori stopped her with a raised hand. 'There's more. You'll change your mind in a moment.'

Kate placed her hand on Tori's crossed leg. 'Never.'

'I went back to Melbourne the minute my uncle died, determined to stay with Jean and help her out. She'd never paid bills or dealt with lawyers. The whole being alone thing terrified her, even though Raymond was so awful. He managed everything while she cooked and cleaned and was his general dogsbody. I took her out to the movies, to lunch and to the art gallery. She'd never been to the gallery. Can you imagine that? We went for walks along the Yarra, ate at cafes and drank wine in the middle of the day. Jean kept telling me to get back to Brisbane and finish uni, but I actually didn't want to. That time with her felt like breathing space. An opportunity to decide what I really wanted to do with my life. I developed the kernel of the idea that became The Treasure Chest.

When Jean died, I was bereft. I'd never felt so alone. After the funeral, I just wandered through the city and planned to drink myself into the relief of oblivion. I found a bar and was about to get myself a beer when I heard someone call my name.

Tori shrank into her knitted cardigan, her hands over her face. She trembled and Kate kneeled on the floor next to her. 'What is it? Can I get you something? Pain relief.'

Tori shook her head. 'It was Daryl. We'd not been close at uni, I never liked the man, but he was pleased to see me, and I have to admit, I was so relieved to see a familiar face. I wanted to tell someone who knew me about Jean dying. We had a few drinks, and he invited me back to his place. He grabbed some kebabs, more beer and I was in a daze, grateful another person was there to make decisions and look after me.'

Tori's shoulders started shaking now. Loud sobs. Her whole body heaved.

'Please, you will hate me. I know.'

Kate tried to hug her. It was awkward with Tori cross-legged on the lounge, knees and elbows poking out.

'One thing led to another. He started kissing me and well, you can imagine the rest.'

'Tori, it happens. You were both alone, found each other.'

Tori shook her head and made no effort to hold back her tears. Her face was red, eyes bloodshot.

'He was married to Shelley. It was maybe one month after that huge bloody event splashed all over the papers, on the front of every daily, on TV. I woke up the next morning, hungover, feeling like crap, and thought, what kind of friend does that? I should never have gone home with him. He'd been selected to play football, was setting up. Shelley was following him in a month or so.'

Tori sat up. Straight-backed, tear-stained, hair matted.

'I realised a few weeks later, just before Shelley was due to arrive, that I was pregnant. Like a complete fool, I went over and told him.'

She collapsed down again, explained what happened. The rape, the demand for her to terminate, to *just get rid of it.*

'So, I sold up, fled, made the decision that no one need ever know. It wouldn't be a good look for a footballer presented to the world as a clean-cut family man and would devastate Shelley. I didn't want my baby growing up with a mother who slept with her friend's husband because she was feeling a bit crappy.'

Kate sat staring at Tori, realisation dawning on her. 'Daryl is Leo's father.'

Tori nodded.

'And I don't suppose Leo knows.'

Tori shook her head. 'No one knows besides you, and Daryl of course.'

The tea grew cold.
Biscuit crumbs were strewn on the plate.
Shadows slipped, moved, and dappled the room in new patterns.

36

'HELLO.'

The long uneasy quiet was interrupted by Indigo and Leo at the door.

Leo was filthy, brimming with excitement and energy, oblivious to the undercurrents in the room.

'We won. Mum, I wish you'd seen my field goal. I really didn't think I'd get it. Everyone stood up and cheered. Mr Brady named me man of the match.'

Kate saw Tori shudder at the name before she pulled herself together.

'Leo, I'm so proud of you. Did you take any snaps?'

She looked at Indigo.

'I was the bloody paparazzi. Here, have a look.'

She scrolled through photographs on her phone. Kate watched Tori's head bent over photos. Tori turned her head at one of Daryl high fiving Leo. Indigo searched Tori's face.

'Is everything okay here? You seem kinda tense.'

Kate nodded and answered rather too quickly. 'Fine, really. We were chatting about old times and got caught up in memories.'

Indigo looked to Tori for confirmation, but she refused to engage. Instead, she changed the topic, her voice shaky. 'You'll be pleased to know I took your advice. Shelley will be helping three mornings a week.'

Kate turned away and watched Leo who was plundering the

fridge, pulling out cheese, milk, ham, all while eating one of her raspberry melting moments. Now that she knew, it seemed obvious. He had Daryl's firm jawline, and his hair grew from the same central spot at the back of his head. Even some of his movements reminded Kate of Daryl. It was a wonder she had never noticed it before.

Tori called out. 'Leo, go and have a shower before you make lunch.'

'But I'm so hungry.'

He grabbed another of Kate's biscuits and folded a piece of bread around a slice of ham.

'I'll be wanting a blow-by-blow account of the match over lunch, but I'd prefer it if you didn't smell like a men's locker room.'

Leo disappeared.

Indigo stood, arms folded. 'Good news about Shelley. She loves working at The Treasure Chest. It's good for her. I suspect with that husband of hers injured, it's wise for her to be out of the house.'

She glanced at her watch. 'I might head over, give her a break.'

Tori nodded. 'I'll bring some lunch over shortly.'

Kate picked up their mugs, placed them on the tray, carried it all over to the kitchen. Her voice was gentle. 'You will have to tell Leo one day. It's much better he hears it from you than Daryl.'

Tori sat hunched over, didn't respond.

Kate sat next to her. 'He's not saying anything now as he wants to be seen as the perfect family man and fathering a child outside marriage doesn't suit his image. If Shelley left him, that would change.'

Tori stared at her, the whites of her eyes visible. 'I can't imagine her leaving him.'

'She mentioned she was not happy.'

Tori buried her face in her hands again. There was a loud thump on the door. They both startled and looked up.

'Anyone home?'

Tori stared at Kate who stood up, her hands trembling. 'Come in.'

Daryl pushed the door open then pulled it shut hard behind him.

He looked at Tori then Kate, his eyes narrowed.

'I just went to pick up my wife and she tells me she's bloody employed by you now.'

Kate's heart thumped so hard she thought it might be visible. She glanced at Tori who looked pale like a ghost. The air was sucked out of the room. It suddenly felt very small. Tori walked over to him, hands on her hips. 'That's right. I didn't like that Shelley was working there for nothing, so I offered her some paid hours.'

Daryl took a step towards Tori. Kate noticed the way the muscle in his jaw twitched madly.

'I was happy for my wife to help while you were recovering from surgery but the bloody reason we moved here was to start afresh and spend more time together. Are you suggesting I can't support my family?'

He stood so close to Tori there was a mere breath between them. Tori crossed her arms and looked Daryl in the eye.

'This is not about you. Shelley loves working at The Treasure Chest. It makes her happy and I need an extra employee.'

Daryl leant towards Tori his voice low now. 'Are you playing games? Trying to destroy my family?'

There was another knock at the door, soft this time.

Daryl paused.

Tori called out, 'Come in.'

Shelley gently pushed the door open and stopped when she saw Daryl. 'Hello, darling. I was just letting Tori know I was done at the shop.'

All three of them looked at her. No one spoke.

Leo emerged, freshly showered, and looked around at the adults standing awkwardly around the room.

'Is anyone else hungry?'

Tori turned, moved towards the kitchen. 'Let's have some lunch.' She turned her gaze to Shelley and added, 'Why don't you join us, and we can talk about your hours at The Treasure Chest? Draw up a contract.'

Kate picked up her bag and avoided looking at Daryl. 'I might just head home and see how Noah is going.'

She watched how Daryl looked from Shelley to Tori. 'We're heading home too.'

Shelley hesitated. When Daryl headed towards the door, she looked back at Tori with an apologetic smile. 'Thanks for everything. I'll let you get on with lunch and see you later in the week.'

She turned and hurried out.

Kate waited till the Bradys left before walking to her Corolla and driving home.

She had barely pulled up at home when her phone rang. When she opened the front door, phone pressed to her ear, she nearly fell backwards when Bear jumped up to greet her, hoping for a walk. It was Tori, her voice faltering. 'I'm going to tell Shelley. I want to tell her before I tell Leo.'

'Do you want me to be there?'

'Would you? Let's all go out together. I suspect she won't want to have anything to do with me after she finds out.'

'You might be surprised.'

Tori hung up and Kate bent down to pat Bear who gave her face a lick. She confided in him while she rubbed his silky ears, his chocolate almond eyes staring into hers. 'Bear, I have made a mess of things and I'm not sure how to fix it. Since Daryl moved here, everything has become complicated.'

37

ON Monday morning Tori insisted on taking Leo to school. She asked Indigo to open at The Treasure Chest.

'Mum, I like it when Indigo takes me. We have milkshakes before she drops me off and I promised to tell her some more stuff about football.'

'It's only today. I'm hoping to catch Shelley.'

'Just text her.'

'It sounds like you're trying to get rid of your mum. I want to see Shelley face-to-face. She's going to be working with me at the shop soon.'

Leo slouched off at the school gate, disappointed. It made Tori smile, and she vowed to become more fluent with the nuances of Australian Rules. When she saw Kate's Corolla squeeze into a spot, Tori waved her over. 'Not a peep from Shelley. She's often late. I've seen her floor that beast of a car down the street as the second bell is ringing.'

Kate did a quick scan, caught sight of Georgie and waved. 'Have you seen Shelley this morning?'

Georgie's eyes darted away. 'This morning?'

She made a show of looking around and shaking her head. 'I can't say I have.'

'Thanks. If you see her, let me know. Tori is giving her some shifts at The Treasure Chest.'

Nodding, Georgie gave an effusive smile. 'Great news. Sorry to rush, but I need to get away this morning.'

Tori watched her leave. 'Georgie-girl seems a bit edgy this morning.'

Kate shrugged. 'Perhaps they stopped making her fave shade of lipstick.'

'That's not very kind.'

Before Kate headed back to her car, Tori grabbed her arm. 'I'm scared. Worried what will happen once Shelley knows, and Leo learns the truth. They will both hate me. I'm terrified of losing him. Daryl can give him everything he dreams of. Opportunities to play football at a higher level, access to exclusive seats.'

Kate hugged her. 'That boy adores you. Daryl is exciting for the moment, but he wasn't there when Leo was sick, afraid of the dark, or starting school. He wasn't the person there reading him stories and watching him take his first step. You will always be his number one.'

Tori tried to push her anxieties down, but they popped up like ping pong balls being held under water. 'Thanks for everything.'

✦

When there was no sign of Shelley, Kate hurried to work, her stomach in knots. If Tori knew Kate had been meeting up with Daryl, she would be furious. As for Shelley, the thought of her finding out made Kate nauseous.

The sensuous pink orchids stood bold and loud in the waiting room and she regretted leaving them there. She hurried to her consulting room and logged on, fingers trembling on the keys. Before starting her session, she rested one hand on her upper abdomen and took a few deep breaths. She forced herself away from her own worries, ready to immerse herself in the problems of others.

The morning of consulting flew past. Kate slipped out of her shoes, pushed her chair back, and pulled her salad out of the fridge. She sat at her desk, speared a piece of chicken and roast tomato when she heard the unmistakable click at the door. Frowning, she pushed the container to one side and pushed her feet back into her shoes when there he was, filling the doorway. She dropped the fork into her pocket, her pulse accelerating. 'Daryl.'

She pushed her chair back a little. He took a step forward.

'God, you look gorgeous today.'

How was it she always felt naked under his scrutiny?

'I'm a bit surprised to see you here.'

Her voice was high pitched and tinny. It skittered around the walls.

'I'd forgotten how beautiful you are.'

He took another step closer. A muscle in his jaw twitched. Kate wondered if he could see her heart banging behind her ribs. She remembered her supervisor recommending that a therapist should always have ready access to an exit. Right now, Daryl was blocking it.

He strolled in and sat in the client's chair then pulled it closer to hers. Their knees nearly touched. She wondered what he would say if he knew she knew he was Leo's father. Kate found her courage. She was not the one with anything to lose. 'This affair you mentioned, did you father any children?'

His jaw tensed, but the rest of him stayed motionless. He let the silence between them elongate before speaking softly. 'I know you still have feelings for me. You're the only one who really understands me.'

His face bent towards her until his breath mingled with hers. She was trapped behind the desk.

'I can see it all now. You are as unhappy as I am. Pushing through. Trying to do the right thing. We belong together, should never have broken up. It's not too late. We can leave all the bullshit behind us.'

He was so close she could see the pores where he shaved this morning. She tried to use her desk to push away and create some space between them when in one fluid movement, he stood and grabbed her shoulders. He tried to kiss her. She wrenched herself free with a strength she did not know she possessed and stood with her back pressed to the wall. 'Leave now.'

Her hair had come loose and was messy around her face. She could feel the hard print where his thumbs had pressed into her flesh.

'I'm not ready to leave just yet. I see now you are part of the conspiracy to deprive me of my son and separate me from my wife.'

He was breathing hard now. His anger was hot on her skin. The hairs on her neck stood to attention.

'Well, I'm not done yet. When I leak that little story to the press, how the mother of my child crossed borders to deprive me of my paternal rights, without leaving a forwarding address, she can play her games in court.'

He leant one hand on the wall next to Kate's head and brought his face close to hers. 'It's not too late for you. I will give you one last chance to leave that runt you hooked up with and come with me. You are so much better than all of them.'

He punched the wall millimetres from her face and left a dent. 'Otherwise, I might be tempted to tell them about the psychologist who tried to fuck me over and used me to get back at my wife.'

He reached for his phone and scrolled through their text exchanges.

Kate wriggled one hand around to the fork in her pocket. Knowing she only had one chance to distract him, she jammed a heel into his foot, swung the fork and only just missed his eye.

He hopped on one foot and grabbed his bleeding temple in the other.

'Fucking cock teaser.'

His yells reverberated around the room and echoed in her ears.

He lunged towards her again, one fist raised. Blood roaring in her ears, she tried to dart around him and escape.

One hand reached to grab her, his other still balled. She turned her face away and readied herself for the impact. It smashed into the wall near the framed family photograph from their trip to Carnarvon Gorge. He snatched it off the hook and hurled it across the room with the full force of his fury. The frame hit the wall like a gunshot and cracked, glass splintering across the floor. Shards scattered between them, large broken pieces like icicles.

Kate held her breath, certain she would be next. He raised his arms, sweat rings visible on his white shirt. He swept his hand across her desk, scattering her lunch, paperweights, and a pot plant, then grabbed her fat diary bursting with notes she had not transferred to client's files. He opened it up and flicked through, some notes drifting to the floor like autumn leaves. Kate stayed pressed against the wall, a stone blocking her windpipe. He pulled out a scrap of paper and taunted her. '*Elsa, take her through rescue breathing again, remind her to keep the inhalation and exhalation the same length.*' Then he turned the diary upside down and confidential notes about her clients fluttered around the room like confetti. 'Who pays for all this bullshit anyway?'

He dropped it with a thud on the floor then turned and kicked the chair until it hit the other wall so hard that the leg snapped. The wall shuddered. A fraction later, her framed qualifications loosened and fell to the ground. He came up close again, the veins in his neck quivering cords. He punched her hard in the sternum, making her crumple forwards.

'I'm not fuckin' done yet. Don't get any ideas.'

Bending down, he picked up her degree, flung it across the room where it landed to the sound of further shattering glass then walked out, a trickle of blood down the side of his face.

The front door slammed and the whole building trembled.

Kate was too scared to move in case he returned. Her phone was in her handbag out of reach. She let the air out of her lungs slowly and scanned the fractured room.

Her legs were shaking. She slid down the wall until her knees hit her chest. Tears slid down her cheeks. Using her hands to push, she forced herself to stand, remembering the resigned curve of Shelley's back when she left Tori's place and followed him home.

Still wobbly, Kate fumbled for her keys, picked up her bag and pulled the door locked behind her. She ran out to her car and drove white knuckled to Shelley's place. She parked, started down the path, noticed the gleam of Daryl's car. The dark windows were like sullen eyes watching her. Stumbling, Kate ran backwards and nearly tripped. She realised how foolish it was to come here alone, scrambled back to her car and urged it home. It shuddered in protest and wheezed to a halt after she roared into her driveway.

Ryan was at the kitchen bench making himself a sandwich, his satchel half open beside him.

'Ryan.'

She glimpsed her bruised and dishevelled reflection. Her shoulder ached and a throb had started in the middle of her chest. He stared at her open-mouthed.

Kate staggered, ignoring Bear who pawed her leg and whimpered. Once Daryl revealed those texts, her career would be history. Ryan would leave and her name would be splashed through the media. Noah and Edie taunted at school, their mum the psychologist who overstepped boundaries and compromised herself.

'I've made a terrible mistake.'

38

KATE stared at the reassuring household chaos, hands trembling. Dishes cluttered the sink, a screwdriver lay inexplicably next to the kettle, and sheet music piled at one end of the bench like driftwood at low tide. Ryan left his sandwich half made and stared at her. 'Did you have an accident? Are you okay?'

When she didn't answer, he beckoned with one hand motioning her to the lounge. 'Come and sit down.'

Kate's legs felt heavy and uncooperative. The ache in her chest throbbed and she wondered if Daryl had fractured her ribs. Bear jumped up, his entire rump wriggling, but his efforts to capture her attention remained unrewarded. She lowered herself onto the lounge and felt the familiar give of the old springs.

Ryan stood loose-limbed and patient and waited for her to speak. He bumped the coffee table and the pile of mail she planned to sort through slid in a jumble to the floor. He left it there. 'Can I get you something? A glass of water?'

She held her head in her hands, her voice muffled. 'It's my fault. I let things get out of control. Daryl came into the clinic and threatened me.'

The whole terrifying scene replayed in her head again. The bulge of Daryl's shoulder, the gleam of a gold cufflink, his scent when he leaned in to kiss her, the chilling sounds of shattering glass. Her body started to shake, and she began to cry.

Ryan pulled up a stool and sat a small distance in front of her, elbows on his knees. 'What the hell was Shelley's husband doing at the clinic? Let me call the police.'

'No!' Kate wiped her nose on her sleeve and rocked back and forth. 'I just didn't expect him. He was so angry.'

Her chest was really hurting now. Her head pulsed.

'Shelley wants to leave him. She wants a divorce.'

'What the hell, Kate? Why does that involve you? We must get the police involved.'

Ryan started to search for his phone. He'd left it somewhere again. Kate grabbed him by the shoulders to stop him. 'Wait, please. I need to talk to Shelley. She wouldn't want the police involved.'

Instead of putting his arms around her the way he used to, he held his hands up in surrender. 'You're not making a lot of sense. If the guy is dangerous and threatens people, we need to report him. I've never seen you like this. Did he hurt you?'

Her thoughts flashed back to the smashed photo, the dent in the wall, and Daryl's hot angry breath on her skin. She had to clean up the clinic, so Ryan didn't see the damage. And of course, there was Shelley's safety to think about.

Kate took a deep breath and winced at the sudden stab in her sternum. 'You need to trust me. Let me talk to Shelley. I know she would hate me if I called the police without telling her first.'

Ryan checked his watch, picked up his keys, and headed towards the door. 'I'm heading to pick up the kids. Just don't do anything rash.'

The front door banged, and she listened to the wheeze of Ryan's car backing out the driveway. Bear whined. She reached down and scratched him behind the ears. Dogs always knew when things weren't right. Gazing into his deep chocolate eyes, she pleaded, 'Oh Bear, please let Shell be safe.'

Kate fumbled through her bag for her phone and tried to call Shelley. No response. She rang Tori and willed her to pick up, wondering how much to tell her. Tori's phone rang out and went to message bank. Kate cursed. Then she remembered Georgie this morning, the odd way she reacted when they asked about Shelley. It was so unlike Georgie not to want to chat. Kate rang her.

'Hello, it's me. Kate.'

'Is everything alright?'

'I'm looking for Shelley. It's urgent. She's not answering her phone.'

There was a hesitation. 'Shelley's away. She pulled the kids from school for two days.'

'Where did she go? I need to speak to her.'

Georgie paused. 'No idea. She should be back in a day or so.'

'It's so important I speak to her. The sooner the better.'

There was another long pause. 'Sorry, Kate, I can't tell you. Shelley wanted some privacy.'

Kate dropped into the lounge, her phone still pressed to her ear. 'Please, Georgie. It sounds dramatic but it's life and death. I must speak to her. She won't answer her phone, and I have tried to drive past her place.'

'I told you already. She's away and switched her phone off for a few days. Leave it for tomorrow when she gets back.'

Kate forced herself to stay calm. Georgie usually couldn't keep a secret for five minutes. There was no other option if Kate was to keep Shelley safe. Kate would have to tell Georgie the truth.

'I did something really stupid. Daryl asked me for help. I have been seeing him as a friend and let him talk to me about the marriage. Shelley doesn't know. He threatened me today and I am worried that he is going to hurt Shelley or his kids. I need to warn her.'

It was a relief to tell someone. There was a sharp intake of breath on the phone. 'I can't believe you were seeing him behind Shelley's back!'

Kate glanced at the digital clock on the oven and hoped Ryan would not get back before she found out where Shelley was. The throat clearing at the other end indicated Georgie was about to speak. 'She's staying at our holiday place at Noosa to sort out some personal issues. I'm not sure what's going on, but she was quite anxious and wanted a couple of days away with the kids.'

Kate knew exactly where the place was. A few years ago, they stayed at the Noosa place during the school holidays. *Mates' rates,* Mark had said handing over the keys. He and Georgie were heading to Japan with the girls and wouldn't be using it. When she saw the price, Kate remembered asking Ryan what the usual rates were. It cost so much more than she expected.

Kate sent a kiss through the phone. 'Thanks so much. I appreciate you telling me. My lips are sealed.' She grabbed her keys from the side table in the hallway and headed for the door just as Ryan's car spluttered into the driveway. Kate cursed under her breath, wishing he had arrived home a few minutes later. She kept her voice light. 'I'm just heading to see Shelley to talk to her. She's having a few days at the coast.'

Kate stopped just before letting Noosa slip from her lips.

'Let me come with you, it's a long drive and you're not yourself. I'll leave the kids with Georgie.'

'No, I need to do this alone. I'll be careful, promise.'

She opened the car door and blew him a kiss. 'Thanks for everything, Ry. I appreciate it.'

She backed out before he insisted on coming. She longed to call out, *I love you* but was no longer confident of his feelings for her.

Kate let Ariana Grande's *No Tears Left to Cry* take her along the highway out of Brisbane. It was not going to be easy telling Shelley about seeing Daryl, especially after their last conversation. Kate's hands gripped the steering wheel, determined to do the right thing and wear the consequences. The time for secrets was over. No more guilt and no more hiding things.

Once the song finished, Kate drove in silence and let her mind rake over all her interactions with Daryl and his behaviour in public. Shelley's quiet submission and her efforts to appease him. So many small cries for help. Kate's eyes filled with tears of anger at her own blind stupidity. There was no excuse for failing to read between the lines and listening to what Shelley was too frightened to say out loud.

The hum of the engine vibrated through the flimsy metal body as Kate worried her way to Noosa. At least Daryl didn't know where Shelley was. Georgie would not betray Shelley's trust in that way, even though she was a huge Daryl fan.

The drive took her just under two hours. She looked out for the turn-off and found it easily. The house was located a short walk from Noosa Main Beach and Hastings Street, a blue-chip location, Mark always called it. The minute Kate pulled up in the driveway, Shelley stepped out the front door wrangling a suitcase. Kate parked and ran up the path, relieved to see Shelley was alone and looked all right.

It was only when up close, she noticed Shelley's eyes narrowed to angry slits. Kate stopped, unable to recall seeing Shelley so angry. She must be furious with Georgie for breaching her confidence. Once Kate explained everything and how she pressured Georgie for information, Shelley would understand. She needed to hear the whole ugly truth whatever the outcome.

Shelley stood behind the suitcase like it was a shield, her voice cold like ice. 'What are you doing here?'

Kate took a step forward. 'I've been trying to ring you...'

Shelley kept both hands on the handle of the case, her lips bloodless and eyes cold. It was the first time Kate recalled seeing her without lipstick and it made her look fragile and childlike. The silence congealed around them. Kate put out a hand to touch Shelley who recoiled. 'I know all about you. You call yourself a friend and all the while you betray me behind my back.'

Kate's lips were dry. It appeared Shelley already knew the truth.

'Daryl told me everything. He showed me your texts.'

Shelley fished in her pocket, held up the pendant with its stars and moon. It glinted accusingly in the late afternoon light. 'He confessed that you two have been having an affair. I never want to see you or have anything to do with you again.'

Kate opened her mouth, shocked, but no words came out.

Meanwhile, Shelley stepped inside dragging the suitcase behind her, then slammed the door hard in Kate's face.

39

TORI felt jittery. She wanted to tell Shelley the truth and get it all over with. She made a start on a velvet jacket promised to a regular client and made a mistake. Swearing, she unpicked it and flung the jacket across the room. Her mouth was dry. She walked to the fridge, poured a glass of water, chugged it down and added a sleeper for good measure. Perhaps a good sleep was the only way to get through the next day.

Tori switched her phone to silent, curled up on the lounge and fell asleep. A brief respite from her white-knuckle anxiety. She awoke to the sound of a car horn and raised voices.

Her heart tripped. Then she realised it was coming from Vincent's.

It took a moment to orientate herself. She realised she was at home, in her unit, safe.

Her heart found its rhythm again.

The pattern of shadows across the room indicated she had slept for a few hours.

She picked up her phone and saw there was a message from Kate. The beat in her chest accelerated. Damn, it had been on silent, so Tori missed the call. Pacing, she called Kate. It rang and rang until Kate's message started. Tori ended the call not wanting to leave a message. It was important to talk and to hear Kate's voice.

The foreboding in Tori's chest grew. Had Kate found Shelley? On impulse, Tori rang Ryan who might be able to give her the heads up about where Kate was and reassure her that everything was alright. She pressed the phone to her ear and willed him to pick up.

'Hello.'

Noah and Edie were chatting in the background. Things sounded normal. Tori hoped she was not overreacting.

'Hi, Ryan. Tori here. I feel a bit weird just ringing out of the blue, but I'm a bit worried about Kate.'

She heard Ryan walking somewhere, the click and catch of a sliding door, the excited sound of Bear in the background.

'Just a tic,' he called out to the kids. 'Grab yourselves a Milo and make a start on your homework.'

The sound of a sliding door jerking shut.

'I'm so glad you called. Daryl turned up to Kate's work today and threatened her. I don't know the details. She refused to tell me what happened. I think he just shouted at her and gave her a scare, but she looked awful and took off in her car to see Shelley somewhere on the coast. She's worried that Daryl will hurt Shelley.'

Tori's intestines knotted, worried she had left things too late. 'Where is Shelley?'

'Somewhere on the coast. Kate is with her right now.'

'And Daryl?'

'No idea.'

Tori pulled her feet up onto the lounge and curled over the phone, her tone guarded. 'Ryan, I don't want to scare you, but I am worried about Kate. I know Daryl. He'll stop at nothing if he thinks that Kate has influenced Shelley to leave the marriage.'

Ryan paused for so long, Tori thought she had lost him. When he started to speak again, there was the hint of anxiety in his tone.

'Kate is not herself, hasn't been for a little while now. I suspect I haven't been much help. She looked terrible when she came home today.'

'Let me see if I can talk to her. We had an intense talk about things the other day. I'll keep you posted.'

Tori put her phone down and wondered why Kate was not

responding when the phone buzzed again.

'Tori, I missed your call. Sorry.'

Kate sounded breathless. Relief made Tori weak. Her hands shook. 'Where are you?'

Hysterical sobs punctuated her sentences. 'I'm worried sick… about… Shelley. So much… has happened.'

More weeping. 'She won't… talk to… me. I'm terrified… he's going… to hurt her and… it's my fault.'

Tori paced, forcing her racing thoughts to slow. 'Listen to me. Where are you? I'll come and help.'

'I'm on the highway.' More sobs. '… heading home. It's been a ghastly day.'

'I'm going to text you every fifteen minutes. Just use your hands free and say okay. Drop in on the way home.'

The sobbing subsided into sniffles. 'Tori, you're going to hate me when you hear what happened.'

'Never. We're besties, remember. I've got your back.'

40

KATE sat in the car in the emergency lane, hazard lights blinking, the sunset dissolving behind her in the rear vision. She blew her nose, wiped her eyes on her sleeve and texted Ryan. *Heading home.*

There was an important job she had to do before heading home. True to her word, Tori sent regular texts. *Hang in there, girl. I'm here for you.* It made Kate smile, after she thought she might never be able to smile again. Images of Artemis flashed through her mind, at times replaced with Shelley hanging off a door. Kate used all the strategies she used to help her clients. She brought her focus back to Tori's messages and tried to appreciate the fading reds and oranges in the darkening sky behind her and the lights of Brisbane beckoning in front of her.

Finally, Kate turned off at the clinic, her breathing calmer, the pain in her chest getting worse. She shot a text to Tori. *Gotta sort something. See you tomorrow.*

Over the next hour, she methodically cleared up her consulting room. The place smelt of pine fresh and bleach. She filled black garbage bags with broken glass wrapped in newspaper and pieces of broken chair. She heaved it outside into the skip for the morning rubbish collection, even though the pain in her sternum made her dizzy. Back inside, she hung a picture over the fist-shaped dent in the wall and rearranged her desk to ensure she had direct access to the door.

Finally, she gathered all the scraps of notes Daryl scattered across the floor, placed them in an envelope and locked them into her filing cabinet, vowing to transfer them to her files this week even if she had to stay up all night. Daryl warned *Don't fuck with me*, and might want to bring her down, but she was determined not to leave any other evidence that questioned her professional integrity.

Kate hefted the orchid into the boot of her car with difficulty, drove to the nearby garden store and dumped it at the now locked gate. She hoped they would look after it and find it a new home. By the time she had finished, the sky was a thick velvet with clouds hiding the stars.

It was just after eight when Kate pulled into the driveway. Familiar, yellow muted light spilt onto the path. She sat in the car, exhausted, and delayed going inside. She was not ready to talk about it all with Ryan and longed for some sign of his unconditional love and support. The quirky humour and spontaneous affection she had fallen in love with was now a distant memory. She couldn't help thinking it was her fault. Unable to delay heading in any longer, she grabbed her handbag from the passenger seat and got out of the car.

When she pushed open the front door, jazz was playing softly in the background and the lingering smells of dinner hung in the hallway. She heard a tap being turned on followed by muffled voices from the bathroom. Ryan's voice, 'Have you finished cleaning your teeth?'

Kate imagined the simple joy of being immersed in all this domesticity without the threat of Daryl looming in the background. She dumped her bag on the kitchen bench, strewn with crumbs, the ends of tomatoes, splotches of mayonnaise and sauce. The dishwasher hummed in the background. Ryan's voice again, 'Is that you, Kate?'

Tears swelled behind her lids. She made sure to keep her tone light.

'Yes, just me.'

What would Ryan think of her when he learnt that she had been Daryl's girlfriend? When he discovered that she agreed to see him and then talked to him over breakfast and lunch at distant cafes? Daryl was a big loose cannon, a potential wrecking ball through her life.

'Give me a sec. Just putting the kids to bed.'

Kate longed to do something normal like hug the children goodnight, but knew she no longer deserved these ordinary, simple pleasures in life. Instead, she poured a large glass of water from the near empty jug left on the bench and drank it in big thirsty gulps. It tasted lukewarm and unsatisfying.

Ryan emerged wearing a hoodie and cargo shorts. 'Can I get you some dinner? I made us burgers.'

Kate realised she was ravenous. 'Yes please.'

He reached into the fridge, pulled out the final patty and lit the gas. He poured oil into the pan and soon the kitchen filled with the spit and smell of frying meat. He assembled the burger without saying a word. A bun, a blob of mayo and sauce, cooked patty, tomato slices, a leaf of lettuce, beetroot, and some grated cheese. He slid it over to her but didn't try to hug or kiss her.

The music stopped. The quiet was tense.

'Thanks.' She took a bite. Meat juice trickled down her chin and she made no effort to wipe it off. Ryan stood, arms folded, leaning against the bench. 'So, are you going to tell me what on earth happened today?'

'It's all a tangled mess. I wouldn't know where to start.'

'The beginning is always a good spot.'

⊕

The next morning, Ryan left early without his usual kiss goodbye. Edie and Noah sensed a quiet strain and got ready for school without any fuss. Kate slipped the family photo from Carnarvon Gorge into her handbag and winced at the flashback of shattering glass. She left messages for all her clients today and advised she was unwell and needed to postpone their appointments. It was possible she would never see any of them again.

When Kate pulled up at the school, the sky was mutinous. She wondered if any of the others would be there, uncertain if she wanted to see them or not. Noah and Edie got out and hoisted satchels onto their backs.

They ran off to join the stream of grey heading to the quadrangle when the familiar black four-wheel drive squealed into the freshly vacated park behind her. Shelley stepped out wearing her white jeans with a pink shirt knotted at the front. She was wearing flats, and it made her look tiny. Kate pressed one hand on her chest to ease the bruising pain that was not alleviated with ibuprofen.

Shelley came up close and Kate stood immobile, swallowed hard.

Shelley pressed a manicured finger in the same spot where Daryl punched her a day earlier. Kate cried out.

'How dare you destroy my family. I trusted you and confided in you.'

Other parents were turning around to look at them. Kate held one hand to her chest, Shelley's hands were on her hips.

When Kate opened her mouth to speak, Shelley screamed at her. 'I'm leaving Daryl. Are you happy now?'

There was a small crowd eavesdropping and Kate hung her head and bit back angry tears. 'Listen, it was not what you think…'

'I'm tired of listening to you. I never, ever want to see you again.'

With that, Shelley turned around, pulled herself up into her beast of a car and squealed out of her park, nearly ramming the car in front of her.

The small gathering of onlookers hurried away, shooing children in front of them, some of them punching messages into their phones.

Kate stood shell-shocked on the footpath a little longer and waited for the heave of the morning rush to thin. Soon there was just a flurry of leaves and wrappers, scattered by a forceful gust of wind. She felt the heavy, grey press of the sky and just as she felt the first spit of rain, she got back into her car and followed the curve of the road to Tori's house.

41

TORI felt groggy after the sleepers she took last night. She had toyed with not taking them, but after yesterday she knew without them, she would be wide awake all night. Now she stood with her hands wrapped around herself in her kitchen and watched the storm roll in. A sudden flash of lightning followed by the rumble of thunder. Soon sheets of rain poured in torrents down the slope of driveway. She shrugged her arms into the bulky woollen jacket draped across the back of a chair.

Just as the kettle reached its piercing crescendo, there was a tap on the door. Tori opened it expecting Kate and there was Indigo, water dripping down her coat, dark hair stuck to her cheeks in black strands. Tori hesitated, knowing Kate would be here any moment and might not want to talk with someone else here.

Another grumble of thunder decided her. 'Perhaps you should come in and have a cuppa.'

Indigo wiped her boots on the welcome mat, slid her arms out of her coat and hung it on one of the hooks; drips puddled the floor. Tori reached for the teapot, a couple of mugs and the tin of leaves. She took comfort from the warm reassurance of a familiar ritual. The rain continued its loud, steady beat outside, and it hammered the roof and rushed down gutters. They had to shout to be heard. Tori motioned for Indigo to sit down at the table and poured her a dark brew, just how she liked it. Their hands brushed. Tori felt it thrill down her arm and pulled away quickly. Indigo lifted the mug in cheers just as there was a loud thump at the door.

Tori scuttled to the door where Kate stood dripping, pale as a ghost. She started to weep.

'Jesus, what's up? Come in.'

Kate stood soggy and didn't even notice Indigo. The heavy rain started to slow to a steady drizzle, the landscape outside a dismal waterlogged grey.

'Have a seat, I'll pour you a cuppa.'

Kate saw Indigo and hesitated. She pulled up a chair at the other end of the table, leaving a trail of wet prints behind her.

Tori poured another mug of tea and pulled up a chair when there was a hammering at the front door again. It exploded and there stood Daryl. He strode in, boots squelching, and pounded a fist on the table, rattling the crockery.

Shocked, they stared at him. Tori saw Indigo edge backwards and eye the glint of kitchen knives lined up in a block.

He leaned on the table with both hands. 'How dare you fucking mess with me, my life, and my family.'

He lunged towards Kate who shrank back. Indigo leapt to her feet. 'Back off, mate.'

Daryl shifted his gaze to her, the muscles below his jaw twitching, his forearms flexed. 'I will once that bitch next to you gives me access to my son.'

Indigo flinched but stood her ground.

Tori dropped her head, stared at the table, whispered, 'He's Leo's father.'

Daryl roared at her, 'I didn't fucking hear you. Say that again.'

Trembling, Tori stood up next to Indigo and drew on her courage. She looked up at Daryl and shouted at him. 'This sorry son of a bitch is Leo's father.'

The words hung in the room. Daryl's muscles tensed like an animal ready to step in for the kill.

Suddenly he tipped up the table and sent everything flying. An avalanche of tea things was momentarily airborne before smashing in a mess of crockery, tea leaves, sugar, and milk across the floor. Kate screamed, the hot tea scorching her thigh.

Daryl stepped closer. She curved away from him.

'As for this bitch, she's a fucking whore.'

He spat at her.

The glob landed on her cheek and slid down her face. 'Thanks to you, my wife wants to leave me, take my kids away, destroy my career and my reputation.'

Nobody breathed.

He crossed his arms, kicked the remains of the teapot across the room. 'Fuck all of you.'

He turned and punched the front door hard on his way out.

They sat in silence for a moment. Indigo spoke first. 'Good for Shelley.'

Her voice was surprisingly calm. 'I might just clean up this mess, get you two something a bit stronger than tea.'

Tori's phone pinged. She grabbed it. 'It's Georgie.'

Tori scanned the message. 'She's letting us know Shelley has decided to leave Daryl and is discussing the details at a family picnic at Drop Beach tomorrow so that shared custody arrangements can be sorted out amicably.'

Indigo swept up crockery and glass then threw the soggy tablecloth into the sink. She stood up. 'Good luck with that.'

Tori and Kate stayed seated.

Indigo pulled up a third chair. 'Anyone up for a trip to the beach tomorrow?'

Kate looked up, her face like a sheet. 'You mean follow them down?'

Indigo nodded. 'I think we should inform the police, report him, let them know about the picnic tomorrow, and then follow at a distance.'

She turned to Kate. 'You should try talking to Shelley again.'

'She refuses to talk to me.'

Tori imagined a couple of hours sitting beside Indigo in the car and her heart did a somersault. 'I think it's a great idea.'

42

BACK at home, Kate pulled out the family photo at Carnarvon Gorge and gazed at it. The holiday had been an impulsive last-minute decision after Ryan saw a picture of the walks and camping area in the weekend supplement. She stared down at his goofy face, the one he wore when he was messing with the kids. Noah's hair stuck up at the front, his dimple danced in his cheek, while Edie was not just smiling but laughing. It was usually impossible to get her to smile for a photo. Holding the picture close, Kate homed in on herself, standing with one arm over Ryan's shoulder, gazing with love down at their children. Ryan had handed his phone to one of the campers and asked him to take a picture of all of them. It was strange to think that this stranger captured a moment of perfection where everyone was so relaxed and happy. The trip felt like a lifetime ago and yet it was barely eighteen months. If only Kate had appreciated the beauty of such pure, simple joys at the time.

She stared out into the drab day, the rain reduced to the drip off the broken guttering, the mood grey and heavy. The new photo frame waited on the bench, the replacement she had purchased after discarding the splintered timber and shattered glass in the skip. She pressed the picture face down against the new, clear glass then eased the backing onto it. It fixed firmly into place, and she propped it against the wall where she could see it while she was cooking and supervising homework.

Daryl's threats and anger echoed in her ears, in a constant replay.

An ugly purple bruise bloomed on her chest, every breath a reminder of his violent outburst. Kate made herself a plate of food using leftovers from the fridge for lunch, then spent half an hour pushing it around her plate. Bear nuzzled into her, his wet nose pressed against her thigh.

When Ryan rang and reminded her the band was playing at The Spiked Echidna tonight and not to wait up, she was relieved. He had not seen the bruise. She had taken great care to cover it with her pyjamas and dressed in the bathroom before he got up. She wondered how long it would take to fade. Time edged into afternoon, an uneasy glide into tomorrow. School pick-up, homework, scrambled eggs for dinner. Once again, she pushed food around the plate then fed it to Bear.

It was past midnight when Ryan stumbled into the bedroom. She heard his clothes drop to the floor and the bed creak when he climbed in. He rolled over away from her. Before long, his breathing softened, and she dared to glance over at his mussed hair and the way his mouth fell open when he slept.

A few hours later, she slid out from under the doona, slipped into her jeans and tiptoed out to the kitchen where she spooned the remains of her yoghurt straight out of the plastic tub. She clattered her spoon into the sink, gave the empty container a rinse and tossed it into the recycling bin.

Tori and Indigo agreed she would take her own car, and they would meet up at Drop Beach and perhaps enjoy lunch at one of the beachside cafes from where they could keep an eye on the Brady family. They agreed to contact the police if Daryl did anything threatening. Tori suspected he might attempt to take the kids and do a runner.

The morning stayed still and quiet. Kate picked up her keys, careful not to let them jangle. She unlocked the door, then on impulse, tiptoed back to the kitchen and tore a blank page from one of Ryan's music books. She scribbled *I love you* between the staves and drew a single smiling sunflower before adding a couple of kisses. Butterflies danced in her belly.

The sky was a pale baby blue, washed clean after yesterday's storm. It was the perfect day for a picnic at the beach. Kate checked the time. It was so early she decided she would get herself a coffee at Vincent's. It was unlikely the Bradys would leave for a while yet.

Morning risers and insomniacs were lined up at the hatch. Kate joined the queue for a takeaway and planned to head straight to Shelley and Daryl's street to keep watch. The agreement was she would text Tori when they left. It was reassuring Indigo would be there as well. Three of them should be enough if Daryl tried anything on.

When Kate hurried back to the car, takeaway in hand, she stopped dead. There was Shelley crossing the road wearing a tight denim skirt teamed with a clinging white sweater and strappy heels. Kate wondered for a moment if there had been a change of plan, that they had decided not to head for a picnic after all. Shelley didn't look dressed for a day at the beach.

Chest aching, Kate made a snap decision to follow Shelley inside. Kate paused at the entrance and scanned the café. There was Shelley at the counter with the young waitress handing her a large white cake box. Kate positioned herself so that Shelley would see her the moment she turned around. When Shelley saw Kate, she startled and nearly dropped the cake.

'Whoa. Careful.' Kate reached forward and steadied the wobbling box with one hand while holding her coffee in the other. She left her hand on the box and half expected Shelley to snatch it away and storm out.

'Shell, have you got a minute? I just want to talk.'

Shelley looked at the door then down at the box in her hands.

'I gotta go. Daryl is keen to head off early. We're going to Drop Beach.'

'It won't take a minute, and then, I promise to leave you alone if that's what you want.'

Shelley wavered, then pulled the box away from Kate and teetered into the café.

When they found a table, Shelley perched on the very edge of the chair, the box between them giving off a sweet tang of lemon. Kate took a sip of her coffee, let the bolus of liquid burn a pathway for her words. She knew she didn't have much time. 'Daryl came to my clinic, asked to see me about his marriage problems. I met with him a few times as a friend and let him talk.'

Shelley sat still, her eyes blue, hard stones.

'It was unprofessional and totally the wrong thing to do. It is something I will always regret, something I now have to live with.'

Shelley stared at Kate without blinking. Kate shook her head. 'I swear, I have not had an affair with him.'

There was a scrape of chairs at the next table, followed by loud voices.

'I know how it must look, those texts arranging café catch-ups, but that is what they were. Nothing happened.'

Shelley's lacquered fingers were still around the box. 'That pendant,' she whispered. 'He told me you gifted it to him, that you wore it when you were together at uni, and you wanted him to have something to remind him of you when you weren't together.'

Tears slid down Kate's cheeks now, thinking of all that she might yet lose, of her oldest friend sitting opposite her thinking the worst. 'Shell, when we were together at uni, I fell pregnant to Daryl. I bought that pendant as a gift to myself. I never told anyone, not even Daryl about the pregnancy, and then I lost the baby. He wanted me to leave my degree, move away with him, and I knew I didn't want that. He reached for it the other day and the chain broke. I let him take it.'

Shelley's blonde head bent forward. 'I always wondered if he still loved you and was pleased when he asked me to move away with him. I left my degree. I just wanted to be with him, to support him and have the happy family life I never had growing up.'

Her voice quavered. 'He has always been edgy, little things really set him off, but it was better when he was away for work more. Now, with his injuries and that incident I mentioned, it's impossible. He gets so angry that sometimes he doesn't talk to me for a week at a time. It frightens me. I want to work again and get out of the house without him checking up on me.'

Kate took a chance and placed a hand over Shelley's.

'Please be careful. When Daryl is angry, he can be unpredictable.'

'The thing is, he adores our kids. He pressured me to have more. I want to reassure him that he can see them regularly. I don't want them growing up without their dad.'

One of the blokes nearby thumped his fist on the table. Kate and Shelley jumped, and their hands flew apart. Shelley stood, clutching the box again. 'I just can't do it anymore. I can't breathe.'

She pushed her chair back in with one foot. 'Today, we'll tell the kids and sort it all out. I've even bought his favourite lemon meringue pie. I gotta go. I've been here far too long already. I told him I was just coming here to pick up something for the picnic.'

Kate wanted to grab Shelley's arm and stop her from going. She wished now she had talked about Daryl's violent outburst at work, and then again at Tori's place. It was too late for that now.

Shelley picked up the box and without even saying goodbye, hurried out.

43

TORI woke feeling light, knowing that she would be going to Drop Beach with her two good friends in case Shelley needed support. It was such a relief that her secret was out in the open, even better than having the cancer removed. And Kate and Indigo not only knew, but neither had judged her or thought any less of her. When she thought about yesterday, she shivered, grateful she had not been alone.

Tori heard the clatter of pans in the kitchen, smelt toast, bacon, and eggs. Indigo had stayed overnight, and Leo was staying with one of his football mates. They were getting dropped off for their game and agreed to bring Leo home late afternoon. It was a relief knowing Daryl wouldn't be at the game today.

Tori missed Leo's Saturday morning energy and enthusiasm and endless patter about football. Letting him go on a sleepover, even for a night, still made her uneasy.

Tori watched Indigo slice an avocado and drizzle lemon over the top. The sourdough popped, and the coffee percolator hissed and spat.

'Morning,' Indigo called out.

There was a sharp edge to the day, a knowledge of what they would do. Yesterday's revelations and violence still reverberated in the room.

'Do you think less of me after learning the truth about Leo?'

Indigo paused with her preparations. 'Whatever happened in the past has gone to make you the woman you are today. I admire your

217

grit, your ability to pick yourself up and go on, despite the shit life has thrown at you.'

'I'm sorry I didn't talk to you about Daryl. I was terrified I might lose Leo. I couldn't bear him spending even part of the week away from me with that man.'

'You don't owe me explanations. It was none of my business.'

'Thanks for everything.'

Indigo put toast and slices of avocado onto plates before she slid bacon and eggs on top. Tori poured coffee. It was so domestic and normal after yesterday afternoon. She realised she was hollow with hunger. It was like her revelations had left a huge, gaping hole and woken her appetite up. The smells and sounds of breakfast were intense, her sensory system, heightened, unburdened by the silence of her past. The phone vibrated. It was Kate. Tori plunged back into the reality of Daryl's threats and their mission for today. *Just saw Shelley at Vincent's heading off soon.*

Fear made her hands and lips tingle.

'You alright?'

Tori nodded. 'Kate just saw Shelley at Vincent's and thinks they might head off soon.'

Indigo nodded. 'We'll be right behind her.'

Tori busied herself mopping up runny yolk with her toast, and wondered whether to contact Leo and wish him well for his game. He was no doubt having a ball staying with a mate, getting to talk football non-stop, and might not appreciate hearing from his mum. She was so relieved Leo hadn't been home when Daryl was here yesterday. Tori dreaded telling Leo the truth about his father.

Tori swirled the last mouthful of coffee around in her mug and drank it. After she gathered the dirty plates and piled them on the sink, Indigo took a step towards her, the space between them charged. Tori breathed in her scent. Sandalwood, cinnamon, the sweet spice of acceptance. Her pulse hummed. Indigo's breath brushed her cheek. The door slapped open.

The two of them jumped away from each other and turned to see who was there. It was Leo, dressed for football.

Tori ran towards him. 'What's happened? Are you okay?'

'Yeah, Mum. I asked them to drive past, so I could say good morning before my game.'

Tori pulled him close, her knees suddenly weak. Indigo rinsed dirty plates and loaded them into the dishwasher.

'I love you, Leo. Now go and kick arse at your game today. Send me a text and let me know how you go. I want all the details.'

She high fived him and he turned and loped down the drive. Tori leant against the doorframe and watched him until he disappeared around the corner.

Kate turned into Shelley and Daryl's street in time to see him throw two boogie boards in the back. He yelled something and Melody rushed out the front door with a pile of towels. Shelley burst out next, hauling an esky that seemed to wrench her arm out of its socket. She left it askew on the driveway and went back in. Kate parked on top of the hill behind the large weeping fig where they would not see her watching them. They looked like a normal family heading to the beach for a picnic. She tried to reconcile what she now knew about Daryl, with the man who was spending the day on the beach with his wife and kids.

When she thought about the dark shadow of him looming over her at the clinic, the way he tipped their world upside down yesterday, she felt a wave of nausea. Bathed in sweat, she opened the car door and retched. An elderly lady on a wheelie walker shuffled past and looked at her with distaste. When there was nothing left to bring up, Kate closed the door and leant her head onto the steering wheel. She reassured herself that they were doing the right thing. Tori and Indigo were coming, the police had been informed, and the chances were, in a few hours, the three of them would enjoy lunch on the esplanade.

Kate saw the big, black four-wheel drive disappear around the corner. She put her foot on the accelerator and urged the old Corolla along, praying it would have the grunt to stay close to their sleek high-powered four-wheel drive. She was careful to stay a few cars behind, knuckles ridged over the steering wheel. The heavy beat of someone else's stereo throbbed through the thin metal shell that separated her from the countless other commuters. She cursed when she reached for her drink bottle and realised she had forgotten to pack it. Vomit and fear tasted sour in her mouth.

Eventually, Daryl turned off. Instead of turning right to Drop Beach where there were picnic spots and patrolled beaches, he turned left towards the cliffs. It was not popular with families as the surf near the rocks was rough with treacherous rips. There was a small horseshoe curve of bay where several popular coastal walks started, and beyond that a treacherous drop with spectacular views. From time to time, fishermen braved the rocks at low tide, but several had been swept away even on calm days.

Kate decided Daryl and Shelley must want privacy. It was understandable that Shelley would prefer to discuss the end of their marriage without the inevitable intrusion by diehard fans wanting Daryl's signature.

Kate slowed down and wondered whether to text Tori who must be close behind. The strip shops had petered out and only two cars separated her from Daryl. For the umpteenth time she wished she had brought her bottle of water. When she navigated a sharp bend, the sun hit the windscreen, blinding her. She took one hand off the steering wheel to open the hinged flap of the visor and block the white ball of light drilling a hole between the sky and the back of her eyeballs.

Her pupils adjusted and she lowered her foot back on the accelerator, panicking when she thought Daryl's car had disappeared. Then she saw him turn sharply at the cliffs. He must have realised he had come too far and was now trying to do a U-turn in the worst possible spot. She wondered what to do as it was now inevitable they would see her. There was nowhere to turn off and escape scrutiny. Kate scrambled for explanations in her head.

She blinked or perhaps she just turned away for a moment.

The black Range Rover sped up and headed for the precipitous drop.

Kate's earlier foreboding exploded in her chest. She jumped out of her car, left the door open and ran towards the strip of grass just as the black car accelerated hard then was airborne.

She reached the verge just in time to see Shelley's blonde ponytail through the side window and one of the twin's little faces, hands pressed up against the glass in a final plea. Everything slowed right down and happened in slow motion. The car tilted in the empty space beyond the cliffs, a slide of heads and boogie boards to the left. Kate imagined she heard Shelley's cry for help. It seemed the whole world tilted on its axis and paused before the inevitable plummet to the turbulent edge of the sea and cliffs below.

Kate scrambled to the crumbling edge and opened her mouth to scream but no sound escaped. Fuelled by adrenaline she ran along the top of the cliffs, searched in vain for handholds or footholds.

Her ears were filled with the hideous sound of metal on rock, the roar of the surf, and the loud slap of waves meeting the cliffs. Kate tried to lower herself over the edge, the hard rock and dirt pressing into her bruised chest. The car dipped and heaved in the churning water, successive waves smashing it repeatedly against the rocks. She thought she saw terrified eyes, but it might have been the glint of sunlight on glass. Kate willed Shelley to wrench open the door, reach in and pull her children to safety, to hang onto the cliff face until Tori and Indigo arrived. They would know what to do.

The car sank deeper, and one side crumpled like a soft drink can. It hovered for a moment, the black roof just above the waterline. Kate pictured herself scrambling down the cliffs and pulling them out, Shelley's hair floating like seaweed, the children pale, with limbs bloodless and cold like alabaster statues. Kate thought she saw a shadow of a little face, then a wave washed over, and the car was swallowed up by the ocean. She dragged herself away from the edge and knelt in the dirt. She dropped her head into her hands and screamed. It echoed around the cliffs, joined the shrill shriek of swooping, diving gulls.

All that remained was the haunting, clear blue sky, the relentless glare of sun, and the white-tipped, indifferent surge of the ocean, its appetite temporarily appeased.

44

KATE didn't notice the elderly couple who were about to set off on one of the walking tracks and now stood transfixed nearby. The swollen white froth of waves had completely swallowed the Bradys and now went back to the task of gnawing and reshaping the cliffs. Kate shivered and felt her body shut down.

She had no idea how much time had passed. It could have been minutes or hours. Clusters of people stood useless at the top, tragedy always a drawcard for curious spectators. They pulled out phones and spoke in hushed tones of disbelief. Kate was half aware of raised voices and feet hurrying along the tiny, dirt track that led to the top of the cliffs. A small crowd stared at the crashing surf below. Several even snapped photographs, giving in to morbid fascination.

The boundary between the irrevocable present and recent events blurred behind Kate's lids, the reality too awful to absorb. A scream clawed at her throat but remained trapped. She shivered and hunched her body against the brisk wind that was gathering pace.

Sirens pierced the air. Kate slammed back into the now, still huddled over in a ball. Dirt and drying grasses were hard and prickly beneath her.

The crowd swelled. Voices sounded loud all around her. She was aware of the bright yellow of a high vis vest and heard a voice.

'Did you see what happened?'

She held her face in her hands, unable to face the growing fear, anger, and disbelief rippling through the throng of helpless onlookers.

Kate imagined a path down to the rocks, a way to release Shelley and the children from their watery prison. She pleaded through her fingers.

'Please help them, please.'

Kate wanted someone to arrange a crew of rescuers in bright yellow dinghies or a helicopter with divers lowered on ropes. She imagined Shelley's made-up face, her blue eyes bulging from holding her breath too long. Why was everyone hesitating? She let out a moan through her fingers. A hand firm grasped her shoulder. 'You all right love? Did you see what happened? Is that your car?'

She kicked her legs out and pushed them all away. The sound of the waves was relentless. Their hard smack against the rocks sent white foams of spray into the air. Scrubby trees bowed before the ceaseless wind that blasted sand against her skin.

'Kate.'

The voice sounded strangely familiar above the shrill sounds of sirens, the rising clatter of voices and press of the growing crowd. Kate's breath was jagged like glass in her throat. That comforting, familiar voice again. 'Are you okay?'

Tori knelt in front of Kate and grabbed her shoulders. She fell forward and the two embraced, tear stained and damp from the spray that burst over the top of the cliffs at irregular intervals.

'I let her die…' Grief swallowed Kate, a black void of failures. Losses too big for tears, a raw pain gouging out her insides, her body numb.

'Hush, we did the best we could. We came.'

Kate was aware of Indigo standing behind Tori. She handed Kate a bottle of water. Tori pulled away, eyes red rimmed.

'Ryan followed us. He rang me just after we left.'

Kate shivered. She was shaking so hard her teeth rattled. When Ryan arrived, he went down on his knees and tried to embrace her. She let her body dissolve against his. Her jumbled and blurred brain cut and pasted images from her past and the present. A collage of all her failures in black and white relief. She remembered her note this morning, wondered if it was too little, too late.

The next few hours were hazy. She found herself in the back of a moving vehicle. Another voice, female this time, hushed her, took her pulse and her blood pressure. She was taken to the local hospital. The dark swirling green of the floor, the plastic chairs and smell of antiseptic made her feel ill. Someone handed her a metal bowl and she vomited again and again. Her mouth tasted sour. She was taken to a small room. Ryan's face was there somewhere. It slid past her, and she wondered how much he knew.

'Cup of tea, love?'

One of the nurses. Short, grey hair, solid build, face indistinct.

Kate shook her head. She could not stop shivering. They handed her a warm blanket. She crouched under it, grateful for its weight and the semi darkness it provided.

She heard other voices. Tori and Indigo.

Ryan said something to them. She thought they might have hugged each other. There were tears. Kate was relieved they had come. Relieved when they left.

The police came in and wanted a statement. The mattress sank beside her. She knew it was Ryan. He put his arm over the blanket and wanted to know how she was. She wondered how many hours had passed. She had lost track of time. All she knew was that Shelley and her kids were gone. That she had failed them.

She answered questions and told them what she had seen as truthfully as she could. Her voice seemed to come from some place far away, like a recording. They all eventually left, and she begged to go home. Ryan filled in more forms and spoke first to one of the doctors and then a nurse. Every second felt like an hour. After the bright fluorescent lights, metallic clatter, and antiseptic smells, it was a relief to be outside. The sky was nearly dark, a veil over the events of the day. People walked in the streets, drove their cars and rushed home like nothing had happened.

Impossible though it seemed, life outside had reverted to normal, indifferent to the horrors of the day. The news came on and as the screaming headline started, Ryan turned it off. His voice was gentle.

'Can I get you something to eat?'

She shook her head. She felt nauseous again and wondered how Ryan had worked out where to come. 'Thanks for coming.'

'You left a note. I rang Tori and she explained what you were both up to. I left the kids with Georgie and was almost here when Indigo rang and told me what happened.'

Kate pulled her knees up to her chest, her feet on the seat. 'It's all my fault. They died and it's all my fault.'

Ryan pulled over onto the verge. 'You're in shock. Just try to sleep. The doctor gave you something to take tonight.' His fingers thrummed on the steering wheel. 'No one could have imagined what would happen, but you tried, you did your best.'

Kate was aware of the seatbelt putting pressure on her bruise. The sky was a dark velvet now with a fragile eggshell moon poised between a sprinkle of stars. In her ears, she could still hear the chaos of voices, the shouts and shrieks and sirens. She smelt the briny salt air, tasted bitterness, and saw shimmers of light in the distance where moonlight danced on the waves. There was a blending of senses. Light, sound, and taste. They all led to the same irreversible reality. A finality from which there was no return.

She wound down the window and let out a wail. It disappeared into the night.

Ryan placed his hand on her thigh, the one scalded by tea. She drew away from him, the image of Daryl tipping the table loud in her head. She let her legs drop to the floor, bent over, and covered her ears with her hands to drown him out. She whispered, 'Ryan. I need to tell you something.'

He switched the engine off. She looked back out of the windscreen at the black curve of sky. He waited for her to continue without speaking. He was good like that.

'I was in a relationship with Daryl years ago. When I was nineteen.' She paused. 'I fell pregnant but never told him. I lost the baby and left him.'

There was silence between them. Each time traffic passed, the car shuddered. Kate stared towards the speckle of lights in the far distance.

'Did you love him?' Ryan's words hung suspended inside the car. The details of those heady days rushed back to Kate like an enormous wave. The way she nearly left uni and sacrificed her own dreams because he wanted her to. The sheer grandiosity of him. She was surprised by the firm certainty with which she replied. 'No. I was infatuated with the idea of him.'

She had craved him and felt pressured to be with him. She learnt about the intoxicating suck and pull of desire. His fingers had whispered her skin to goosebumps, his tongue spoke of arousal and need. It was more carnal than love. Love was what she shared with Ryan. A quiet intimacy interwoven between the mundane; the inevitable dirty washing, endless chores, and unpaid bills. Love was brief moments of romance dotted between disagreements and compromise. It happened when you least expected it and made you soft and warm inside. Love was support through the tough times, negotiation, and at times, misunderstanding. There was no cruelty, coercion, or manipulation. It was a place to feel safe and comfortable, where you could be yourself and let your hair down knowing the other person was still there for you. It was being there for them and listening, just the way Ryan was listening now. Without judgement or recrimination.

Kate thought about Tori's secrets held close for so long and finally confessed. The three of them had been connected through their vulnerabilities and were torn apart by their silence and secrets. She shuddered and felt grateful for the life she had chosen instead.

Kate knew now she wanted Ryan to know everything. There was no more room for half-truths, lies, and secrets. She had to wear the consequences of the truth.

'Daryl came to my clinic earlier this year and asked to see me about his marriage. They were having problems.' Kate put her head in her hands and started to sob. 'I agreed. I met up with him as a friend a few times.'

Ryan stayed very still. The quiet became a sound of its own. She was aware of his warmth beside her, conscious of his breathing. She started to shiver again. Eventually, Ryan leant towards her, touched her arm. 'I think I was part of the problem. I was not there for you.'

Ryan kept his hand on her arm. 'You can't fix everything. Sometimes we try our hardest and it's not enough.' He gave her arm a squeeze. 'But you know, you did your best and that's enough for the people who love you.'

They drove home in a silence that washed over Kate like warm water. Her skin felt grimy with the events of the day, and she was grateful for Ryan's quiet acceptance, his ability to receive information without probing further.

She pulled her knees up, wrapped her arms around them, and rested her head against the window. The steady rattle and hum of the car dulled her senses. The dark swallowed up the black day until there was no further light to reveal things.

45

A few weeks later, Kate was curled up on Tori's lounge, a new teapot poised between them on the coffee table. She used the remote to switch off the television, refusing to watch the news bulletins that replayed scenes from that devastating day. She complained to Tori, 'I think they have interviewed everyone Shelley ever knew. Her mother, her former employer, old university friends, school friends and neighbours she has not seen for years.'

'I guess everyone wants a fresh take, some explanation of how a perfect family like the Bradys managed to hide a dark secret like that. I mean, there were stories about them in glossy magazines, in the newspaper, and Daryl always liked to be surrounded by his wife and daughters. No one wants to believe the truth.'

Kate frowned, thought back to that ghastly day when she found Artemis bloodied and hanging from Bea's front door.

'I saw another woman before all of this happened, who died just before Shelley and her children were murdered. Do you remember the cat I asked Georgie to pin up at the school because it was lost?'

Tori nodded. 'Did she ever find the cat?'

Kate teared up again. 'Her partner killed the cat.'

Kate was shaking again, tears welling up. Tori came over, put an arm around her and handed her the tissues. They had used up several boxes in the last few weeks.

When Kate's sobs subsided, she blew her nose hard, kept talking. 'The thing is, she rang me, told me she was leaving, and I grew suspicious. It was all odd and didn't sound right. It turns out, she had jumped from the balcony of a high-rise hotel. She saw that as the only option left to her.'

Kate's lip trembled. 'The awful truth is she won't even make the statistics of women who are victims of abuse. She ended her life so he is not to blame. I went to the funeral, and it made me sad how few people were there. I think she had been isolated from family and friends. Bea found solace and love with her cat, Artemis. Her partner, Jake, deliberately killed the last thing that brought her joy.'

'Oh, Kate, why didn't you come and talk to me?'

'I wanted to talk to you and to Ryan, but the opportunity never arose. We all got pulled into the riptide of Daryl's destruction. I shelved Bea somewhere and never managed to do anything about it. And now I wonder, how many women are there who disappear, not only when they are alive, but after they die? Their stories of horror, endurance, and courage are buried, and their partners get away with murder – literally.'

'Well, it's a good thing Shelley's story is casting a fresh light on things. Perhaps, just perhaps, things might shift a little. I fall apart whenever I see a picture of her smiling from some magazine or newspaper, surrounded by her daughters.'

'She warned us, you know. In lots of small ways. I was too blind to see it and to respond. I just wish I'd let her know we would have her back if anything happened. We should get everyone together, while it's fresh in the public's mind. Do something to stop something like this happening again. We need to bring the whole thing centre stage and make people aware of how they can help. The thing with Shelley is that she was beautiful and well-known, a loving mother and wife, so her loss has had a huge impact on people.'

Kate reached for her mug of lukewarm tea, held it in both hands and took a sip.

'Some journo suggested that Shelley drove Daryl to it. Can you imagine? I was livid. He suggested that she didn't support his career, and it drove him to desperation. He has since retracted his obnoxious statement. He apologised but explained he was taken out of context blah, blah, blah.'

Tori stared into the distance and plucked at a loose thread in a cushion. 'I still have to tell Leo. I need to find my moment. After what happened, he might really hate me.'

'Leo adores you. He will learn what his mother did for him. How tough she was to leave and raise him in a safe and loving environment on her own.'

'Not on my own, Kate. With lots of support from you, Georgie, and now Indigo.'

They heard the front door open. 'Hello. Anyone home? I've just locked up the shop for the night and thought I might grab us a take-away.'

'Indigo,' they said together.

Tori added. 'Great idea. Let's invite the others and add in a couple of bottles of wine.'

Kate called Ryan; Tori invited Georgie and Mark. Everyone arrived with kids in tow. They all jammed into Tori's tiny place, half of them squashed on the lounge and others lolling on big cushions. Tori set up a movie on her computer in Leo's room for the kids, then pulled his door shut.

Kate raised her glass and tapped the side with a spoon to get everyone's attention. 'We want to create a legacy and do something to support women like Shelley and her children. And women like Bea who often go unnoticed.' Kate wiped her eyes. 'And Artemis. Some women stay because there is nowhere to go if you have a pet, and they know their beloved pet may not survive if it is left behind.'

Everyone was keen to be involved and to do something positive. Kate continued. 'We want to change attitudes so that women in relationships with men like Daryl find the courage to speak out. It's important to educate men and women that it is not okay to control another person, to monitor where they go and what they do. Coercive control is harder to recognise because the damage is often invisible. The bruises are on the inside.'

Georgie suggested having a launch at Vincent's. Ryan offered to bring the band along to kick off some fundraising. They talked late into the night. Ideas flowed, a timetable was drawn up, and a date for the launch set.

It turned out they had underestimated the public response. One wall of the café had pictures of Shelley and the girls, and another had a picture of Bea and Artemis. Vincent had cleared the tables, and the school loaned him chairs for the event. The café was jam packed and staff could barely keep pace with drinks and nibbles. Once the inside was full, at least as many stood outside in solidarity. The children handed out small paper sunflowers. The tag dangling off the stem had the phone number for Dorothy's Place on one side and the words, *we've got your back,* on the other. Some people asked for a whole bunch.

Kate stared out at the sea of faces. 'I think I've changed my mind.'

Tori gave her a shove. 'Go on, you can do this. Just think of Shelley and her kids, remember Bea and Artemis.'

Kate's hands shook. Just when she wondered if she would manage to hold it together, she felt a hand on her back and turned around. It was Peg, Bea's neighbour, bent over and dressed in a bright yellow dress with a sunflower in her silvery hair.

Kate gave her a hug and held her for a long time. No words were needed. A comfortable chair was dragged to the very front where Vincent had set up a small podium with a microphone. Kate caught Tori's eye then smiled at Ryan and Georgie and nodded at Indigo. She left her notes on the seat and instead spoke from the heart, standing next to an enormous vase of sunflowers nestled in a large earthenware pot.

'The Daryl we saw was charming. A sports star who gave his time to support younger players. His face smiled from magazine covers, always with his beautiful wife, Shelley, and his three daughters. There was another side to him. Angry, aggressive, and jealous. Some of us witnessed this side of him but did not come forward. No one ever called him to account. It allowed him the freedom to make Shelley's life hell. He controlled everything she did. He prevented her from working, and kept a track of where she went and whom she saw. When she decided to leave him, she wanted to do the right thing and allow him to see his children. Her wish was to separate amicably. I spoke to her right here on the morning before she died. She even bought his favourite dessert to take with them on that fatal picnic.'

Kate faltered, tears slid down her face. 'Daryl was so charismatic, it was impossible to believe the dark secrets he disguised with his success. We blinded ourselves to the truth, making it impossible for Shelley to speak up about her husband. I was one of those women, one of her close friends who didn't probe below the surface.'

Vincent had thoughtfully placed tissues on some of the chairs. There was a lot of nose-blowing and crying. The smiling face of Shelley looked down on the crowded room. Kate paused before she continued. 'I want to speak about another woman, Bea, who is less well known. You may have noticed the cat on the wall. Artemis was Bea's beloved companion. Her partner killed the cat in the most brutal way. Artemis brought love, companionship, and joy to a life eroded by domestic violence and coercion. Bea came to me for help when Artemis was lost. She was devastated. Her partner had recently been released from prison and threatened her as soon as he was released. Ironically, he had been sentenced after he assaulted somebody in the street and rendered them unconscious. He had been assaulting Bea for years behind closed doors without consequence.'

Kate wiped tears from her cheeks and looked around the room. 'Following the murder of Artemis, Bea no longer saw any hope she would ever escape her partner. She took her own life.'

Kate looked down at Peg and acknowledged her with a small nod. 'We need to stand as a community to end the silence, the shame, and the fear that lead women like Bea to such utter despair.'

Kate scanned the faces in the crowd. Based on the statistics, one in six women in the room was the victim of domestic violence, one in four the victim of emotional abuse. She pushed her shoulders back and continued. 'There are so many stories, so many women who do not feel safe at home, who face a daily threat to their lives. I spent a lot of my childhood crouched in the dark safety of my wardrobe and remember what that was like. Domestic abuse in all its ugly forms affects all of us. It is up to each one of us to notice, to check in with our friends, our neighbours, family. We need to stand together and end the world of silence that protects and enables perpetrators to continue their reign of terror in our homes – physical, mental, and emotional. Dorothy's Place is a tiny oasis providing refuge for those impacted by domestic abuse. Today, we would like to support this haven, so that more women will have a safe place to go should they need it. Together with my friend, Tori, I invite everyone here to donate their time, money, and goodwill, to make domestic violence in all its ugly forms a thing of the past.'

By the end of that evening there were already hundreds of stories about first-hand experience of abuse on the Dorothy's Place social media feed. Money poured in and Mark and Georgie offered their skills to manage the funds. Others offered to help. Kate was keen to expand Dorothy's Place. A date was set for a further meeting to discuss how this vision could be realised.

The following weekend, a few of them drove down to Drop Beach. There was still a collection of teddy bears, cards, and fading bouquets of flowers at the site. Clutches of people stopped to pause and reflect, wondering anew how it had happened to a *nice family like that*. Daryl's former football team arranged to have a bench installed and it was inscribed in memory of Shelley and the children. They donated generously to Dorothy's Place and invited Kate to come and run a series of seminars about domestic abuse and how to watch out for friends and neighbours and others in the community.

Before she left, Kate reached in her bag, pulled out the old photograph of herself with Daryl, and tore it in four. She walked to the spot where Daryl drove his family to their deaths. She flung the fragments over the cliff. They fluttered, dipped, and swirled in the breezes, until eventually they dived and disappeared into the dark, turbulent waters below.

Tori pulled Kate aside. 'It's time. I'm planning to stay on a bit longer with Leo, maybe grab a couple of burgers and sit right here on the bench and tell him the truth. Kate gave her a hug. They stood like that for a while. The breeze tugged at Kate's scarf and blew Tori's hair across her face.

Once the others had gone, Tori beckoned to Leo. 'Let's go for a walk along the clifftops. It's time I told you about your father.'

Afterwards, the two of them sat on the new bench, staring out to sea. Leo had listened and stayed surprisingly quiet while they ate their burgers and watched a V of birds soar overhead. Eventually, he asked her, 'Did you love him?'

Tori shook her head. 'No, I was lonely and alone. I just wanted some company because I was so sad.'

'Did he hurt you?'

Tori bit her lip. She had put a great deal of thought into what she might tell Leo.

'He did hurt me, but I left. I think he was scared too. Sometimes people do bad things when really, they are hurting inside.'

They watched the light shifting on the ocean, the way it tipped into the curve of the horizon.

'Did he love me?'

'I think he was very proud of you. I'm not sure what love meant to him.'

Another pause. The squall of seagulls and distant rumble of surf.

'Did you regret having me?'

Tori turned and embraced him hard, her face pressed into his hair, her arms tight around his lanky frame. 'I never, not for one minute, regretted having you. It is the very best thing I have ever done, the thing that has made me proudest. I love you, Leo, with all my heart.'

The birds now in the distance broke away from their formation, dipped and soared in the currents, their wings spread wide.

46

A month later, Kate drew up a list of things she wanted to discuss with Ryan. *I am turning into Georgie*, she thought to herself when she saw the dot points. She wanted to find some sort of compromise where Ryan spent time on his music while she worked less hours at the clinic and maybe volunteered more at Dorothy's Place.

Ryan looked nervous when he saw her list. 'Should I book somewhere for dinner?'

Kate shook her head. 'I would rather you did your chilli crab, and we ate right here at home. Georgie offered to take the kids.'

Kate had forgotten what a great cook Ryan was when he put his mind to it. They sat opposite each other, sticky fingered, while a couple of candles flickered between them. It reminded Kate of the good old days when they spent the afternoon cooking, enjoyed a long lazy dinner then cleared up together before reaching for each other. A lump formed in her throat. She didn't want to cry this evening. She had shed enough tears in the past weeks to last a lifetime.

Just as she was thinking how handsome Ryan was, he reached over and put his hand over hers. She sensed he was nervous too. It felt like an early date, getting to know each other all over again. Kate fizzed a little inside, that heady mix of hope and anxiety.

When they finished their meal, Ryan poured them each a final glass of wine. He took her by the hand, and they settled on the couch. When he turned to face her, worry creased his forehead. 'Why didn't you tell me about Daryl?' He paused… 'Before the tragedy.'

Kate wondered the same thing herself. 'I honestly don't know, Ry. I think I got so caught up with keeping my head above water, with work, the kids and everything, that I just lost sight of the important things.'

She thought back to the party when she saw Shelley and tried to avoid Daryl, the way he showed up at her clinic, begged for her help. When she remembered how she agreed to see him, while he simultaneously tried to unsettle Tori and made Shelley's life hell, Kate's fingernails dug into her palm. 'I guess he made me feel important and special. He convinced me I was doing a good job. I turned a blind eye to the things I didn't want to see and convinced myself I was saving Shelley's marriage.'

Ryan leant over and pulled her into his arms. 'I am sorry. I was so caught up with the band, with my own big dream, that I just let you carry the whole load at home. The finances, the kids, the household. I was selfish and didn't consider how it might impact the family.'

The couch sighed when Kate shifted her weight to snuggle closer to Ryan. It felt so good, so right to be here and feel her body pressed against his.

He cleared his throat. 'Miss Nightingale is leaving. I applied for her job. I had the interview a few weeks ago and I think I have a good chance. I would like to keep doing some gigs at The Spiked Echidna, but no more weddings. It would mean a regular income again.'

Kate softened against him. She had wanted to discuss finances and her list, but did not want to sound like she was obsessed with money again. She locked her hands behind his neck and breathed him in, absorbed the curve of his neck and familiar stippled jaw.

'One other thing.' He slid out from beneath her arms, knelt at her feet and fumbled in his pocket. He pulled out a simple white and rose coated silver ring. 'Kate Simpson, from the minute you pulled my keys out of the sand, you had the keys to my heart. I have left this much too long. Will you marry me?'

Looking at the man she loved knelt before her, Kate teared up.

'Mr Ryan Murphy, nothing would bring me greater pleasure than to accept your proposal.'

Her slid the ring onto her finger and pulled her close.

He drew her up from the lounge and into his arms. Holding her lightly around the waist, he started humming The Waif's *London Still*, slowly whirling her around the floor in a waltz. In the semi-darkness they gradually moved around the furniture and towards the bedroom.

✢

Leo asked if he could sleep over at his friend's place again and watch a movie, so Tori found herself alone with Indigo. Tori spent time making a rich, spicy curry and Indigo helped her to chop and dice vegetables, to cook rice until the grains were soft, fragrant pillows.

They ate with soft music in the background, the smell of food spicy and satisfying. There was a strange sense that the world was revolving past them, that the two of them were the centre of its revolution. The last of the evening sun set the sky on fire.

Tori knew Indigo would stay the night.

ACKNOWLEDGEMENTS

It is surprisingly difficult to write acknowledgements as there are so many people involved over several years. No book ends up in readers' hands without a team of people to help with its creation. My sincere apologies in advance to anyone I have neglected to mention. In future, I will keep a running list of everyone as I write, research, edit, and rewrite my books.

I was overjoyed when I received the phone call informing me that I had a contract for my first novel. It was a combination of shock, joy, and disbelief. I didn't believe I would ever get one of my books published so writing acknowledgements for a second book feels surreal. I finished writing *A World of Silence* long before I wrote *The Truth about My Daughter*. The first draft was completed two weeks before the horrific murder of Hannah Clarke and her three beautiful children. It seemed wrong to attempt to publish a book about coercive control when we were all reeling from the horror of that event.

I have completed so many drafts of this book, I have lost count. I am incredibly grateful to the many people who helped bring this novel to the world. My first writing mentor, Kelly Rigby, helped with the earliest drafts. My ever-patient editor, Lauren Elise Daniels, challenged me to completely rewrite the original which was so tough. Thank you for your faith in my words and for believing I could shape my shitty first (second, third…) drafts into a novel.

I would like to thank Fiona W who not only did a sensitivity read and provided valuable information about how domestic violence is reported but shared the story which appears in the first chapter where Bea (not her real name) came home to a knife in her front door. The rest of Bea's story is entirely fictional.

Thanks to Clare Kildea for her insights about life on the festival circuit for a band. Any inaccuracies about life living with or being a musician are entirely mine.

Coercive control is now taken seriously with a move from an incident-based approach to one that criminalises ongoing patterns of abusive behaviour. Journalist and author, Madonna King, wrote a comprehensive article about coercive control after interviewing the family and close friends of Hannah Clarke, highlighting how easy it is for a perpetrator's behaviour to go unrecognised. The behaviours and patterns of secrecy and control explored in this article were used to make the themes of my novel as authentic as possible. King's piece was published on 20 November 2020 in *Good Weekend.*

I was shocked to hear from several early readers of my novel who reached out to let me know that they too had been victims of abuse and not spoken to anybody about it. One close friend confessed her eldest daughter had been strangled when she attempted to leave her abuser. I also want to acknowledge the many women who have seen me as patients and entrusted me with their stories after years of enduring intimate partner violence and/or coercive control. I know there are many more who are yet to talk about what they are enduring daily.

I devoured Jess Hill's outstanding book, *See What You Made Me Do,* in a single weekend and it affirmed everything I have experienced working as a GP with women who are the victims of abuse. Thank you for writing this comprehensive resource that is a must read for anybody working with victims or perpetrators of abuse. I referred to this book often while writing and rewriting my fictional novel.

Thank you to Di Farmer, member for Bulimba, who organised an informative evening about coercive control where she invited Sue and Lloyd Clarke to speak after they had been nominated as Queensland Australians of the Year. I attended with several of my patients and was inspired by the courage shown by Hannah's parents who, despite unimaginable losses, have dedicated themselves to end coercive control through their foundation, Small Steps for Hannah. Do support this fabulous foundation. You will save a woman's life.

Thank you to my niece, Rochelle, who once gifted me a tee with the message – *Hey Girl, I got your back.* Every woman needs this tee. It embodies the message in *A World of Silence.*

Thank you to the gorgeous women in my writing group, Brisbane

Scribes. Early harsh critique of this novel was much needed and appreciated. Jenny Adams and Jane Connolly read an earlier version and gave comprehensive feedback, much of which made it into the final novel. Tatia Power's honesty telling me to rewrite a difficult scene was invaluable. We still laugh about one particularly clumsy phrase, and I am grateful for her frank feedback. Female friendships are very special, and I love the robust discussions about books, writing and yes, politics that take place when this group of women get together each month. Thank you to Bernie Condren, Marnie Bolton, Rachel Millar, and Carolyn Martinez for being part of the Scribes. You gals are the best and, left alone with a bottle of wine or two, we could solve the problems of the world. While the book deals with some dark themes, at its heart, it is about female friendships and how powerful these can be when we support each other.

Thank you to The Writers' Studio, Sydney, where I began my writing journey. Your ongoing support makes my heart sing and my pen fly. Thank you also to the Queensland Writers Centre for the many events that have helped me to hone my craft. Thank you to the Australian Writers Centre for your comprehensive online courses. I have done several of them. My website was created after following the step-by-step course by Michelle Barraclough with some help from my son, Jonathan. Meeting Valerie Khoo when I volunteered at the Northern Beaches Readers Festival and gifting her a copy of my debut novel was very special. Thanks for your support of the Australian writing community, Valerie.

Thank you to the incredible team at Hawkeye Publishing. Carolyn, Anne, Meesha, Isabelle, Rikki, and Lara, I am humbled that you selected my book amongst the huge number of manuscripts that are submitted. I feel very proud to be part of the Hawkeye family. I would like to thank Kaity Tran for the gorgeous cover that is perfect for my novel. I really love it.

Most of all, I want to thank you, the reader. A book is simply a dead tree until it comes alive in a reader's imagination. If this book has raised challenging issues for you or someone you love, do reach out and seek help and support. It is out there.

To transform our social narratives around misogyny requires a concerted, collective effort to change the conversations we have at home, at work, and in our leisure time. Raising men who respect women and regard sexism in all its forms as abhorrent begins at home and needs to be taken up by schools, workplaces, and the wider community, until it becomes the accepted norm. While sexist comments and behaviour form part of our collective consciousness, women will remain silent when they find themselves victims of sexual abuse.

I imagine a world where a young man who tells a sexist joke or makes salacious remarks about a young woman is forced to hang his head in shame after being pulled into line by his friends. That the fear of being outcast and ridiculed by his peers results in a shift in his language and behaviour.

Last but not least, I would like to thank my family who never complain when I disappear for hours on end to write, research, and edit my next novel, and never doubt my ability to pull it all together. Your support, encouragement, and love make it possible to follow my dreams.

ABOUT THE AUTHOR

Jo Skinner is a Brisbane based GP who writes contemporary women's fiction as well as freelance non-fiction articles about women's issues and mental health. She also has a distance running habit. When she is not working or writing you will find her accruing kilometres while plotting her next story.

Jo was once asked if she was a GP who writes or a writer who is a GP. It is an impossible question to answer as she is passionate about both. Her love of writing came first with her first story published when she was in primary school. She has never forgotten the thrill of her story winning a competition and being included in a time capsule.

Her stories have long and shortlisted in competitions and been published in anthologies. Her non-fiction work is regularly published in women's magazines and medical journals. Her great love is writing contemporary women's fiction. *A World of Silence* was completed before her debut novel, *The Truth about My Daughter,* and longlisted in the Hawkeye Manuscript Development Prize.

Jo is married with three children.

You can find her at johannaskinner.com.

BOOK CLUB QUESTIONS

1. What do you think of the character Georgie? Do you know anyone just like Georgie?

2. What are some of the red flags suggesting that Daryl is not the good father and husband he appears to be?

3. How does a childhood impacted by abuse affect someone long term? How does it affect Kate? Daryl? Shelley? Tori?

4. Georgie asks, 'Why doesn't she just leave?' when she learns about Bea. Have you ever asked this? Why do we stay with people who hurt us physically, emotionally, and sexually?

5. Is Ryan a good man? Why? Why not?

6. Why doesn't Tori tell Leo about his father? Did she do the right thing?

7. What role does Indigo play in Tori's life? How important is she to Tori's character arc?

8. Animals play an important role in this novel. What is the significance of Artemis' death?

9. What role does Bear play?

10. Should Kate have spoken to Daryl as a friend? Did she breach her professional boundaries?

11. At what point could the trajectory of the novel have changed? What did you think about the ending?

Book reviews can make or break a book. If you liked what you read today,
please do consider posting a review on Goodreads or your favourite forum.
A World of Silence is available at hawkeyebooks.com.au
and all good bookstores and libraries.

If you enjoyed *A World of Silence*, we believe you'll also enjoy:

The Truth About My Daughter by Jo Skinner
Forgotten by Casey Nott
Returning to Adelaide and *Me That You See* by Anne Freeman
Rosanna by Annie O'Moon-Browning
New Year's Eve by Sarah Todman
Where There is a Will by Michel Vimal du Monteil
Big Music by Gillian Wills